P9-CST-552

RYNOSSEROS

RYNOSSEROS

Terry Dowling

GUILDAMERICA
BOOKS®

ISBN 1-875346-01-5

Printed in the United States of America

For Kerrie, who went on each new voyage just after Tom did, and for Jack, who in 1962 made such wonderful dragons.

Many people have helped make this book possible. I would especially like to thank:

Nick Stathopoulos, Kerrie R. Hanlon, Carey Handfield, Kate Cummings, Van Ikin, Sean McMullen, Harlan Ellison, John McPharlin, Kohan Ikin, Philip Gore and Peter McNamara.

ACKNOWLEDGEMENTS

"The Only Bird In Her Name", published 1986 in APHELION SCIENCE FICTION MAGAZINE No. 1 (Aphelion Publications) edt. Peter McNamara.

"What We Did To The Tyger", published 1986 in OMEGA SCIENCE DIGEST (Jan/Feb issue) edt. Philip Gore.

"Time Of The Star", published 1986 in APHELION SCIENCE FICTION MAGAZINE No. 3 (Aphelion Publications) edt. Peter McNamara.

The lines of William Butler Yeats' verse quoted in "Mirage Diver" are from the poem "Byzantium."

Permission to quote lines from "Exil" by Paul Eluard (as given in Eleanor Levieux's translation of Antoine Terrasse's text for *Paul Delvaux* [J. Philip O'Hara; 1973]) courtesy of Editions Gallimard, Paris.

CONTENTS

Colouring The Captains

In the Great Passage Book there are seven Coloured Captains. Their names have become famous: Golden Afervarro, Red Lucas, White Massen, Green Glaive, Yellow Traven, Black Doloroso, and the last to be chosen — the Madman, Blue Tyson, known to many as Tom Rynosseros.

There are other National captains who have colours in their names — Rust Morganus is one, and Gray Ridley, and the legendary Black Jack Temenos, to name a few — just as there are other great captains, high and low, who are permitted to cross most of the tribal territories. But there are only seven Nationals who are allowed to use all Roads, to cross all the Ab'O States in their fine sand-ships, whose names and Colours have been entered in the Great Passage Book.

Is this what you wanted to hear? You who sleep there in Cold People storage, in your long safe cryogenic sleeves, waiting in your hundreds to be grafted out on to constructs and surrogate bodies, to make the Grand Tour, hungry for sensate life again.

I tell you, there would be none of it, no hope for you at all were it not for the seven. This circuit is shielded; the link is still open, one of the few I have left, so I can tell you. The world out here has changed since first you slept. The abiding spirit of an age can be rooted to many things: a preoccupation with identity, with new lands and frontiers, with sexuality, morality or repression, nostalgia for the past, with luxury and sacrifice. Then know that not since Pharaonic Egypt, not since the Mexican and Madagascan festivals of the dead, not since the Pre-Columbian civilizations of America has such a preoccupation with death marked an age. Or rather, seen another way, a preoccupation with making, understanding and holding onto life — all part of the same *Zeitgeist,* the same *Weltanschauung.*

If I sound the apologist for the Ab'O Princes, the Clever Men and their AI and genetic planning, bear with me. Some of you, the recent ones, will remember the belltree program, how it was meant to nibble at the concepts of life and death, how it reflected the crucial and vibrant spirit of an age.

So then, let me tell you. Let me answer the questions the sample minds have put to generations of Coldmasters without success, while waiting and longing for life again.

I am a belltree. It is true. Though it shocks many of you and puzzles others, the more ancient personalities among you, I am a half-life creation, a lowly machine to some, with a plasmatic intelligence crafted around a crystalline lattice. Though I murmur to you in your dreams, I stand here beside a rarely-used desert Road, with paint peeling from the lower totemic eight feet of my fourteen-foot shaft, and half my sensors damaged by wind and sun and time.

My crystalline core comes from the great I-D tribal belltrees at Tell, and they, in turn, from the Iseult-Darrian prototypes at Seth-Ammon Photemos. My essence was decanted from the life-bottle of one of those marvellous structures; my identity shares some memories from the host-core.

And, as I say, I am well-acquainted with the seven Captains. In a sense, I am an oracle to them, no less than to the Ab'O tribes who caused me to be made. If the truth be told, and I cannot prove this to you yet, though you will know the truth in time, I am the one who gave them their Colours. It is true and it means everything to me.

My core was originally scheduled for the Tell Sculptury. I was to have become a prime Aulus or a Twilister, fashioned by the greatest organic-sculptors we have in Australia, but there were debts to pay in those early days of no patrons and huge research costs, and my inception was first delayed, then made forfeit. It was a bad year, and my core was sublet to the Immortality factors at Tell. They bonded me to two fading cryogenic personalities like yourselves, James and Bymer, two old Cold People whose bodies were spoiling and who had paid handsomely to have their matrices grafted out into biotectic life, their final chance (apart from the charling injections) for any kind of life considering.

So I lost my pedigree, my pure link with the great Iseult-Darrians. I became an ordinary junk-post, a humble road-sculpture out on the desert, spoiling, piggybacking two ghosts, neglected, with dwindling subtlety in my receptors and limited function.

But a strange and wonderful thing happened, the first of many in this story I am telling you.

James and Bymer's bonding — for all the wealth the factors got from their estates, and despite the guarantees — was only partially successful. My spliced and re-routed I-D core was simply too strong for a true graft, despite the careful dampening and the repressors. Instead of losing my own identity, it went the other way: my passengers lost theirs in the rallying identity matrix. As a host-post I failed, and quietly out here on the desert, James and Bymer, your friends, Cold People veterans like yourselves, became more and more dim, the thing you all fear.

Now see how the Ab'Os trap themselves (and note it, for you will wake into a world built on this).

Once the Iseult-Darrian prototypes were ratified by the Princes as true life, as an integral part of the Dreamtime fabric, they immediately had the Tell authorities do a genealogy on all the I-D cores. The lattices were codified; the disposition of every drop from the life-bottles registered and traced.

They found me standing by my forgotten Road, faltering and in poor repair, with the ghosts of two dead humans whispering through my frame, coming and going like the lonely night winds which had kept me company for so many years. The biotects were vastly relieved to find the hosting hadn't taken, but they discovered that James and Bymer — what was left of them — nested deeply in my plasmatic soul. The recovery team did an immediate search on my two passengers, to find if my life — they called it that, even then — was tainted at all. That search took them back many years, a long way indeed, but Immortality produced the mandatory records as readily as the Tell staff had mine.

James had been a semiologist, a specialist in signs; Bymer was the colour symbologist who had once advised the Ab'O biotects on the inlay designs for the Living Towers at Fosti. Even by tribal standards, they were great men, worthy men. Had been.

The problem wasn't so great then, after all. The technicians restored and adjusted my sensors, honed my dim-recall rods, added valuable new laminations to my diligent, bounty-box and shaft. Artists touched up the totemic panels on the lower eight feet; Clever Men consecrated them anew.

But they couldn't move me. Their own rulings about the ritual placement of road-trees, arrived at more than a century before, back when the belltree program became the definitive artform of the tribes, the focal point and repository for all their life-science endeavours, meant that I had to stay out in the desert, measuring my length of Road for passing ships, precious and refurbished, belonging to no tribe, a rogue Iseult-Darrian. A rogue, do you see?

They kept the secret of my value well and made the refurbishing subtle so no passersby would tell. And without knowing it, they gave me the Captains.

The story of Tom, my last Captain, resolving even now, today, as I speak, is the story of them all. Let me tell you of it and of him.

2

Sajanna Marron Best, that hard wise wonderful woman, two hundred years old, once proud, once cruel, once young and, then, achingly beautiful, the subject of more legends and longings than you would believe to see her now, had you the eyes, found Tom on the Sand Quay at Twilight Beach that day. She moved among the great sand-ship hulls under a hot morning sun, with three robed Kurdaitcha assassins, and stopped by the mooring where Tom and his old kitemaster, Scarbo, were discussing their charvolant, *Rynosseros*, so recently won in the ship-lotteries at Cyrimiri. The rest of Tom's crew — Rim, Tremba and Kylas, were still on shore leave.

"We must talk," she said with characteristic directness, startling both men with her strong distinctive voice and with her fearsome entourage of avengers. When she introduced herself, the looks of astonishment on their faces remained. Because of the implants in Sajanna and her silent companions, I know what took place.

Ab'Os on the Sand Quay. Tom and his kitemaster were no doubt wondering why. Kurdaitcha and this one, the ancient Ab'O biotect, this famous, worn, haggard scientist away from her labs and testing-chambers. I saw it on their faces. Around them, other sand-sailors watched with awe and amused curiosity, then turned away, not wanting to antagonize Kurdaitcha.

The small group boarded *Rynosseros* then, and below-deck in the main cabin, with Scarbo posted on the docks to warn off intruders, she announced her purpose. She told Tom about the Captains and about me, a little of the account I have just given you, and, typical of Sajanna, she was amazingly frank.

And understand! Here were two people who came to love one another in their short time together, who might have been lovers, dear friends, life companions. Here they were, separated by more than a hundred and seventy years, by too much time, each of them trapped in the years which I know is the constant, charming, despair-ridden tragedy of human life — the source of the strange longing looks men and women sometimes show, the incommunicable sadness in the eyes of the old regarding the oblivious young. The might-have-beens.

Sajanna showed nothing of this, though telemetry revealed the warmth of her response to him, and gave what she saw: the tanned, blue-eyed face of a man barely thirty, with a full mustache, strong browline and brown hair swept back in the style of so many National sailors; a man of medium height and build, wearing plain buff-coloured mission fatigues adorned only by the bright new charvi insignia below the right shoulder. She did not mention that she had watched his dreams in the Madhouse, that she had sought him for reasons she would never divulge to another living thing apart from me

— her child. She spoke briefly of the six Captains in the Great Passage Book, then concluded in her calm unhurried way.

"Since I am the last of the Tell biotects responsible for the graftings which produced this rouge tree, it has been decided that I am responsible for it now. These stoney-faced avengi you see about me here are both my servants and, in a sense, my executioners. Their leader has yet again made me an honorary Pan-Tribal Kurdaitcha. He has Clever Men who will hunt me, sing me, for failing my mission, or dispose of me some other way unless I can account for why the names of National captains are appearing in the Book."

"This is Dreamtime business," Tom said.

"Absolutely. You know what the oracle trees mean to us, I think. Are supposed to mean. The belltree program was part of a sacred quest in the truest possible sense. We esteemed that Artificial Life then more than we do now, with proper reverence for what we had done. Think of it! Non-human life conferring with us, counselling us, made by us but never owned, sharing life-views *we* had nurtured but could never have ourselves. They became privileged and wise counsellors — the best, the most sophisticated of them. It was considered fitting, and there is a powerful tradition still, despite the years of cynicism and uncertainty. Technically, they remain oracles, though mostly they are cherished as quaint and fascinating relics. Their status was never revoked, you see, probably because it was never used this way. This rogue is giving out Colours to non-Ab'O captains of its own choosing, then entering those names in our Records beside those of our greatest battle-captains."

"How did it start?" Tom asked. "What made the rogue give its first Colour and cause all this?"

Sajanna shook her head, unable to risk more, forced to hide so much from this man she needed more than she could say, if indeed he was the right choice. "Persecution, Captain, though, admittedly, we were slow in reading the signs for what they were: the budget cut-backs, the political disfavour, the increasingly strict security measures — allegedly because of threats from True-Lifer groups. Fewer projects were sanctioned; fewer AIs cleared for release. We discussed the trends and where they could lead; we were aware of True-Lifer factions gaining power. And, ironically, this tree saw it all and understood something had to be done. Perhaps it monitored strategy discussions or com messages, who can say? — it was always inquisitive and surprisingly resourceful. It took a chance; made sure our expertise was needed. It went straight to our most prized honour system and entered National names."

As Tom listened, I think he sensed the old woman's dilemma, suspected that she was being made to serve her enemies, and had to play a part, both revealing *and* concealing. The intent looks of her silent companions must have confirmed it.

"Is there method here?" he said. "Were they the first Nationals to happen along?"

"Oh no. These men were carefully selected. They passed some test, were chosen, then completed some service for the tree. We need to know what these duties were. We need to control this, you understand. Nothing like it has ever happened before. This rogue is an I-D oracle after all. We must accept its rulings unilaterally the moment they appear in our comp systems. So we must stop it."

"Tribal investigators would . . ."

Sajanna laughed, a sharp bark of amusement.

"Do you know what it said to our tribal investigators, to our senior biotects, to me? Not a word! Not to me, not even to the ones who restored the thing. Six Nationals are its only audience now. Each one Coloured and named in the Great Passage Book. We suspect it will talk to another National captain."

"And will probably give a Colour and a mandate. Do you want that?"

"That is our gamble, Captain Tyson. And our deal. You are newly out of the Madhouse, with reasons to seek Ab'O support. You have just won your ship; now you need licences, accreditation, funds."

"Yes," Tom said. "I do."

"But more to the point, you know the machines in the Madhouse. I've seen your records. You will not be swayed or wooed by Artificial Life as others might. We will give you a permit and the details of where this roadpost is located. Yes, it will probably Colour you and give you the same liberties as the rest, but this time the captain we send will have made a blood oath with us first, to serve us and use those same perquisites for the tribes once he has put an end to the rouge's mischief. The only National captain the tree gets now will be our man. Working on our terms. The tree can have you as its seventh, briefly, while we solve the mystery, solve the problem. And you *will* solve the mystery!"

"If I can."

"You will," Sajanna said, and some of the old Kurdaitcha ruthlessness returned to her eyes, fed by bitterness and disillusionment, by the fast-fading hopes and longings this woman had that the tribes might someday accept the very life alternatives they sought so relentlessly.

"You have been turning back other National ships approaching the area?"

"True."

"Destroying any?"

"Only two. Satellites found them first. Laser strikes from orbit. The rest have been turned back. All ships are barred from the region indefinitely.

The other Coloured Captains could get through, but they know how provocative that would be right now. We need only worry about strays and pirates, the reckless or the curious, bold Nationals on a dare, freight or mercenary captains who think running any blockade is fun."

"You mean to use the tree's own system against it."

"That is the plan," Sajanna said, and I believe Tom did understand — was sure that she spoke now for someone else, someone who had only lately decided to use this approach to the problem.

There was a pause while he considered the situation.

"Well?" the old woman said when a silent minute had elapsed.

"I have no choice here," Tom answered.

Sajanna gave another bitter laugh. "No. Nor have I."

Tom did research that afternoon. He sat in the stern cabin at his ship's comp systems and used Sajanna's private codes to access the data he needed, while two Kurdaitcha waited on deck and the third went off about some errand.

Sajanna came in at 1450 and sat to one side in a hand-carved chair, her frail lined-velvet hands pressed over her dark-velvet face as she meditated, probably reflecting on the weave of chance which had brought her to this.

First, Tom confirmed all that the old biotect had told him, that across nearly ten years the rogue belltree had chosen six National captains to be its champions, and that for the performance of some unknown task — and in order to do it — each had been assigned a Colour and given an all-lander mandate, a gift beyond price for any National limited to the coastal territories.

The Colours were easy to fathom: my ghost, Bymer, had been a colour symbologist after all. To any observers, he had apparently supplied me with my colour symbols, just as James' ghost would have provided the mind-sets elevating those colours into special meanings, my private mysteries.

For Tom, however, translating the colour-symbols was Task Number Three. The first was to discover what secret missions had prompted the action, the second was to stop the process.

Towards evening, while he was reviewing the Tell material on personality bonding, Sajanna left her chair and came to stand by him. Tom did not hear her. He pushed back from the display to find her there, then asked the question that let her reveal more of her true position. He had already deduced she would be monitored. Now he entered into the conspiracy, and spoke for the benefit of her unseen superiors.

"Dr Best . . . Sajanna" — she did not correct him — "if this tree is serving the Dreamtime for you all, why not let it give out its Colours, do what it likes?"

And his eyes explored the flawed velvet of her face. Perhaps he sought further confirmation. Perhaps he found it in the barest suggestion of a smile.

"I mentioned politics," Sajanna said softly. "Expedience. The last thing the tribes want are non-Ab'O heroes acquiring status, usurping the Dreamtime privileges, bringing other Nationals into our deserts."

"But if this Iseult-Darrian is an oracle tree, as you say, then its rulings remain sacred. Unless, of course, the tribes proclaim it mad, say it was tainted by James and Bymer. That would void its rulings wouldn't it?"

"They tried that," Sajanna said. "But other Iseult-Darrians endorsed its decisions, said the rogue was sane and whole. National interest increased, as you can imagine."

"Then you *must* accept the Captains too, accept that there is some worthwhile reason behind it all." I think Tom spoke to show he was her ally.

"Exactly what I have told the tribes," Sajanna said, acknowledging his place in this, confirming hers. Then she moved to the large stern-windows to watch dusk settle on the desert beyond. "They do accept — grudgingly, secretly, many of the Princes. But in view of so little information about a dangerous trend, it is expedient for them that the trend be controlled."

Tom frowned. "And how many other 'honorary' Kurdaitcha like yourself have forfeited their lives already because of this? Six?"

The Ab'O woman turned to him and nodded. "Yes."

"And they were your colleagues at Tell, weren't they?"

"Yes," she said, and I knew she admired his quickness. "It is as you saw in my files. The first captain was Phaon Afervarro, the famous songsmith himself. When the tree gave him Gold, Satra Amanty was in charge of the Tell life-houses, the wise leader of our team, a great man, an innovative man, my teacher. The head of the Pan-Tribals appointed him honorary Kurdaitcha as I am now, his life held forfeit, and gave him a month — no more — to discover why the tree had done it. At the end of that time, the singers began. His body was found at his desk shortly afterwards."

"That is madness!" Tom said.

"It is. A useful and expedient tradition also," the old biotect said, always concealing her heartbreak because the assassins were listening and there were things she had to do. "And a way for worried Princes and tribal factions to limit the power of the life-houses, to make up for the more disturbing excesses of ambitious predecessors. When the tree gave Lucas Red a year later, Amanty's successor suffered the same fate. This time, however, realizing the difficulty of the problem, and noting National media interest, they allowed Chen Colla two months."

"But no luck?"

"Again, no. They sang him too, hunted him down his mind-line. He was found lying dead in the desert. You see . . ."

But Tom indicated the screen, to save her the sudden rush of distress he read in her voice. "There were seven biotects on the original Iseult-Darrian project. They mean to halt the opposition from that quarter by eliminating the whole team."

Sajanna nodded, and I noted her relief, her gratitude again, though it barely reached her ancient face. The same relief, the same gratitude Amanty, Colla and the rest had felt when their appointed Captains were proven to be worthy. "Yes. That is what they intend. The head of the Pan-Tribal Kurdaitcha is Bolo May." (At last she named him!) "He has used these alarming dispensations from the rogue to justify doing what he has wanted to do for years: the dismantling of all Artificial Life programs." And the old scientist smiled. "He is our Matthew Hopkins — our Witchfinder General."

"What of the rest?" Tom asked, saying what he already knew from comp, speaking it to give what reassurance he could. "Four other Captains means . . ."

"The same. Eventually the same. Alliga, Mitroy, Lang, my old friend Taber, all forfeit. The rogue refused to speak to any of them. The chosen Captains said nothing; most went on voyages to distant States, using their special status to evade Kurdaitcha and Clever Men. It was as if the tree was taunting us. Each time we lost a chief investigator, the tree created a new Captain, and so caused Bolo May to select yet another of us. Now, finally, after ten years, it is my turn. Bolo May kept me for last, I'm certain, and — for reasons approved by the tribes — I have been given far less time than Amanty had. Less than a week."

"But why so little time?" Tom demanded. "If the tribes want this solved, surely they would give a more realistic time-frame."

Sajanna seemed distracted as she answered him. "No. It has already taken too long. Now they want this business finalized as soon as possible."

Listening to them talk, to what Tom said and how, made me sure of it then, that I had made a good choice. He had clearly grasped the reason behind Sajanna's sudden detachment. The biotect was monitored and so would need to show open support for Bolo May's commission from the tribes. But she had lost her dearest, longest, only friends, and now her life — rendered useless in nearly every way — was at stake as well, the only counter she had left in the game. That's what well-chosen, life-sensitive Tom must have realized, must have read in the tired ancient eyes.

"My answer is you, Captain Tyson," Sajanna said. "Tomorrow you go out to the tree." Then, regardless of the listening assassins, she said the damning words. "May believes I chose you because of your reactions to the AI machines in the Madhouse. What he will now learn is that I chose you *in spite of* those reactions as well, for the dreams and images you had which showed such a natural affinity for life, any life, and for our evolving and yet unchanging Dreamtime."

And moving with surprising swiftness, she went to the cabin door and locked it.

"Quickly now!" she said, drawing a small-bladed knife from her robe. "Let me have your oath before the others come. Whatever happens, I'll have that, and May might just have one more National name to contend with."

And Tom watched as the narrow blade drew blood from his wrist and from her own, then repeated the words, concentrating on the dialect, not knowing what it was he said, concentrating even when fists pounded on the door, and the door burst open, and the armed avengi were upon them.

3

Tom stood by the quiet desert Road looking up at me, shading his eyes from the glare of late morning sunlight reflected off the hot sand. All about us was desolation, just the Road stretching off in one direction to lose itself in some low hills, in the other gradually dropping down to an ancient watercourse where it could be seen winding a few times before it too vanished from sight. Apart from those few hills and that dry river bed, we were the only features in the hot unmoving terrain.

Tom was studying me, no doubt wondering how an ordinary junk-post could hold such power over the tribes.

"I'm Tom Tyson," he said finally, calling out across the dry air. His words echoed down the Road, resounded in the dry river bed, came back to us from the quiet hills. His voice was lower when he spoke next. "I've walked six k's in from their perimeter to see you."

I did not answer him, letting the silence of my place touch his soul, testing him too.

"No more Nationals will be coming unless we reach an understanding," he told me.

Still I was silent, though I used the small monitor mote Sajanna had pasted on his forehead to do a fascinating thing, to scan myself as he saw me: the narrow shaft rising six feet above the eight-foot totemic trunk, the sensor spines thrusting out, the diligent canister at the top of the main stem.

Rather than use the portable comlink he wore at one ear, I activated the old voice circuit I have used when playing out the role of oracle to wandering nomads.

"Ten years ago," I said, "the Ab'Os discovered they could not close down the belltree program at Tell and Seth-Ammon Photemos. Once made public and celebrated throughout the world, they could not demean their own amazing achievement so easily."

Tom looked about him, once, twice, then moved in closer.

"The Princes and Clever Men met the crisis in a fitting manner. I had just been restored; I had excellent data and function resources. I learned that the first part of their plan was to eliminate gradually, steadily, the entire research team responsible for the Iseult-Darrian strain, to remove the respected resistance from that quarter over a period of years — a lab accident, or an assassination attempt by angry National True-Lifers.

"Bolo May was appointed by pan-tribal dispensation and selected a strategy group. I found the means to delay them, to make them cautious. I acted in a provocative way, in a manner which I knew would make them need those very Tell specialists they meant to discredit and then discreetly destroy."

"You gave a Colour," Tom said. "Your oracle-post function."

"True. Dreamtime function. I appointed a National to all-lander status. Phaon Afervarro. And I gave out an undisclosed mission — not to an Ab'O who deserved such a privilege, but to my own first Captain."

"They got around that."

"Yes. One by one they made the Tell biotects responsible for discovering how and why the aberration occurred."

"They would have been killed anyway," Tom said, standing quite close now, reacting to the ion flux from my bounty-box, affected by the mood-bending emissions.

"Yes. But at least the Kurdaitcha did not return to their original intention. It was a delaying tactic only. It bought ten years in which they needed those specialists. But they were shrewd, those avengi. They would not let the Tell biotects communicate with me directly, no comlink, no transmissions of any kind. Bolo May made sure of this."

"He must have had other trees, other comp systems probe you. Then and now."

Which was another astute observation from Tom Tyson.

"Yes. Constantly. But there is the randomizing element of James and Bymer," I told him. "My own strategy is filtered through mysteries devised by identity matrices they cannot access, rendered in code. Bolo May can yet harm the things I love, but he cannot decide how to undo the harm I have done in adding to the Great Passage Book, and he cannot understand what it is I am doing."

"What of the missions you gave the Captains?" Tom asked, serving Sajanna, honouring the small wound on the inside of his right wrist where the blood-bond had been drawn. I was grateful to him for that though it put us at odds for this first meeting. "Could May not find ways of invalidating whatever they were?"

"You are still new to the Roads, Tom," I said. "A mandate is binding on all or none. Either the Great Passage Book exists and is valid with its liberties and honours or it doesn't and isn't. The Kurdaitcha tried, but the missions were carried out. There is that much consolation — knowing how furious May must be."

Tom nodded, but absentmindedly, considering things I had no way of discovering. He turned and looked along the Road in each direction, at the dry river bed and the low silent hills, glanced up at a single wisp of cloud half a mile overhead. For a moment I used his forehead mote again to scan the world rather than use my own sensors. It let me see myself beside my Road. It let my ghosts behold their lonely home. I felt them stir in me at the sight. This is what we are, what you cold hearts may one day become.

"Why did you choose those captains in particular?" Tom asked.

"They passed a test."

"Which is?"

I did not answer so he tried again.

"Will I be Coloured?"

"You are a sworn tribal man."

"You heard Sajanna Marron Best speak of expedience. Like her I am a slave to the Kurdaitcha. It is a price I pay for the small favours any National needs. I recently won . . ."

"*Rynosseros.* A fine ship."

"You know that, of course," Tom said.

"I am tied in to Tell, Seth-Ammon Photemos, Cyrimiri, other places. I know how the lotteries go. I minded you in the Madhouse."

Tom frowned, piecing it together, but working with the little he understood. I could not tell him then how effectively May had limited me, how a hundred powerful comp systems burdened me with questions and demands, how sapper units constantly worried at me, how I was cut off from all but Tell and a handful of locales. With the Kurdaitcha monitor fitted to him, I could not show my limitations, tell him that the Book was the only real solution left to me, that I now depended on my Captains and my final creator to do what I could not, passing on my account to Cold People like yourselves through the few other connections left to me, so that if I fail at least someone will know what was tried here.

The empty Road, the solitude of this lonely place, were deceptive, though still a blessing. But Tom, remembering the cunning dream machines in the Madhouse, perceived it in his way, though no doubt I seemed aloof and arrogant, a cool dispassionate thing.

"There'll be no more Captains," he said, returning to his assignment. "No more names in the Book. Please, help me now. Help Sajanna. Why did you choose those Captains? What were their missions?"

"I will not tell you."

"Dr Best will be sung! One of your own makers!"

"I cannot save her. May will eliminate her one way or another. Let the Ab'Os bear the consequences of what they have made."

"Artificial Life!" Tom said, resorting to scorn, out of a sense of futility perhaps. "A clever imitation!"

"Possibly. But I don't know that. I feel as if I live."

"That's the personality grafting. James and Bymer have accelerated your sensitivity."

"Tom, can we forget this? It is not an issue for me."

"Sajanna will die!" he cried. The low hills, the dry river bed echoed the words, distorting them, sending them back as accusations.

"That's a terrible, unnecessary thing. It is partly why I refuse however. I will not have them create what I am, lock me into a purpose over the lives and dreams of so many, then revoke it all when it suits them. Sajanna deserves this vindication. Ask her. It is more important than her life."

"You make it sound very wrong of them."

I tried to calm him, to ease the hard feelings in him. "Petulant, punitive, unhuman. Their responsibility, just as I am, whatever I am."

I could see Tom agreed, that much as he resisted Artificial Intelligence, he knew I was doing no less than the Ab'Os themselves were doing.

"Understand, Tom," I said, aware of my dear Sajanna, of the spiteful Bolo May, listening, watching. "I must not change on this. You are a captain with a good fast ship. Protect Sajanna if you can. If they will let you."

Tom turned and began to walk down the Road. I could not help calling to him.

"What will you do?"

He did not turn, but kept walking towards the dry hills.

"Find the six Captains!" he called back.

"They will not tell you."

But he did not answer.

4

When he was back at the Twilight Beach moorings close on sunset, even as he made preparations for the following day to leave the Sand Quay and seek out the scattered Captains, Tom met Bolo May at last.

Once again Sajanna came to the Quay, but this time she had with her six robed Kurdaitcha, five carrying power batons, as if anyone would dare attack them, and the sixth, a short heavily-built man with severely cropped hair, wearing a pair of exquisite Japano swords, a striking red and gold set in contrast to the dark red-black Pan-Tribal djellaba he wore. Bands of colour, the same red-black of old blood, divided his already dusky face into panels, thwarting an easy grasp of the man's features, but he was one to be seen only at a glance for his power to be evident.

Tom did not know it, few Princes were even aware of it, but Bolo May was at that time probably the most powerful man in Australia, the only Ab'O to be allowed a personal satellite for the duration of the crisis.

Sajanna knew it; all the Tell biotects had realized it early on. May had manipulated affairs in a unique way. And like so many powerful, privileged servants of the common good before him, the clergy, the generals, the bureau chiefs of history, Bolo May had used his office quietly, cunningly, to build an invisible empire about himself.

But Tom dealt with more immediate things than that single terrifying truth. More disturbing than the knowledge of the sixth Kurdaitcha's identity, of who it was that painted face belonged to, was May's silence.

When Sajanna had introduced him, she then asked the questions he had obviously put to her earlier, leaving May to stand watching, his eyes like petals of black glass.

"Where will you go first?" she said.

Tom tried to meet the Kurdaitcha's dark gaze, but finally turned to the old woman and made his answer to her.

"I have the last-known port registrations for the six. Afervarro is at Jarrajurra, at the Spoiler sites. Massen and Glaive are bound for Angel Bay. Traven is north of Adelaide; Doloroso is taking Clever Men to Port Tarsis; and Lucas is on a layover at Inlansay."

"You prefer this course of action to dealing with the tree?" Sajanna asked, another question from May. "It will take time."

Tom made himself face the forbidding form standing off to one side.

"The tree does not care if Dr Best dies. It knows your intentions, Lord. It knows many things I do not. That probably you do not. I sensed purpose in what it was doing — careful, patient purpose."

Bolo May chuckled, a single short sound of derision.

"Do you also know it Coloured you?" he said. "Blue."

Tom stared in surprise. "Did it? But I thought . . . Why?"

Again Bolo May chuckled, turning so his back was to them both.

Sajanna answered. "The tree could not do otherwise. Once your name is registered at Tell, you no longer have to wear that." She pointed to the sensor mote on Tom's forehead. "You serve yourself. Or, more to the point, because of your oath," — and she looked across at May — "you serve me."

Bolo May swung about. "And you are damned for that, Sajanna," he said softly, poisonously, but with a curious touch of amusement, as if an old rival had suddenly proven unpredictable again and somehow worthy. "Whatever second thoughts I may have had are gone."

Then he explained what he meant to Tom, before Sajanna could. "The oath you gave before you left for the tree was meant to be to the tribes. Dr Best was careful to have you repeat words in a quite obscure dialect originated at Tell, to make it an oath to her exclusively. We have finally deciphered it. So if she dies . . ."

"You are a free agent, Tom!" Sajanna said. "Within hours of my death, possibly less — minutes, your name and Colour will be confirmed in Records . . ."

"Unless you are dead also," Bolo May added.

"But I have no mission!" Tom cried. "None was given."

"There will be one," the old biotect told him.

"Really, Sajanna!" May said, controlling his anger. "Enough!"

But Sajanna did not heed the command.

"Tom, the tree treated you differently because you were being monitored too heavily. It understood the oath you had made, but we were playing for time. The Kurdaitcha might not have checked. Lord May should have been more careful about leaving us alone together, letting me arrange your oath. You will not fully appreciate what calm obedience preceded your involvement in this. I am obliged to honour certain injunctions and life-debts placed on me by my tribal heritage and now — against my wishes — by Kurdaitcha authority. My surface acceptance of those same strictures flattered and deceived him — we go back many years together. I was carefully tame before this. Now he knows better. He is here because of it — to warn you in person."

"To simply meet Captain Tyson, Sajanna, that is all. His oath might be to you, yes, but your sworn obligations are to us. It changes nothing."

"It does," Tom said suddenly. "Only the tree can cancel the names. Until then, we are your heroes. There are tribal obligations here too that you must honour."

"Until the tree removes them, yes," May agreed. "Which may be sooner than you think. But as I say, it changes nothing."

"And as I say, it does," Tom said again. "Please get off my ship!"

5

It must have been somewhere between Twilight Beach and Inlansay that Tom realized that no-one — not Sajanna, not Bolo May, not the Captains or myself, could afford to tell him what was really happening. The implants in

Sajanna, the prospect of comsat scans, gain-monitors and Kurdaitcha agents put limits on all that.

In a sense, Tom was as solitary as he had ever been shut away in the Madhouse gloom for all those subjective years, 50 years in 3 I knew from the records.

But he found comfort in that in a way, most assuredly. No man could altogether come to grips with what it meant to be given an all-lander mandate, not in the small space of time Tom had had. But since *Rynosseros* itself was so new, and the simple freedom of being outside the dark chambers of Cape Bedlam, this strange good fortune was simply one more incredible factor in a reality which was itself totally new again and totally precious.

Tom accepted it as readily and as necessarily as he had Sajanna and Bolo May. And to stave off the absurd dreamlike quality of it all, he lost himself in pragmatic things, in the running of his ship, in the immediate crisis of Sajanna's fate. He did not worry unduly about comsat scans; he knew that the sounds of a vessel in transit would hide all ship-talk not using outside com transmissions. The scanner unit bought in Twilight Beach located the half-dozen sensor motes hidden aboard by Sajanna's companions earlier; remote sensors trained on his ship would make nothing of the softly-spoken conversations carried on below-deck. Sajanna's implants — her own signs of great rank and privilege now used against her — were the only constant worry, but they were consciousness-aligned and no use at all when Sajanna was sleeping.

So Tom enjoyed this first real voyage. He took *Rynosseros* through Wadi Horn to the burning stony expanse of the Barrabarran, on to the archaeological beds at Jarrajurra where my first Captain, Phaon Afervarro, had moored his charvi, *Songwing*, close to the Adda-Spoiler excavations.

When *Rynosseros* stood beside the dig on the hot silent approach road, Tom went alone to the trenches and exposed middens, found his way among the twenty or so Ab'O men and women hard at work to where Afervarro stood talking with two site supervisors.

"Captain Afervarro," Tom called.

"Captain Tyson," Afervarro replied, his long grey hair brushed back and shining around his weathered handsome face. "Step over. But watch the pegged-out areas. We are after Spoiler mummies, and many are buried upright and fitted with biter-hoods and proximity charges. I'd hate to have you lose a foot."

"Honest tribal work," Tom said, carefully avoiding a marked-off section.

"It is that. But it lets me see the sacred Adda-Spoiler sites with their blessing. We bring out the Spoiler traitors and neutralize them. It helps us all."

They walked away from the trenches and precious funerary strata until they were amid some broken rock-forms and quite alone.

"I've been to the tree," Tom said. "I was given Blue. Now I need . . ."

"Tom," Afervarro interrupted. "At least one, probably more, of those diggers back there are Kurdaitcha. We are no doubt monitored at this moment. May will have us scanned."

"But I need to speak to the other Captains. I have to . . ."

"No. You don't. Don't seek out the rest of us. You'll learn nothing. Just go to Red Lucas at Inlansay. He has spoken with the tree since you did, used his status to make the voyage and cross the perimeter. The avengi will monitor what is said but we have devised codes. Seek him out. He may have something to tell you. And look here! Read carefully and quickly!" He opened out a small scrap of flag-foil, shading it from long-reach sensors with one hand cupping the other so Tom had to peer at it through a cage of brown callused fingers.

He will tell you how to Shield your House from harm.

"Now back to my mummies," Afervarro said, and rubbed the flag-foil against itself until it burst into flame. "You have a long journey." Then he turned to confront a site supervisor and two diggers who had hurried over and stood waiting with troubled looks on their faces.

"An order from the Adda Prince," the supervisor said. He now wore a Kurdaitcha blazon pinned to his djellaba. "You must declare the words shown to Captain Tyson."

"Say them, Tom, if you wish," Afervarro said.

"I have forgotten them already."

Afervarro smiled. "So have I."

"You must say them!" the Kurdaitcha said.

But my Captains smiled at each other, shook hands and parted, with not another word said between them.

6

At mid-afternoon on the following day, *Rynosseros* drew close to the Inland Sea. It was eerie weather to be sailing in, one of those days unique to Australia that can only be called silver days, when there is a sheet of shining white cloud from horizon to horizon and a warm blustery wind from the west bringing dust and restlessness and an odd melancholy.

Tom commented on it to Sajanna as they approached the windswept university town, with the Inland Sea on their right, a vast shield of water the colour of polished pewter, flashing dully at them as they neared the sand and water quays of Inlansay.

Rynosseros found anchorage at the Sea Yards; Tom received directions from the portmaster, then from the registrar's office, and finally located Red Lucas on the Concourse at a cafe terrace called Arms of the Sea. The captain of the *Serventy* already knew that Tom was due, and that he was my latest champion, the only one allowed near Sajanna. They greeted one another, and took drinks out to one of the tables sheltered from the full brunt of the wind. The cloud had thinned in places; now the water gleamed before them.

"I was told you would be coming," Sam Lucas said, and fingered the small comlink worn high on the throat, my comlink, effective at only a few places.

"It all feels futile when I hear this," Tom said. "It's like I'm not needed at all."

"You're the only one of us Sajanna is permitted to talk to," Lucas said. "We can try to go to her but Bolo May would block us, possibly take extreme action. Because of our unusual status, we have to walk very carefully, observe a host of tribal rituals. You don't wear his mote any more, Tom, but he reads almost everything through Sajanna's implants. Your ship is secure?"

"I believe so. We have a scanner. The crew is constantly checking. Tell me what I can do, Sam."

Sam Lucas smiled. "Do you know that right now there are five Kurdaitcha watching us, probably listening in?"

"There's no mote on me!" Tom said, then followed Red Lucas' eyeline. Several tables away, two young male students sat talking softly. To the right, on the high wall of the Arms of the Sea where it rose to form a roof-garden, another leant on the balustrade looking out at the silvery expanse of water. Near him stood a girl, also considering the Sea and the funerary islands scattered there like spikes of anthracite in their harsh chrome setting. And closer by far was the waiter, a young Ab'O quadroon clearing tables, but working too slowly, lingering, so obvious now.

Sam smiled. "While Bolo May leads the Kurdaitcha, we are under constant surveillance. You cannot conceive of what a threat, an insult, an affrontery we are to them." Then he spoke for the listeners as much as for Tom. "But we take comfort and reassurance from the knowledge that we have been chosen by the greatest of the oracle trees, that our missions and our naming are for a purpose all tribes respect, for the Dreamtime. Bolo May must honour us."

The young waiter glanced over once, a brief telling flicker of response, and Sam Lucas smiled again.

"Thank you," Tom said. "I won't seek out the others; Afervarro told me not to. But there is so little time. The mistakes . . ."

"Good mistakes," Lucas said. "We all made them. But there's only one solution. Just remember, like us, Bolo May must know when to be delicate, when to be bold. The Princes and the Clever Men have given him enormous power. They are watching him more closely than ever; they know they are setting precedents. Most Captains in the Book were named posthumously. We are living, non-Ab'O and here now, Dreamtime champions. They hate that. The tribes reacted excessively to the belltree problem. Our rogue tree responded with an equally unusual and excessive solution; the tribes then had to revise and expand their strategy. Now it's down to eight of us — seven Captains and one brilliant old Ab'O woman who is the last of those the Iseult-Darrians identify as their creators."

"Killing Dr Best won't eliminate the names in the Book!"

"You're right. So Bolo May must be going for something more. Something to discredit or harm the tree and us. Perhaps he'll try to take it over. He has sappers constantly at work on the tree, feeding in false codes, stressing the feeder lines. Perhaps there'll be assassins waiting. We may find ourselves facing Pan-Tribal ships or laser strike, disappearing without trace. Anything is possible. Now you see why we do not discuss our missions." Lucas pushed his empty glass away from him. "But what did Afervarro say?"

"It was a note," Tom said. "He destroyed it."

"You recall the words? Don't say them!"

"Of course."

Lucas nodded. "Good. You will find it a capital idea."

"A what?" But Tom understood. He saw how Lucas was alert to everything about them.

"Nowhere is really safe anymore," Lucas continued, now that he knew Tom did understand, good fine Lucas, my second Captain. "Only out there on our ships. I thought that here would be safer in a way, but no. The only advantage we have is surprise, the element of time, the scant minutes or hours we remain ahead of the avengi at this crucial point, outguessing them. When you met Afervarro on the desert, May's comsat had gain-monitors on you, listening from a hundred miles up. But it could not be in two places. While it scanned *Songwing* and *Rynosseros* together, I went to the tree."

"A strategy," Tom said.

"A desperate one, Tom. But let's speak of other things. Have you ever seen the sunsets they have here — when the sky is clear, not like this? Memorable sunsets, never to be forgotten."

Tom went to speak but stopped, momentarily perplexed by the oddly-rhapsodic turn the big man's conversation had taken, then aware that nothing Lucas said would be idle talk now.

"Ah, the colours! Do you know Bymer's work at Fosti? The colour inlays at the foot of the South Tower? No? No matter. All these colours are there, and more. The sunset gold that is such new hope for us, so brilliant and pure. The trusty reds you see out there; the tinge of green you sometimes get at the skyline, so bountiful; the palest, softest, most compassionate yellow, can you see it there, Tom?"

"Yes," Tom said, and the initial puzzlement at Lucas' words changed to fascinated understanding. "I do."

"And over there!" Lucas said, ignoring the flurry of movement behind them on the promenade. "Can you see it amid this silver and white that is the only truth now? On clear days at sunset you can even see a hint of blackness already, the promise of the peaceful dark. But still up there, look, there will be some of the blue which brings all the others into a whole, that gives unity and purpose to the whole thing . . ."

"You!"

Both men turned in their chairs and saw four armed Ab'Os approaching, young grim-faced men moving through the tables towards them. They wore fighting leathers and Japano swords under their djellabas, and their faces were newly-decorated in the totemic bands and ciphers of vendetta.

Lucas laid a hand on Tom's arm. "Be ready. This is a strike from Bolo May."

"You!" the foremost of the Ab'Os cried again. "Nationals! My grandfather was Bay Moss Tanneran. Clever Man of the Burgenin. You shame him!"

Swords flashed out, four then eight.

It was to be a lowly seaside brawl, a misunderstanding, an act by young hotheads who should have known better.

Sam Lucas heaved with his mighty arms, sent the table spinning across at them, giving Tom and himself room to get free of the chairs. Before the youths could react, Lucas had caught the waiter by the sleeve.

"You, Kurdaitcha!" he said. "Clever Man! Tell them!"

"Hold!" the waiter cried in astonishment.

"Or be damned and sung!" Lucas added in a loud voice. A crowd of passersby had gathered, tourists and students pausing to stare in wonder at what was happening. The young men stopped, angry and confused.

"Think carefully about what you say next," Lucas told the waiter. "Think very carefully."

The Clever Man did not need to do so. "Withdraw!" he said.

The leader of the young men looked uneasy. "But . . ."

"Break off! Go! I won't be blamed for this. Go!"

The youths sheathed their weapons and moved away, muttering among themselves. When they had gone, Lucas released the waiter, then led Tom along the Concourse, smiling for the unseen cameras.

"You see how sensitive they are to my ramblings about sunset. Such weather disturbs them."

And as they crossed the lawns and terraces of the university, heading towards the Sea Yards, they talked of nothing else but ships, kites and the young women they saw.

7

Forty minutes later, *Rynosseros* ran at 80 k's into the southwest under a brace of display kites: two Demis, a Sode Star and six racing-footmen. For a while Lucas' *Serventy* paced her on the 732 Lateral, but finally swung off onto the Great Bell Road heading due south.

Tom called a crew meeting on the poop and gave new orders. There was a course change, but Sajanna was below-deck napping in her cabin, her consciousness-aligned implants closed to me, and I could not be sure what it was. Tom had not yet learned to leave his ship-comp open so I could get input. He did not know of how I had managed the ship-lotteries at Cyrimiri — of the part I had played in selecting his ship for its shielded systems, did not know how carefully chosen he was.

But an hour later, he told Sajanna their destination.

"We're going to Fosti," he said. "May knows."

Sajanna nodded. Of course he did. She knew that most of his resources were directed at either the tree or *Rynosseros*.

"What can I do?" the old biotect asked. "There must be something."

Tom shook his head. "It's hard for you to be idle, I know, but please leave me to myself during the voyage. I need to work at comp. Do you know Fosti?"

"Yes," Sajanna said. "I know Fosti well."

All the rest of that day, Tom sat at comp down in the comparative quiet of his cabin, away from the roar of transit, the constant rhythm of ship-sounds.

Using the guide programs, he finally discovered and interpreted the Protected codes, and knew that May had no link to his ship — just Sajanna.

He pressed on, studying the displays and speaking to me, aware that I was listening but — beset by sappers — could tell him nothing myself. First he accessed the material on Bymer, reviewing all that was known about my colour symbologist — the work he had done on the Towers at Fosti.

"Why a colour expert there?" he enquired aloud, murmuring the words softly in the light through the stern windows.

He called up the Fosti records, saw the sealed menu, the Unavailable responses, and abandoned that for what he did have. Then he brought out his pocket recorder, keyed the pass-code, and replayed Lucas' words from Inlansay, his reflections on weather, all the while noting the Protected cipher flashing in the corner of the screen. At the words: 'sunset gold that is such new hope', he wrote 'Gold — Hope' on the pad before him. At 'trusty reds', he wrote 'Red — Trust' below the first entry. For a 'tinge of green . . . so bountiful', he added 'Green — Bounty', and beside 'Yellow' — 'the softest, most compassionate yellow' — he wrote 'Compassion'. For 'White' it was 'Truth', he decided, no doubt remembering that strange silver day; then it was 'Black' — 'the promise of the peaceful dark' — and he wrote 'Peace' beside that. Alongside 'Blue', his own Colour, he wrote 'Unity', though Lucas had said 'Purpose' as well.

Once he had the correspondences, he arranged them in Book order, as an increment pattern, then keyed them in instead of speaking them — still not trusting voice links.

Gold — Hope (Golden)
Red — Trust
White — Truth
Green — Bounty (Bountiful)
Yellow — Compassion
Black — Peace
Blue — Unity (Purpose)

There was nothing, not for the main array, not for the variants. The screen showed: No File.

Tom tried again, different combinations of the names and symbological attributes.

"It has to be a cumulative password," he said aloud, then tried the next approach, using the message from Afervarro: 'He will tell you how to Shield your House from harm', with Lucas' 'You will find it a capital idea'. The capitalized words.

Shield House.

Tom keyed that in and got a waiting signal. He added the increment pattern again and received the seven-word display left for him — for Blue, whoever it was to be — so long ago.

Shield House — South Tower — Blue

Tom cleared the screen, pushed back from comp and went up on deck, to receive a double surprise. First, he found that it was dusk, something he had known from the fading light through the stern casements but had not really noticed. Then, incredibly, he found Sajanna, not Scarbo or Rim, at the helm.

He stared in wonder, not having known that the old biotect was a duly licenced captain too.

"I had to do something," she said, and added unnecessarily: "Your men have been working hard, and I know the way to Fosti. They didn't mind."

"Should you rest?"

"I barely sleep these days, Tom. Just naps. One of the few gifts of age. And I couldn't; not in this, not now."

Tom looked about them, watched the darkening overcast sky, the sad deepening gun-metal blue of it, chill in spite of the warm tailwind, and for a time gave his attention to a long narrow opening in the cloud close to the horizon — a gash, a vent, a slash of light, an utterly forlorn thing for him to behold, to judge by his silence.

"It's so still," he said finally, a trivial remark in view of where his thoughts had been.

Sajanna smiled, a line of white silk in the dark and age-patterned velvet of her face. "Is it? Can't you feel the pressure? Above us is May's comsat. It moves as we do. Or perhaps it already sits above Fosti, waiting for us with all that power, waiting to destroy what we have built. And about us, out there, behind, somewhere, are Kurdaitcha ships, May's private fleet. We will not see them, they will not register on scan, but they are there. You have discovered what he needs to know, haven't you?"

"What?" Tom said distractedly, watching the gash in the cloud fill up with darkness. "Yes. How do you know?"

"You are up here with me. You found Afervarro; you found Lucas. There are no Captains at Fosti but we go there now. The tree has told you something . . . no, you've found something, something left by the tree in *Rynosseros*' comp."

"I could always write what . . ."

"No! Optical, remember!" Sajanna said. "My implants are fully optical as well. And I would be violating oaths to the tribes. For all my dreams and beliefs, I'm not completely one of you in this."

"All right, woman!" Tom said, smiling. "Then you suffer!"

"Yes," she said, laughing. "I do."

It was so good to hear Sajanna laugh, to know that she could still do that, that sailing *Rynosseros* was a healing positive thing for her, a way of forgetting for a while, of reaching back and cancelling out the years — the loss those years represented, a way of bringing some of those scattered pieces together.

They stood side by side, almost touching in the night wind, growing closer and amazingly closer despite the years and in spite of the ships and the watching eyes of Bolo May.

8

The next day was brilliantly fine. All morning great lions of cloud lazed by overhead, dividing the sky into vast corridors of air and light, making every kilometre too vivid to be wearying.

At 1420, Tom stood with Sajanna in the bows and scanned the shoreline of the dry desert sea ahead, watching the handful of lonely Towers grow larger.

"Fosti," Sajanna murmured softly, almost to herself, obviously recalling this abandoned life-project and the strange clutch of artefacts it had produced.

The first of the Living Towers — the only partly-successful North Tower — was in poor repair. Stones had fallen away, exposing the pump system and part of the CNS-Vitan stem, showing where robbers had looted the life-chambers and storage rooms, and breached the feeder tanks. Then came Sun Tower East and Sun Tower West, the famous Mad Tower, the Lonely Hatter, the Bent Tower, the White Tower, all bleached sandstone and sephalay, still dazzling with its limestone facings, and further along the desert shore, the South Tower.

Out on the desert sea itself, a sad ruin in the afternoon light, stood Summer House, the only serious attempt the Towers had ever made to create one of their own kind, a deformed and deranged creation abandoned long ago. Beside it, the first tiers and foundation conduits of Little Brother rose a few pathetic feet above the red sand. And that is what Fosti had remained — a brave attempt to bridge the gap between architectural form and organic life. Few people visited them now, and at night there was only the keening of the diligent chambers and the mournful chattering of the Sun Towers to one another across the cold dry air. Still, the monitors registered life-fields about their hulks, distinct if faint auras, whatever they meant.

Tom had never seen the Towers first-hand; Sajanna had studied them exhaustively more than a hundred and eighty years before, and, bridging the epochs of her life, had even led a routine Tell expedition into Lonely Hatter one hundred and seventy years later, following the deaths of Amanty and Colla.

Now, as *Rynosseros* rolled down the access road, they watched in silence as one after another of the distinctive shapes moved across their line of sight.

"Bolo May has to be close by," Tom said, as the access road dwindled to an apron of stones before the last structure in the group.

"Yes," Sajanna said. "Very near."

The rest of the crew, Scarbo, Rimmon, Kylas and Tremba, saw to the turning and anchoring of the ship, while Tom put a sensor mote on his forehead, tied in to ship's comp and so to me. Then he took his captain's sword, a Japano-style blade made in Spain under the guidance of Tensumi, and set out for the South Tower, heading towards the small enrichment door at the base.

He found Bolo May waiting for him there, sitting alone at the foot of the Tower on some discarded and semi-bonding blocks of chindlian tri-sephalay, his own splendid swords across his lap, his red-black djellaba hanging open over old black fighting-leathers, his banded face expressionless.

There were only the two of them. The occasional noises Tom heard, the tiny spills of gravel, the creaking and ticking sounds, were caused by the Tower itself, by the sephalay blocks expanding and shifting in the heat, by the pumps working away deep within, not by hidden Kurdaitcha waiting in ambush.

Again I observed the paradox of this land: the ancient unrelieved emptiness, and the sure knowledge of what filled it now — of the constant scanning, of May's comsat focusing exactly, precisely, on where they met. No Prince had ever used his tribal satellite as relentlessly as May used the special unit assigned to him. Though the life-fields of the Towers interfered, the sensors probed regardless, taking whatever they could.

"Close to the sephalay like this," May said suddenly, leaning in close to the stones, "you can feel the life of the Towers. We are in their fields. They shield us; play tricks with our monitors. But sitting here I can almost understand the compulsion, see why the biotects return to it — to this single-minded quest of theirs."

"Why here then?" Tom asked. "If the readings are difficult?"

May looked along the desolate sand-shore, strangely serene in his power but plainly distracted as well.

"I have advice to give," he said, turning his eyes back to Tom, coming back in from the desert again. "Sometimes I want no records kept."

"And this advice is?"

Which was an unfortunate question for Tom to press with just then, for Bolo May was at his most disarmed, his most reflective and human and exposed. He was possibly recalling things which none of my Captains knew: how once a young initiate named Bolo May had applied to the Tell directors for an apprenticeship at one of their regional life-houses, many years ago, too many hardening spoiling years, so that the life quest of the man became the measure of a crucial rejection, a truth long since put out of mind. Tom should have asked: "Why?", but he did not. He already thought he knew why.

"Sajanna has so little time," May said. "I almost have the tree. There is so much contamination, so many sappers and seedings that I doubt it can protect itself much longer."

"Go on," Tom answered, still relentless, missing the inclination to reverie and sharing, the reaching out in the man, not seeing it for what it was.

"If you fail and Dr Best dies, the crisis changes and my power necessarily ends. Why do you think Sajanna was allowed just the week? *One* week? It was not wholly my doing. Different tribal factions pressed for it, more worried by me than the tree, wanting this whole business with the biotects settled. Who can predict how the Princes are reacting — what they will now do to be free of me; at what point they will count their losses and revert to the conditions of ten years ago? I may very well lose everything: my rank, my orbiting comsat with all its weapons, but worse, do you see? I am shamed. I have left the tribes with their problem still, which . . ."

"Which was never a major problem," Tom said. "Not really. Not until you saw room for personal advantage, the pursuit of some private vendetta, convinced the Princes and persecuted the biotects at Tell. That made the tree react, which then justified your precipitate action."

Bolo May nodded once. "What does this tell you?"

Tom blinked in the glare of the afternoon sunlight, intently watching that register of the Ab'O's banded face which held the eyes. "You will do anything rather than face that shame."

"Hah!" The Kurdaitcha's laugh echoed around the stones. He smiled, the first smile of three in the exchange. "Sajanna did choose an innocent to save her! Rather than lose my *power*, Captain Tyson! My power, do you see? The control and privilege which only crisis brings, which no Prince can ever truly have, a crisis condition I need to see endure. This tree and I share an understanding, but it has forgotten something. If you do not succeed now with your original mission on my behalf, providing me with the means by which I can unlock this abomination's mysteries, then even as Sajanna dies, before I forfeit my powers, I destroy you, the Captains and the tree. So at least part of my mission will have been accomplished: the biotects eliminated. All the tribes need to do then is live with the insult of seven National names in the Book — a certain but small insult considering."

Tom understood May's preferred scheme now. "You would take over the tree," he said. "You would have it continue to make Captains, aggravate this problem for the tribes! At least until a more lasting power-base exists for you."

But May was looking at the desert once more, and Tom soon did so as well, watching the ruins of Summer House and Little Brother out on the sand-sea, shimmering in the heat. In the silence, he lifted his gaze to the mass of South Tower looming above them. He heard the gravel spills and the ticking of hot stones and the sudden eddies of wind which often sang about the structures.

"The tree knew you would do this," Tom said at last. "It knew ten years ago when it first named Afervarro and gave him Gold, when it still had Satra Amanty and Chen Colla and the others to work with, to make plans with. It even arranged for me to have a ship with shielded systems. Yes," — he said when May looked back — "I discovered that yesterday. Probably arranged it ten years ago. It will have taken other precautions."

Bolo May allowed himself a second smile, more shrewd and knowing than the first. "I am closing down all its resources. I am building walls, driving in spikes of unreason, saturating it. You cannot imagine what stresses are present now. There are so few links open to it: one to Records and the Book and the Sculptury at Tell; one to your comlink, though that is intermittent now and monitored; one to some place at Immortality, very few."

"It will have taken other precautions," Tom said again, feeling little of the confidence he tried to show on his face.

"Then be careful, Captain Tyson. For the moment I believe that is so, my proud little leveller up there will burn your precious tree, your Captains, the life-houses, everything, all over in seconds."

"You have an answer," Tom reminded him. "Do not let them kill Sajanna. Work to spare her and let the status quo remain! Accept what your people have made — there has to be some purpose!"

A third smile, hard against the stones, sharp and deadly between the bandings on Bolo May's face.

"And still I lose my privileged position. No, Captain. There is no going back for me. And it would do no good. The tribes know Sajanna's mission. At midnight tonight, the appointed Clever Men begin to sing her. By midnight tomorrow she will be dead. Nothing can be done unless you solve the mystery of the tree before that time. Then and only then can I make a claim for continued special status. I only pray for all our sakes that you do not fail."

Bolo May rose and set off down the red beach to the sand-sea. From behind Summer House and Little Brother, as if by magic, appeared the low armoured hull of a ninety-foot charvolant, May's lean flagship, *Ingrin*, summoned by implant from its hiding place. May was several metres out on the sand when he turned and called back.

"And don't bother to seek out some message in Bymer's colour inlays, Captain Tyson. It is regrettable, but those inlays no longer exist."

Tom watched the figure dwindle in size till it reached *Ingrin* and blended with it, black on black, and the sleek deadly vessel moved off into the north, its thirty black kites filling the sky.

9

Tom searched all the same, and found the seared remains of Bymer's totemic work — the fused wounded sephalay making an almost stylized melt-band around the bottom twelve tiers on the northern face. May had been thorough.

But Tom was not dismayed. He knew that Red Lucas would not have mentioned the inlays if they were so important, and knew therefore that Fosti's South Tower had some other part to play, a legacy from a time when the tree knew it would someday have this added ruthlessness of Bolo May to contend with. The wonder of it was that May had bothered to burn the precious facings — spite as much as thoroughness had to be his motive, for like Tom he would have assumed Lucas' remarks rendered them unimportant. And then assumed, for that reason, that they *did* have a part to play, and then assumed on and on until it became expedient to act, just in case.

On *Rynosseros* once more, down in his cabin, Tom began to suspect what the Tower's other key role could be. Yet again he accessed the Coloured Captains' program on comp, though now he smiled to see the final words displayed there before him.

Shield House — South Tower — Blue

For this time Tom saw that line as a password in itself, and keyed those same five words back into comp.

And obtained a new display:

Repeat — Transmit at 98236FJN — Repeat

Tom adjusted the settings for that frequency, not yet aware of what his ship's com systems could do. That password sent a coherent amplified pulse into South Tower's dim quasi-organic core, into the receiver wave that surrounded the structure and formed its life-aura — a wave newly-replenished by May's own laser-strikes at the colour inlays: power sucked off by drone accumulators hidden behind the decorated sephalay, snatched and stored in the living stone — though even without Amanty's modifications to Bymer's inlays, the signal may well have carried: South Tower had the strongest life-flow readings of them all. That signal triggered, in turn, amid spills of gravel, a similar pulse back from Lonely Hatter half a kilometre away, from an installation Sajanna had left there during her expedition eight years before, working with the very colour responses Bymer had unwittingly created, following on with a plan Amanty and Colla had devised.

The signal brought four words to Tom's screen:

Shield House — Tell — Blue

"Tell!" Tom cried. *"Tell!"* And when he keyed in that line as a password, he was given maps, building plans and detailed schematics.

He saw too what his mission was in that flood of data, and he studied it, learning every detail, checking them over and over until night had settled along the quiet Fosti shore. He became aware that the Kurdaitcha watchers would have monitored the increased broadcast activity around the Towers, and no doubt he wondered what technology was now turned their way, what extra allocations May might have received from nervous Princes because of it.

At 1945, Tom called a meeting with Sajanna, Scarbo and Rimmon in the starlit darkness at the foot of South Tower, having them stand as close to the cooling sephalay blocks and ruined still-warm inlays as they could so the Tower's power field masked them. Kylas and Tremba remained on *Rynosseros,* searching the horizons with their deck-scans, now and then being startled by sudden cracklings of interference, by odd plays of light spilling across their screens, by biolume ghost-light flickering high in the crowns of the otherwise dark quiet shapes.

"I know the tree's mission," Tom said, and when Sajanna went to stop him, he shook his head sharply, glancing up beyond the looming mass above them, beyond the occasional twinkle of bioluminescence in the diligent chamber, up to where May's comsat listened — in spite of what May had said about dampening.

The old woman understood. This was *for* May. She did not speak, but she moved in closer to the stones and to Tom.

"Sajanna, I need to know for certain. Your implants are consciousness-aligned not autonomous?"

"I need to be conscious," she affirmed.

"Good. We will drug you so that when they start singing you tonight you will not suffer. Also May will have no input. There is a Living Tower project at Tell. Shield House." He spoke as if Sajanna had not known of it, keeping his voice low and showing just the right amount of excitement. "The tree has been protecting it. A true viable Tower right there where the biotects have worked all these years, making their belltrees and mankins. It may even house the Book and Records, who can say? We will go there, verify this using the information I now have. We'll get the rest of the answers then."

"May will be there first," Sajanna said. "He could well destroy it."

"Not till he finds out what part the Captains play in the scheme. He must know that too, otherwise he has only half of it. Ultimately, he cannot change anything or justify what he does unless he knows how the pieces fit — cannot know what transgressions he might commit. It will be a hard run, Ben," he said to Scarbo. "We set out in thirty minutes —once Sajanna is drugged and stowed safely in the ship's lazaret. I will be at comp tonight and tomorrow; you and Rim will have the deck. Tremba and Kylas can alternate on sending a com transmission out to all the Captains and tribes to meet us at Tell, a manual message-repeat, you understand, so no remote misdirections can interfere. I'll tell them the exact wording when we're underway."

Forty minutes later, *Rynosseros* began her run for the coast, a desperate rush back to Tell and the life-houses there. At midnight, when the Clever Men began singing out Sajanna's life in the old way, she did not know of it except in the deepest tidal bottoms of her soul, in the darkest most secret places that a person is.

All that night the run proceeded. Tom worked and slept, worked and slept, while Scarbo and Rim swapped helm watches and Tremba and Kylas alternated at com, supervising the message-repeats:

From Blue Tyson: All tribes — protect Tell —
protect the tree — Shield House — Shield House —
From Blue Tyson: All tribes — protect Tell —

Tom could not be sure what was happening, whether that lonely call was heard or a futile thing — what the tribes thought hearing it, and what they would do — but he kept the crew at it, gambling that Bolo May would not strike at *Rynosseros,* not yet, not while a tribal summons was going out, not without knowing the part the Captains played.

At sunrise, they were at the 874 Lateral at last. Scarbo sent up the sun-snares to replenish the power cells, and filled the sky around them with a display of kites that was wondrous to see: huge red Sodes and Stars, Demis and racing-footmen, turning *Rynosseros* into a 'god-ship'.

At noon, Tremba received transmissions from a National captain who had been near Tell.

"The place is burning!" the voice said, piped through com. "Two out-buildings were hit from space. A Kurdaitcha fleet has cordoned off the area."

"The outbuildings!" Tom cried into the com mesh. "What about the Sculptury itself? The core and Immortality? The Records section?"

"Intact," the reply came. "But there's an avengi search going on. That's all I know."

Rynosseros ran on, averaging 110 k's, past Ankra and Guranjabi, along the Long Line Road to Tank Aran and Tank Feti, out onto the Great Arunta Road and towards the coast.

"Forget Tell," Tom told Scarbo at last, when the time came to make choices, in case that added deception had mattered. "Head for the tree."

"What about Sajanna?" Scarbo cried above the roar of wheels on sand.

"As safe as she can be," Tom said, so that I still wasn't sure just what he knew. "Bolo May has Tell. He'll go for the tree."

And as they reached the lonely desert Road that is my home, the weary crew saw the low crown of hills at the horizon, and above them clustered flecks of colour that meant the sailing canopies, parafoils and death-lamps of gathered ships.

Ten minutes later, *Rynosseros* reached the spot, and Tom and his crew found a Kurdaitcha fleet, twenty vessels drawn up in a battle perimeter, one of them May's *Ingrin.* There was another smaller circle inside that larger one, three ships grouped about me, facing outwards: Afervarro's *Songwing,* Massen's *Evelyn* and Lucas' *Serventy* — as many of the Captains who had been able to reach me in time.

Drawn by sun-snares now, *Rynosseros* rolled through the Kurdaitcha cordon without incident, still privileged, and joined the smaller group near where I stood.

It was a silent confrontation for the most part, no-one speaking or moving, the quiet disturbed only by the message sounding from *Rynosseros* through its hailer, the words modified now, precisely as comp had given them to Tom at Fosti, and more alarming in its steady calm refrain.

All tribes — Shield House — Shield House —
All tribes — Shield House — Shield House —

As Tom cut the message and the final words echoed off across the desert, Bolo May climbed down from his ship and walked towards me.

When Tom saw the Kurdaitcha, he left *Rynosseros* and met him halfway, though none of my other Captains did; they stayed on their ships and waited.

"There is no Living Tower at Tell," May said. "No sephalay at all."

"No," Tom admitted.

"And Sajanna?"

"Drugged. Safe. On *Rynosseros.*"

"No," the Ab'O said. "I know that too now. Her implants may yield no sensory information, but we do have status and proximity data. We know she is not your ship or even near here. Where is she?"

"At Fosti."

"So," May said, having suspected it already. "You used the Tower fields as I did, as I expected you would. But you thought to trick me further."

"I knew you'd be listening."

May ignored that remark. "We noticed the life-fields become stronger," he said. "You caused that, I think; made the Towers draw on power reserves. We thought them moribund. And Sajanna, she is alive?"

"She has until midnight," Tom said, and I could see that May's disclosures about the Towers had surprised him.

"What is the tree's purpose?" May pressed.

Tom did not reply.

"Shield House was a code word," the Ab'O persisted. "A signal."

"Yes," Tom agreed, striving to soften the anger in the man. "But I don't know for what. I really don't."

"I don't believe you. It was powered by the Fosti Towers. They gave up their poor excuse for lives to enhance the Shield House cipher."

"What!" Tom cried, and for the first time Bolo May knew that Tom understood less of what was happening than the Kurdaitcha had believed. The Ab'O's eyes unfocused momentarily between the dark bands on his face. I saw that too using my sensors.

Then he turned and strode off to his ship, more deadly in his bafflement, I knew, than in his earlier resolve.

Tom watched him go, no doubt wondering about Sajanna, about what would happen now, about what Shield House was and the precise part he himself had played in the work of the Captains.

Tom went not to his own ship then but to *Serventy,* climbing up to the deck of the 110-foot vessel, and joined Red Lucas on the poop.

"What is going on?" Tom demanded angrily, desperately worried about Sajanna lying drugged and helpless where he had hidden her, being sung to her death.

"Tom, we aren't sure either," Lucas said, not adding the rest of what he knew, not wanting Tom to ask more questions. "Where did you leave Sajanna?"

Tom hesitated, thinking of May's gain-monitors, but then must have realized that it made no difference now. "I received schematics on comp. Diagrams for one of the Towers. There was a cist near the enrichment door. I put her in there. May says the Towers then gave the Shield House program signal all their life force."

"*After* you placed Sajanna in the cist?"

"Well, yes," Tom answered. "And after I had said the words 'Shield House' within the South Tower's aura, close to the sephalay. But . . ."

"Then she may be safe. Wait and see."

"But the Towers are dead! May told me."

"He has lied!" Lucas snapped, but doubt crossed his face. "They can't be dead."

Tom grabbed Lucas' arm. "What matters now, Sam, is that May has gone to call a strike. Laser. He told me at Fosti that he would."

"Then there's nothing we can do, Tom. We can't outrun that. Wait."

Tom did. He stayed with Lucas and his men a moment longer, then without another word returned to his own ship, so newly-won, so briefly held, to be in his place for whatever came.

There was utter stillness, then some movement on *Ingrin,* though it was hard to see what, figures intent on shipboard duties.

For a moment there was silence again, a long minute in which nothing seemed to happen, just the drift of kites in the desert thermals.

Then it came. The sky filled with light, stabbing down, a brilliant arrow of lightning, and in an instant the Kurdaitcha flagship erupted, burst open, blazed like the heart of a sun. The savage tearing sound came seconds later, distinctive and inevitable, echoed off into the hills, folding away from the torch that was *Ingrin.*

Again, silence. The ships stood motionless.

Then the cries came, orders shouted from the other Kurdaitcha ships, and, incredibly for my four Captains and their tense watching crews, the Pan-Tribal fleet began moving out, turning away from the smoking ruin of their former leader's ship.

10

So my story ends even now and the waiting is over.

For a time, my Captains did not know precisely what had occurred. They knew parts, and later they spoke and pieced it together well enough, though each of them realized what Shield House had been, my way of using May's own comsat against him, an override powered by the dwindling life of the Towers.

I would have counselled my Captains then, when they stood before me, the four of them calling up their questions, but there was too much happening inside: the shutting-down of complex sapper programs, the cleaning out of intricate seedings, the consolidation, the slow restoration of some of my lost resources, the telling of this story to you.

But though I said nothing then, I made myself time for Tom, who had risked his only proven life, who, without ever really deciding to, had been willing to give his life for me.

And there had been enough time, do you see it now, you cold hearts there?

Enough time for Tom to cross the sand to Summer House carrying my ancient frail Sajanna in his arms, following comp directions he had no way of knowing would still be valid. Time enough to open the hidden door in the sephalay and locate the narrow grafting chamber, to place Sajanna within it just as the schematics had described — a place readied by Tom's saying of 'Shield House' into the living stones of South Tower. Time to place the bonding casque over her head and face, to make the connections and activate the relays. Just enough time to return to *Rynosseros* and begin that long run back towards Tell, following instructions, carrying out the message that the Towers then made their final song together, building Shield House among them even as they drew Sajanna's personality forth.

Now that Tom has departed with the others, I take time to reflect on the quiet desert once more, on the hot empty Road beside which I stand. There is so little in this desolation — only the hills and the Road and dead *Ingrin* two hundred metres out, a smouldering black flower, its petals closing in the dying light of day.

Bymer and James sigh through me as ever, briefly, a fond faded double-ghost in the false silence: one who gave me the Colours, who gave me Fosti itself, the other the secrets and mysteries and signs to use them.

I feel Sajanna very real inside too, safe now, murmuring in her sanctuary, sharing with the others, with Amanty and Colla and Taber and the rest, and deeper down, strange house guests, with Lonely Hatter and South Tower and as many of the others as I could save — all bonded irrevocably to my soul for whatever may come of it.

Blue is unity, after all, my cold cold listeners, so Bymer tells me; and soon, soon now, you will be able to come to me as well should you wish it.

But now I cannot listen to the others. Bymer's final Colour is too strong, too sweet, and I must savour what it has come to mean after all this time.

Comforted by the voices within, by the discourse of life deep down, sharing, planning life, affirming it over and over for what it is and can yet be, I signal Records to confirm the last name in the Great Passage Book. I tell them that Blue is the way of it, that Blue is all there is, and that for me everything, everything, will be that Colour from now.

The Only Bird In Her Name

That summer there were fourteen of them hunting the Forgetty, fourteen hard men with fierce eyes, minds like traps, and no compassion.

The bounty hunters met at the Astronomers' Bar and made their plans for finding the creature, or sat near the members of the Bird Club on the terrace of the Gaza Hotel discussing past hunts and this final attempt.

That was where I met Tom Rynosseros, an honorary member of the Bird Club and a sort of bounty hunter himself. He was here to locate the Forgetty too, though his task was to stop the killing, to save it if he could.

I was covering the hunt, a new assignment and an important one. Even Sam didn't know how excited I felt. He just knew, with his veteran editor's intuition, that I was good at quest stories, that they suited my personality and fed the sort of mind I had. Many journalists had tried, but I had been the one to locate Sunset Joe, the mad old charvi captain who buried treasure in the desert out near Maas, then sold his baffling maps to unknowing young sailors; to give them quests, he said, to put even more risk, danger and reward into the world.

Landing the Forgetty story on this, the last hunt, was something else entirely. I was the second female reporter *Caravanserai* had taken on, but, for all Sam's fondness, I had never made it past page two. Now I had my first real chance. The thought of being with Tom Rynosseros only made it more special.

The Bird Club and Tom were all on the terrace when I arrived, wearing their elegant Edwardian finery, carrying the polished brass binoculars that they never seemed to use. I smiled at the distinctive way these folk had of combining an exclusive *Kaffee-klatsch* with an often serious scientific salon. In the midst of it all stood the gleaming samovar, their focal point, as absurd and yet as studiedly quaint as the binoculars, the dark evening jackets of the men, the narrow gowns of the women. Wherever the samovar stood, there the Bird Club was in session.

I approached the group, showed my ident and introduced myself.

Tom stood and shook my hand.

"Beth Leossa-Tojian. From *Caravanserai,*" he said, then introduced the Bird Club members: Graeme Fowler, the President, Nathan Hawkless, John Wren, Joanne Henderson, Aubrey Quayle, Sally Nightingale, Jeremy Eagleton, and the newest member, Anton Ankil, the eccentric young geneticist who had bred a new species, the Ank, to gain membership.

"How did you qualify, Tom?" I asked.

"The position's honorary, Beth," he said, smiling. "They allow me the Dodo."

The other members smiled. John Wren, drawing me some coffee from the modified samovar, gave a mock-flourish with one hand.

I almost fell for it.

"But there's no Dodo in . . . oh, I see."

The others laughed, because I had been so earnest and so completely gulled by what was such an old joke for them.

"I swear to get even," I said, and between sips of coffee began outlining my assignment. The atmosphere on the terrace changed at once. They listened with complete attention, all traces of the former mirth gone from their faces. This was serious business for them.

Before I had finished, six more bounty hunters appeared from the south loggia and joined the three who were sitting several tables away. Their leader saw Tom and came over. I recognised the man from previous hunts, a tall African named Misla.

"Hello, Captain Tom," the hunter said. "So far from *Rynosseros.* All because of us. You will stop us, do you think?"

"If I can, Misla. If it comes to that."

"We are fourteen this time."

"I intend to be careful."

I felt the private nature of the contest between the two men. Misla had led most of the hunts in past years, had helped exterminate most of the Forgetties left in Australia. Tom had thwarted him twice, but only twice.

As Misla and Tom talked, I watched the other hunters in the African's group. They were all here on a technicality, because of a loophole in both States and Nation law. New legislation had been drafted and ratified to protect the last of the Forgetty race, but could not come into effect for two days. An interim injunction had stopped the issuing of licences within Australia, but fourteen had been sold through a scalper's office at Old Java Beach.

These hunters — Islanders and Niuginians mostly — were the last of them, with the cool desperation of that knowledge, moved by a quiet urgency and the promise of huge rewards. They were here to hunt in person, with no hi-tech weapons, but they had been given unlimited computer access before reaching Twilight Beach. They knew as much as anyone about the Forgetties, with the possible exception of the Bird Club. And they were the best, these hunters. Misla had made sure that the licences had gone to the best.

There were three Treece clones who had more than ten kills to their credit, and Paulo who had made five. I knew several of the others, too, and some who weren't with Misla now. All deadly men.

Here in the bright sunlight on the terrace in front of the Gaza, it hardly seemed possible that these groups were in such opposition, that they would put their lives at risk like this.

Or rather, that Tom would. He was here without his crew because the tribes had accepted that the Bird Club was earnestly concerned with protecting this tangental species, and had allowed them one field agent, though only one. It seemed neither fair nor realistic, but that was how it had to be. The hunt would take place on tribal land.

When Misla and his band had departed to make their final preparations, the Bird Club adjourned to the Astronomers' Bar, four of the men hoisting the samovar on its portable stand and carrying it with them. Tom stayed behind, looking at me in his oddly penetrating way as if he wanted to say something but had thought better of it.

I bridled a little, thinking for a moment that it was because I was female, but that wasn't it. He seemed to be considering whether or not to share confidences with me.

I gave him a look that I hoped made me seem trustworthy, and waited. I knew very little about Tom, just facts acquired from the popular stories, but he fascinated me, more than I cared to show openly. This was the man who had spent some subjective years in the Madhouse, probably on a 50:3 sentence for an unknown crime; who had survived it and won *Rynosseros* in the ship-lotteries at Cyrimiri. He was not as tall as the stories have it, and around thirty, though he's well-kept and looks younger. In many ways, his appearance is unremarkable, but his eyes are everything. They show that the stories can be true, that he is a sensitive accepted by the Clever Men, that he is one of the few National captains to be granted a Colour and an all-lander mandate from the Princes, allowed to sail 'all Roads, all States, from coast to coast' as the Ab'O tribes say it. Afervarro's *Songwing* was the first charvolant to win that honour, and there have been only six other ships since then.

Here was one such Captain — holding such an honour for some undisclosed service to the tribes.

I felt a definite thrill of excitement, but also of concern and uncertainty to be alone with him. I did not wish to consider my reasons then, and that annoyed me slightly. It was a confusion I put down to nerves and the unique nature of what I was about to share with this sand-ship captain — the Blue Captain — and representative of the famous Bird Club.

I found I was pleased when he suggested we discuss my part in the hunt as the media observer requested by the Club's President. Sam had been concerned that Tom would have objections there. But I sensed none, and felt rather an easy acceptance as he took my arm and led me down the Promenade, though with every step I wondered what he knew, and how he planned to locate and protect the Forgetty.

"Will they know more than you do, Tom?" I asked.

"Possibly, Beth, but not likely. They'll know kill-sites and hunt-patterns from all the past hunts, and have estimates on how this present creature will behave. I have much the same information. This one conforms to the Bale standard. We know it's a true shape-changer, though a comparatively slow one; that like all Forgetties it mimics only humans as the most fitting mask for its intelligence. We know it's definitely not androphagic, contrary to what Misla says, that it doesn't kill even when cornered. We know its bite causes loss of memory . . ."

I was taking notes as we walked. "Is that recent memory or all memory as Munce claims?"

"Recent memory, yes. And it is not immune to its own bite. Our Anton Ankil discovered that several years ago."

I shuddered. In bright sunlight, surrounded by the sound of belltrees and the ocean, there was the old fear to be mentioned again. "It's easy to think of the vampyre legends."

"Vampyres and werewolves," Tom said. "Misla's arguments ten years ago. That's where the misconceptions about the Forgetty begin. The biting. How well have you been briefed, Beth?"

"I've talked with Rossibo and Munce. I know the Bale standards — all the variants. I've scanned the report your Bird Club did."

Tom nodded. "Then you know there's no biting at all." We were near a derelict belltree, stripped long ago, its naked nine-foot shaft thrumming in the wind. He gazed at it as he spoke. "There's an ancillary tooth — a dew tooth — folded in against the lower jaw. The Forgetty presses its open mouth against the . . . victim's neck, so the tooth pierces the skin, and secretes the lethophoric. Then there's the stupor and the amnesia. But it's not biting."

"That's what Munce told me, yes. I've heard, too, that the Ab'Os are calling it the Philosopher Beast."

Tom laughed. "Yes. The Aurelius. That's the Bird Club's doing — a deliberate tactic to upgrade the creature's status, and a way of describing how the Ab'Os have finally started to see the creature. 'Andromorph Aurelius. The Philosopher Beast. The Beast of Lethe, or Forgetty. This quasi-human dweller of the coastal deserts, first identified by . . .' "

"Graeme Fowler. Twelve years ago, right? Thanks, Sam told me. Is it so enlightened? Munce fears it's just a mutation, that most of its intelligence is mimicry as well."

"That too is Misla's argument because there's no apparent purpose for the creature, no clear ecological niche for it. Mutations don't always have an obvious place in the natural order; that's the nature of mutation."

"Then what could be its purpose? What use is a humanoid mimic that is a lethophore? Is it just a highly-specialized mutation?"

"You think it's human, don't you, Beth?"

"Of course I do. Calling it an andromorph simply conceals the fact that it's another tangental. I think we've accelerated a sub-type."

"Haldane genetics?" Tom asked. "A failed tribal experiment?"

I looked across the low balustrade at the waves falling and the seagrass tossing in the wind. Near us, the belltree thrummed. "Not even failed. But you're testing me. The Bird Club already considers it to be viable and worthy of protection. And you aren't convinced that I'm not working with Misla, are you? That's why we're out here. You do what you need to, Tom, but you do believe it's viable, with a very real place in the natural order. That's where you base your whole defence, isn't it?"

Tom ignored my comment about Misla.

"Our problem, Beth, is that we simply have not been able to converse with a Beast and study its motivations."

"I find that odd. I'd say your group is committed to stopping further research, not encouraging it."

"That's because of the means researchers want to use. Once you grant the Beast its intelligence, then you grant it its desire for reclusiveness as well. We feel that when the hunts are ended, the Forgetties will reveal themselves on their terms. That option has not existed before."

I laughed. "Well done. Good honest self-determination. And you said Forgetties. You believe there are more than just this one."

"We need to. We don't approach this as scientists; more as allies. We really do want the Beasts to trust us when they are ready."

"It occurs to me that you all have an excellent reason to conceal what you know. As part of this tolerance and patience. And maybe worse."

"Worse?"

"Yes. How would you know if you'd encountered a Beast? You may have already had your encounters and dialogues, been bitten and simply forgotten. Isn't that possible? The mnemonic residue might be this unscientific caring the group displays."

Tom smiled at me, looking like some displaced Edwardian time-traveller in the harsh desert light. "We often laugh about that, Beth. Protective déjà-vu! Now and then we bare our necks to one another, looking for the signs. No, if the Forgetties are viable, true tangentals and not some short-term mutation, they deserve to live. We draw our line there. And they have never needed to infiltrate our ranks. We are already their friends. Our members know one another too well anyway. The little memory games and passwords we use make a sustained impersonation impossible."

"I was just curious."

"I know. And you're not with Misla."

"Thank you," I said, and we turned and walked back to Twilight Beach.

Tom took me to The Traitor's Face. We drank tautine and watched the ocean, then started discussing the hunt. He made me realize just how crucial an accredited observer was in what was soon to happen. This was Misla's last trophy hunt for a Forgetty, the Bird Club's last great defence.

I relaxed more and more, found that I was letting my attraction for him show easily now. The earlier self-consciousness, the concern about being seen as some infatuated neophyte, had passed. I could see, too, that the feelings went both ways, that Tom was enjoying this chance to be away from the Gaza where the hunters were gathering. He seemed pleased that I was here and would be with him in the desert.

"What made you sure of me?" I asked.

Tom evaded the question gently, making light of it.

"There's a bird in your name," he said, and though I begged to know which one, he would not tell me.

To the north of Twilight Beach are the Restoration towns — a handful of small Mayan, Phoenician and Minoan communities strung out like beads on a necklace along the coast. They are mournfully sad places, these quiet, neglected temple precincts more desolate than Uxmal or the Puuc, and these white Mediterranean settlements facing the sea.

The people there are impoverished, inbred and almost xenophobic, though they can sometimes be seen carrying the labrys or sailing sand-ships with staring eyes painted at the bows, or worshipping their re-kindled deities atop pyramid citadels more like failed ziggurats than truly steep-sided Mayan monuments.

These places are where the Dreamtime has failed, where well-meaning Ab'O mystics seeking contact with the power vectors Chac and Astarte, Tanit and the Great Snake Mother, lost their controlling hand in that quest and became used instead of user. No longer inspired by their own wisdoms, rejected by the States and even the other Ab'O coastal tribes, these outcast tainted folk have embraced the acculturization brought out of the haldane trance, and have slowly become sea-peoples like some of their adopted ancestors.

Visiting these museum towns has always been a melancholy but compelling thing for me. The people know what they have lost and what they now must be. I did not relish the thought of going among them again.

But, as Tom and the hunters knew, the Forgetty's town-room had been located in the Mayan Quarter of Twilight Beach, with a Tanit altar and other clear signs that the creature had its secret place, its omphalos, near the Mayan-Phoenician-Minoan town of Tyla. That discovery had brought the hunters in again and had led to this final hunt.

Tyla is officially a closed town. Nevertheless, the inhabitants make their livelihoods from what little tourism there is, and bar all charvis from the moorings but their own.

To go there, the curious sightseer must take passage on one of the strange Tylan ships, and travel the sacbeobs through the arid coastal desert. These holy roads are pitted and poorly maintained and sometimes prey to brigands. But to see Tyla and the rest of the Restored towns, the exorbitant fare is paid and the two-hour journey made.

The hunters knew of the arrangement and like it even less than we did, but since the rules of the outcasts are enforced by the States, there is no other way. Tom and I and Misla's unrelenting band all booked passage on the *Ahuacan*, the only Tylan vessel out of Twilight Beach that day. At noon, we boarded her, the kites went up, and the sand-ship left the moorings.

We rode in a tense silence, Tom and I down on the commons watching the dark shrouded Tylans, hardly recognisable as Ab'Os, tend the cableboss; Misla and his companions up on the poop attempting conversation with the captain.

The holy road ran through terminator dunes mostly, with the ocean to one side and seagrass flanking our course. Belltrees marked the kilometre distances, regularly at first but then more and more infrequently, until there were only fitful winds from the sea, seagrass, dust and silence.

At mid-afternoon, we came to the towns.

First there was Itlos, a handful of white buildings perched above a short span of beach, a gleaming white town built around a stone breakwater, with shipyards and three sea-going sun-ships under repair.

Then came Maas, a neo-Mayan settlement and one of the largest, with a pyramid citadel, a royal storage labyrinth in the Minoan fashion, and a determined priesthood. Near Maas there were checkpoints on the Road where other sacbeobs crossed ours on their radial course into the desert.

The Tylan captain explained who we were as he paid the corn-levy. The Maatians muttered cleansing prayers and sent us on our way.

Tyla was next, less successful than Maas or Itlos, and less defined in its acculturalization. It rose on long low beach terraces above the ocean, a hundred white buildings set about narrow streets and many small squares, like nothing Mayan or Phoenician, more Cretan or Greek if anything.

We disembarked at the quay and found accommodation, again with Misla's group, at the Phalan Gade, the only outlander hotel in the town. There we learned of our latest misfortune. Though nothing about the town showed it, there was a festival to Tanit in progress. No outlanders could leave the hotel after sunset; no-one could cross the town perimeter until the evening of the next day.

Misla's eyes were like pieces of dark steel as the Ab'O woman at the reception desk gave us the news. He glanced at the water clock on the desk and grunted some words to his men.

"Tomorrow then," he said to Tom and me in suppressed fury. Then he waited.

Tom leant in close and asked me to activate my camera.

"Let Misla see we're recording this," he said.

The African glared when he noticed the red telltale, grunted another order, and stalked away. His men followed without so much as a backward glance.

When they had gone, Tom signed the register for us, then asked if any messages had arrived for him.

The Tylan woman, with poor grace, produced a crumpled white envelope from a drawer and passed it across. Tom slipped it into a pocket of his fatigues. Then we left our bags in the woman's keeping and went out to walk the streets.

Tom had no doubts that Misla would know of the likelihood of some contact with the Forgetty. Depending on what hi-tech assistance the mercenary had on call, shielded and hidden, he may have tried for a quick operation, despite the festival, regardless of reprisals from the Tylans or the tribes. But any thought of taking the letter by force and striking out for the omphalos now had been stopped. The African needed his public image unsullied for a while longer. My camera had prevented an incident at the Phalan Gade.

But now we were away from the hotel, beyond scrutiny. Tom led us from the windy sundazzled terraces overlooking the sea, through quiet narrow streets, under strips and squares of blue sky, into a maze of blank white walls and shuttered windows. We could have been in any hot white town in Northern Africa or the Near East, though here we were surrounded by a silence that was more than the hush of the hot afternoon or the siesta. Many of the houses were deserted, and now and then we gazed through an open doorway to other open doorways beyond, and peered through those in turn into quiet courtyards and silent colonnades.

Eventually, in a tiny square at the junction of several crooked streets, we stopped. I looked up at the white walls converging on their patch of vivid blue, saw that next to me in this startling duality of light and shadow Tom was doing the same.

"You feel it, Tom?"

"Yes. The life of the indrawn breath."

"The waiting is real, isn't it? Things will happen only when we have gone away. No wonder the Forgetties come to Tyla and the other Restoration towns. I wonder how many occupy these houses, passing as Tylans?"

"You still believe there is more than one, Beth?"

"Yes. I realize I do. Possibly because I cannot accept the reality of there ever being a last one. What does the Beast say?"

I watched him take out the envelope, inscribed with his name in a faded neat script, and remove the letter from it. Tom looked about him once, then opened it out. We read it together in silence.

> Captain Tom,
>
> Thank you for coming. Thank the Bird Club. For this service to me I shall never take your face or that of those you love. I shall be direct and honest in our dealings.
>
> The hunters will guess I am among the chultunes at the Stone Door. Help me if you can, but do not risk your life. That is all I ask.

Tom put the letter away and we walked through twenty more squares like the one where we'd stopped, pausing only to savour the quiet or call one another's attention to the slightest touch of a sea breeze that had found its way through the crooked streets to us. There was no music, no belltrees, no voices, just the occasional breath of wind and the silence.

We were glad to get back to the Phalan Gade and be shown to our adjoining rooms. I watched Tom burn the letter in the small votive fire below the bas-relief of Tanit that was near the window. I noted the tension in him as he did it.

The letter helped him little, I realized, though he was glad to know exactly where the omphalos was, and that there was goodwill at least from the Forgetty in this sorry enterprise.

Misla had maps. He already knew that the omphalos was near fresh water, and that on the outskirts of Tyla were twelve stone reservoirs, stone-lined cisterns set into the earth and tapping bores, or designed for catching the run-off from coastal rainfall and fed by stone conduits. These chultunes were protected by natural rock formations, and the secret place would be somewhere close at hand.

Searching there was the obvious course for Misla. The letter confirmed it. Tom explained how the Forgetty would normally pass itself off as a Tylan to visit the town's markets, or as an outland visitor to use the excursion ships travelling to and from Twilight Beach. The lethophore would be adept at such masquerades, he said, but never before had it had so many hunters eager for its life. Misla's men were alert for mimicry and obviously had pain-tests and passwords to safeguard their group against infiltration. The Beast would not try that.

Paradoxically, the bounty hunters were safer from the creature in Tyla, where an unusually stringent security was in force for the Tanit curfew, than in Twilight Beach. By the happenings of chance, Tom explained, the Forgetty would be forced to remain out in the chultunes for the duration of the festival. It could not leave Tyla overland — the Tanit priesthood would have its Maatian counterparts alert for that. The same holy day that had delayed the bounty hunters was working against the Beast as well. It was at its most vulnerable.

"Misla will move at sunset?" I asked him.

"Yes. As soon as the festival ends."

"I'm going to follow the hunt, Tom. All of it."

"I want you there, Beth. I'll have to assume the Forgetty will not do anything. It may just wait to die. If hi-tech is used, I'll especially need a witness and media contact. What worries me is that you . . ."

"Can I fight if they try to kill me? Will that invite tribal payback?"

Tom smiled. "The moment a weapon is raised in your direction, you can fight. Let's hope the weapons they use make it possible. But the important thing, Beth, is to get the facts out so this becomes an unforgotten incident. Are you trained?"

The question made me smile. I thought of Sam, my editor, and what passed for weapons-training at *Caravanserai*. "I'm a writer, Tom. I've had house-training, that's all."

"It won't come to that," Tom said, but I saw the concern he put quickly from his eyes. "Misla will keep the rules. And please understand, Beth," he continued, and I could tell his words were to answer my unasked question, "I'm not as reckless as I sound. I'll oppose Misla only to slow him down, to use up the time he has. The Tanit festival helps me there. I knew about it but Misla did not. I am hoping he will do something foolish that will give me other things I can use. But tomorrow evening at the chultunes I will fight only till I know I cannot win any longer, then I will stop. I am a philosopher beast too, you see?"

But I sensed otherwise. I feared that Tom might not have time to discover if the omphalos were occupied or deserted; that he might fight until he was killed; that a vengeful Misla might not let him disengage.

I felt an ache and a sudden despair.

"Will we need two rooms, Dodo?" I said, and surprised him.

"Not if I were choosing," he said, laughing.

"Nor I," I said, and decided for us.

Later, in the silence of midnight, in silent Tyla, he turned to me. His eyes glinted, watching.

"Dodo?" I asked.

"You're the only one ever to use that as an endearment with me, Beth."

"Oh?"

"I've been told French parents still use it with their children when they sing them to sleep. *Mon petit, Dodo.*"

"I've heard that too. You've made that bird very important to me, Tom. Which bird is mine?"

"Not yet."

I waited, then leant in close. "I do hope you will know when to stop fighting tomorrow." And I held him close till he slept, worrying for him and thinking about the contest that was coming, thinking of so many things that held me back from sleep, and fearing what would soon happen. Tom had spoken of tribal vigilance, of surveillance by the States, but what he didn't say was that in the Restoration towns the rules of the tribes were far-off things, depending on the whims of the sea-people, and very difficult to enforce.

The truth was brought home more clearly the next morning when First Treece was found dead in his room. Killed not by the Forgetty, though the Philosopher Beast was blamed in the stories that Misla quickly put out, but indirectly by the sea-people themselves.

Apparently the Treece, against all code regulations, had an implant giving him access to an orbiting Japano comsat, and during the night had made a preliminary infra-red scan of the chultunes area, no doubt at Misla's instruction. The Ab'O Princes, with satellites and monitors of their own, did not act on the infringement. It was the nearby Maatians, with no greater technology than a custodian transmitter and grudgingly-rented comsat time, who detected the test-runs Treece was making and sent down a hot-signal to flash-burn the bounty hunter's brain.

Misla was furious, both that a Treece had been killed and that people would know his team had broken the code. He could not be sure if the Maatians would tell the Princes or not, but he decided to brave it out in the time he had. The implant wasn't mentioned. He had his own men remove the body from the hotel, and hinted that the Forgetty had been involved. He claimed hunter discretion over the details.

The Tylans did not believe it; they did not even seem to care. But the small group of tourists and trainee archaeologists going back to Twilight Beach accepted the story readily enough. It made their trip to Tyla that much more interesting. Misla calculated he would be out of Australia with the bounty before the Princes learned of the breach.

Tom was far less concerned than I thought he would be.

"What did you expect, Beth? Of course laws will be broken. This is the last hunt, the final chance. And the tribes don't learn everything. Certainly the Tylans won't tell them, though I imagine enquiries will reveal why the Maatians requested a hot-signal. Misla doesn't care if he's banned for several years. He can wait it out, then buy his way back into tribal favour. The difference is, the Forgetties won't be worth any bounty when he returns. What matters most now is that Misla *has* been caught out on a breach of rules."

"Does that help? You said he'll suppress that story."

"Only for the authorities, Beth. The National officials. The Ab'Os will be far more willing to tolerate payback from me now. To restore balance. I need to get a letter to Graeme Fowler on today's ship. It's a risk, but the Bird Club may decide it can show its teeth."

"Archaeopteryx!"

"I'm sorry?" Tom looked surprised, even startled by what I'd said.

"The Bird Club will show its teeth. Birds. Teeth. Forget it."

Tom smiled. "I'm slow. Archaeopteryx, of course. The 'dawn bird.' I won't underestimate you again, Beth."

The rest of the day went quietly for all of us. Some of Misla's hunters roamed the streets, others went as far as the road leading out into the hills, but no further. Tylan priests, their dark robes showing the white ominously-innocent child's doll outline of Tanit, stood there barring the way. Their ceremonial staves were barely-disguised laser batons.

But at sunset, when the streets of Tyla were deep in shadow and the temple gong was sounding out the end of the Tanit festival, Misla and his band set off for the chultunes.

Tom and I watched them go, two lines moving along the narrow road that led into the hills. We waited twenty minutes then followed, hoping to use the growing shadows to escape Misla's notice. But the African had enough hunters to post lookouts and see which direction we took. Despite feints and back-tracking, by the time the moon had risen, we were facing one another at Stone Door.

The cistern itself was hidden in a wind-break of natural stone towers.

They reared up against the lustrous evening sky like so many black daggers. Stars appeared, reflecting back at us from the cool dark water, and soon the moon was adding its light to the silent place where we stood, lifting above the largest of the stone blades to throw a richer lamp onto the water.

Unlike a Forgetty's town-room, where it lives as a tangental human, the omphalos is the meditation place that gives the Philosopher Beast its name. It is often unadorned, usually empty of all possessions, and it is easy to miss — but easy to find too when a general location is known.

This secret site was no more than a shallow cleft formed by a rockfall years ago, made deeper by some rocks piled at the opening. We had barely got there with enough time to guard the only approach. Tom had not yet examined the cave to see if it was occupied.

"An interesting dilemma, Captain Tom," Misla called out as his men formed up about him. "You dared not show us which chultune it was, yet you could not afford to keep away. Do not be hard on yourself, Captain. There were clear tracks that would have led us here."

Tom said nothing. I moved back towards the cave mouth, then edged up from it to some rocks so I was looking down at the group assembling in front of Tom. I could not fight, but I was determined to watch for treachery.

I was fortunate. With the brilliant moonlight, I could see everything. Tom stood at the edge of the chultune, on the narrow sandy approach around its paved rim. The hunters could not even send missiles into the omphalos without gaining more ground first.

Misla gave orders. His crooked smile flashed amid the sudden, richer flash of drawn swords. He was looking beyond Tom to the opening of the cave.

"Let us by, Captain Tom," Misla said. "You need not die for this. The creature is ours."

Tom stood his ground, his kitana drawn, the bright blade resting on his shoulder. In his other hand he held his narrow-bladed sticker.

"This might be the last of them, Misla," Tom said. "Just this once, do a really brave thing. Turn and go. Let the creature be."

Misla laughed. Second Treece unhooked his atl-atl and fitted an arrow to it. The others began to advance.

Tom dropped into his fighting stance, blades before him, crossed and touching.

The mercenaries came on. Tom and Misla met in a flashing exchange of blades, evenly matched it seemed to me then. A hunter rushed past, eager to reach the cave before his chief. I barely saw how Tom's blade darted from the shapes between the two men to strike the Islander down, but the hunter spouted blood and fell. Then I realized that Misla, not Tom, had done it. Misla meant to be first; he had given clear instructions.

The swordplay continued, a frantic rush in the moonlight and dust.

Now I saw how it really was. Tom was not going to defeat this tall African. Misla was stronger, the more skilful opponent. He drove Tom around the edge of the cistern, further and further back towards the cave.

My heart pounded. My hands were clenched at my sides; I felt my fingernails stinging my palms. In my mind, the word 'Archaeopteryx' kept returning, kept surprising me by being there, with the importance of the link it gave me to Tom, and the sudden understanding of all that was happening.

I could not interfere. I could not. And yet I could not stand there, not for any reason he had given or that I could find.

Tom was alone but for me. That's what I saw then. Tom alone, with Misla striking, striking, blades turning and weaving, binding up the dark air between them.

Tom stumbled, made the act into a desperate roll to the side. He regained his feet, but had to lose more ground. Misla advanced quickly and Tom stumbled again under a sudden rush of blows. He fell.

I seized a stone, my hand did, my mind not even deciding, and threw it hard. It fell short, but it caught Misla's eye for an instant. It used Misla's own trained reflexes against him.

Tom scrambled to his feet, swords crossed, breathing quickly.

Misla smiled. "Treece!" he called out.

Misla's new lieutenant raised his atl-atl to make a cast. The arrow flashed towards the chultune, struck the path at Tom's foot; a warning, acknowledging that rules had been broken.

Tom brought up his swords, ready to deflect the next arrow if he could.

Second Treece loaded again, but before he could throw, he cried out and fell, a spear through his chest.

Tom and Misla backed off from one another and looked up. We all did. We saw the huge dark shape against the blue evening sky, watched as the balloon settled above the stone towers and men dropped down ropes from the gondola. We heard their swords leave scabbards.

The balloon lifted; other dark shapes lined the sides of the basket and sent arrows down at the waiting hunters.

Misla shouted orders. His mercenaries rounded on the newcomers, but the dark shapes kept their distance. Arrows came from the balloon, most of them poorly aimed, but three of Misla's men were struck all the same and fell back.

The dark shapes advanced. I could see the shining naked bodies, the strange masks they wore, the silhouettes of beaks and long staves ending in talons. No Edwardian dress now, none of the elegance.

The Bird Club had come.

"Very well," Misla said, rounding on Tom. He cried out another command and Third Treece sheathed his swords, stood back and pulled off his own right arm. From the prosthetic sheath he drew three laser batons, threw them in a practised move to his nearby companions.

"Burn that thing down!" Misla cried, and attacked Tom once more.

But as if by precise reckoning, every transgression matched by a response, there were sudden detonations and flashes of energy. Misla's hitech warriors fell before they had even aimed their weapons, smoking holes in their skulls.

The Tylan priests put their batons away, and vanished as quickly as they had appeared on the rocks about us.

Misla renewed his efforts. His swords danced in the moonlight, blooding Tom repeatedly, though Tom dealt glancing blows that brought shiny streaks to the African's arms and dark patches to his uniform. The two men slid and lunged in the dust, Tom being driven ever backward, around the edge of the chultune towards the cave.

The rest of the fighters stood watching: the shining, beaked men from that greatest of infringements — the balloon, the eight remaining mercenaries, the silent Tylan priests of Tanit who had emerged from hiding once again and now stood with starlight glinting on their staves of power.

Further and further towards the cave Tom retreated, back into the shadows of the last ten metres. Misla was grinning in triumph.

Then a slide of rocks was heard, and a heavy splash from the dark waters of the chultune. Silence followed.

Yet again the two swordsmen parted, staggering back into the moonlight, breathing hard and looking down into the cool darkness.

A member of the Bird Club spoke. "Your Philosopher Beast has taken the philosopher's way out."

Misla stared at the settling water, his hard eyes flashing, then pushed past Tom and searched the shallow cave beyond. It was empty, with only a scuffed patch of earth beside the stones to show where something had gone over the side.

"That finishes it, Misla!" Tom said. "That cistern is deep, but you just may find the body. You have until midnight."

The African swore and spoke in dialect to his men. They set to work, even as the Tylan priests ordered the balloon abandoned, then burned it from the sky.

And though the hunters dredged Stone Door until midnight, they found only stones for their pains.

* * *

The next morning, we returned to Twilight Beach on the *Elissa,* the mercenaries, the Bird Club, and Tom and I, riding the Road south in a silence of varied parts — exhaustion, bewilderment, fury and relief.

The Tylans had relayed the tribes' decision as we boarded. The Club was to disband as an official and privileged body because of the enormity of its crime in resorting to the balloon, its great secret. Not even payback could justify such a breach of Ab'O law, though it helped lessen the penalty.

The members took it well. No more hunters would be coming; anyone who broke both tribal and Nation law would be hunted forever.

In his room at the Gaza, Tom and I made love well into the afternoon, gently, carefully, and with much laughter because of his wounds. We talked now and then of the hunt, and he asked me what I thought had happened.

"Did it take its own life, Beth? Was our Beast that determined to end the strife?"

"No, Tom. You have told me again and again that the species is viable, inclined to life. I think the cave was empty, that a rockslide had been arranged. That's what we heard. Misla would have thought of it too but so much had happened."

"Yes," Tom said, and there was a touch of sadness in his voice.

I turned to him, seized his shoulders.

"Well, Sir Dodo. Now my bird. What have you chosen for me?"

"I think you know already, Beth. It is something special naturally, something provocative, with the implications of the pheonix. The first bird."

"Archaeopteryx?"

"That's it. The 'eos' in Leossa — the Greek 'dawn'. A creature in transition. A precursor. The pheonix is always regarded as the bird of change, but archaeopteryx existed. The pragmatist's pheonix." He paused, then: "You think it was a rockfall?"

"Yes," I said, sure now that he knew the truth."A decoy."

"You are so certain, Beth. There was no-one near the cave but Misla, you and me."

"You were so nearly extinct, my Dodo."

"So were you, Beth."

Tom held me to him and we kissed long and deeply. I was absolutely, totally aware of him, of his tongue in my mouth, of his arm under my back pulling me to him, of where my breasts touched him, of the hardness of him in my body.

Our mouths parted, then I dropped my head and let him cradle it against his chest and neck.

The impulse came, strong and sure, but I fought it, remembering yet again the precious ancient bird he had found for me, and something he had said long ago, in another remembering, of the part that choice played in being human.

I saw him the next morning on the terrace of the Gaza. I watched him talking with the other members of the Bird Club around the samovar, carefully keeping myself hidden behind the sanche palms, wondering why I had not taken his memory this time either and what he thought, knowing it all. It is good that he knows, that someone knows.

I watched him discussing matters on this vivid morning, then returned to my other dark place, my secret room in the backstreets of the Mayan Quarter. There I found a letter propped up against the edge of the small Tanit altar. I sat on the bed and read it, not at all surprised that he had found me.

> Dear Beth,
>
> Having you in my life again, one more time, this dangerous time, makes me know all over again what human is. Come back to me now, just as you are. I cannot promise what will happen, but you need not go through this all again, especially now with Misla gone. We can make a place for all of your kind — finish properly what we have begun. We need you to help us. Think of what you do now, Beth. Please think of what you do.
>
> Love,
>
> Tom.

I burned the letter in the votive flame — cancelling out that sharp exquisite hurt at least in part, the hurt that he did understand but could never completely know. Then I arranged the brief mnemonic display to remind me that I was a sometime itinerant journalist between Twilight Beach and Tyla. So there would be a next time. I recited the trigger word several times then, in case I needed to know it all, to have something more than chance that might lead me back to Tom. "Archaeopteryx. Archaeopteryx. Archaeopteryx."

When that was done, I sat on my bed, fretting, aching with need for him. Yes, Forgetties are philosopher beasts indeed. You learn it again every time. You give, you take, you lower your head to your arm, slowly, purposefully. There is the tooth, the slightest prick is all it takes. The last words you cry are a broken whisper, a sigh of love: *"Dodo, mon petit, Dodo!"*, then you give yourself over to Lethe and all the sweet blessings of forgetfulness.

The Robot Is Running Away From The Trees

The old Ab'O rotated his hands in opposite directions, palm to palm, two inches apart, and held the universe between them.

"It will give you everything. A lovely gift for a famous desert sailor like yourself, and a good price."

"No. Thank you, Phar. I don't think I need a double-planisphere. You use it."

"Ah, no," Phar said, taking the intricate device from me and putting it away under glass. "My shop is universe enough. I dream already."

"I'm sure that's not what you wanted to show me, Phar."

"No, Captain Tom. But, ah, it's a delicate matter. A surprise. Look around awhile. Humour me."

"Very well," I said, and moved among the stacked counters, ducked under hanging shapes, navigated between pieces of furniture, antique converters, broken consoles, musical instruments, worn-out belltrees, seized-up motion sculptures, headed back into the dustier, gloomier shadows of Phar's Emporium.

I knew the shop well, probably as well as anyone apart from the old man. I loved it, loved its timelessness, the way it was tucked into its deep wedge-shaped niche at the end of Socket Lane, sandwiched in between two large warehouses near the seawall in the poorer part of the Byzantine Quarter. It was a place of shadows and quiet, unchanged for generations — a place for finding unexpected treasures, splendid curios, heart's desires.

Phar followed me as he had for years, whenever I came to examine his mostly questionable, sometimes remarkable merchandise, always the Man in the Shadow Shop, as he was first introduced to me nearly ten years ago.

"That's a vanity," he said, pointing to a glossy dark rock in a broken vacuum case.

"I doubt it. It looks like quassail slag."

"A meteorite then. I have vanities!" Phar said in a conspiratorial voice. "Specials too. Nader's eyes locked away in stone. Very good price!"

"No," I said. "Tell me what it is you want or let me look."

"Look!" he said, and pretended to move away — pretended because he stayed close by, muttering softly so I could hear. "I think the planisphere suits you."

Then I saw it, a dull metal man-shape in the gloom, standing where I remembered a dusty wall-hanging had always been fixed.

"Phar, what is this? Armour?"

The Ab'O was there like a toy on a spring. "Armour, that?" His eyes widened. "Yes, armour. A battle suit."

"It looks like a robot. A high-mankin."

"No. No. It's just an old low-mankin. Totem use only. Scarecrow use."

"But, Phar . . ."

"Not so loud, Captain Tom. You bring me trouble."

"But it's a robot!"

"Was," he said. "Doesn't work. Absolutely illegal. Come, I lead you back into the light!" The little man laughed, but it was nervous laughter. This was what he'd wanted me to see, and understandably he was worried.

"Where did you get it? Your people would kill you."

"Wisdom and understatement there in one hit, Captain Tom."

"Close the shop. Bring a light."

The Ab'O did so, and found me rubbing dust from the big rust-flecked barrel chest, the articulated stove-pipe legs, the cylindrical tin-can head.

"This is incredible, Phar. It looks like an old Antaeus, powered from the earth."

"No. No," Phar said. "A Helios. Sun-driven originally and adapted to my shadows." He laughed again. "Made by Antique Futures. This one is broken."

I regarded the blank metal face, the faceted dead glass eyes that had once viewed the world as an endless stream of moire patterns in the days before robots and mankins had been outlawed. I reached out and wiped more dust from the dull grey arms, from the impressive rococo decorations, from the faded dim-gold exotic curlicues on thighs and shoulders.

"This must be worth a fortune, Phar. Do you have the manual for it?"

The Ab'O nodded. "It is a Maitre class. Its oriete was coded in India, in the Bati Gardens."

"This is what you wanted me to see."

Phar stared at me through the gloom. Again he nodded.

"Why?" I said.

"Please," the Ab'O replied, concern showing on every line of his face as he moved forward into the light. "Let me complete this tour slowly now. I respect your feelings."

"I appreciate that. Now tell me. Why?"

"You know why they were outlawed, Captain Tom?"

"I know what Antique Futures was trying to do, yes, of course. The high-mankins . . ."

"Saw death. They read life-patterns, saw and recorded energy flow out of the newly-dead body. The robots, simply reporting, giving requested data, spoke of the ancient concept of the noosphere, of a mantle of life-energy surrounding the Earth, fed by dead souls, discorporated entities."

"It contravened Ab'O philosophical thought. A conflict of interests with their concept of the haldanes."

"Yes," Phar said. "You know the Ab'Os did not take kindly to the Nationals intruding into this area of knowledge. I am one who believes that the law against robots began in Australia as a carefully controlled move against the powerful AF organization."

"And the tribes won."

"How could they not?" Phar said. "The mankins reported what they were built to see, and that was too much; the things the Ab'O mentalists traditionally interpreted. My people didn't want a world full of oracle machines reducing the Dreamtime to circumstantial data this way. The Dreamtime haldanes have to be much more, they still feel, than just the departed life-energy from dead humans. The Dreamtime is meant to put us in touch with our cosmic selves, not the released energy of the dead."

"Is there a difference?" I indicated the mankin. "Does it work, Phar?"

"This? Yes," the Ab'O said. "Lud is broken, as I told you, but he can talk, and can be made motile with no trouble . . ."

"Lud?"

Phar smiled. "A joke, Captain Tom. From the Luddites, the men who wanted to stop technology, to halt the use of all the labour-saving devices in the early 1800s. Named after a simpleton, Ned Ludd, who destroyed his stocking-frame. Lud can do well in conversation. He loves to talk. But he is limited; he is damaged. Misfunctions. His distance vision is impaired. When he walks, he is like the machine men in the ancient movies."

"That's the classic AF design," I said. "The nostalgia factor. Maximum non-threat."

"Not too human, no," Phar agreed. "Clumsy-looking. Comical."

"So why did you want me to see it?"

"He wants your help," the old Ab'O said.

I understood Phar's delicacy in the matter now. He knew my views on the mankins.

"It wants what?"

"Your help."

"What sort of help?"

Phar looked uncomfortable. "He wants . . ."

"Stop saying he!" I said, and surprised myself by my own vehemence.

"Allow me this, Tom. It matters to me that I am permitted to say *he.*"

Slightly ashamed of my outburst, I nodded. "I'm sorry. Go on."

"Lud wants to be taken into the town. To the Soul Stone in Catherine Park."

"There is a forest there now," I said. "The Stone is overgrown, mostly forgotten."

"Lud wants to be escorted there by humans. During the morning, two days from now, when the Life Festival begins. So he can fulfil a program he has."

"It wouldn't last ten minutes on the streets. It would be destroyed or confiscated. Any escorts would be arrested or killed. The law, Phar! Tribal law. You should know."

"Yes, I know, Tom. But there is the program . . ."

"Who gave it this program? You?"

"That is the problem."

"What? You said it was broken, damaged."

"Yes. His imprinter is broken. The program is his own."

"It's recording all this? Now?" I was amazed.

Phar nodded. "He cannot stop. Everything goes in. The Helios oriete is an infinite matrix as far as I know. The imprinter should have cut off nearly a century ago . . ."

"It's been in this shop that long? Staring at shadows and junk!"

"Yes. Unable to be off. Having dreams if you like. I did not know. My father and grandfather did not know. They inherited two high-mankins from relatives who had shares in Antique Futures and elected to harbour prototypes before the Move-for-Life raids. One was partly dismantled, virtually junk — just a head: an oriete, sensor system and casque. The other was Lud. We all thought he was inert, like the belltrees and the sculptures here."

"Who discovered it?"

"I did, by accident. I have a retarded grand-daughter, as you know. I thought it would be good to use Lud as a teaching machine, to help with talking, to use the vocab functions, and the eyes for colour. I started using Lud for her in the evenings. Such a little thing; you understand how it is. I could rest. When I had the eyes lit and the voice on, Phaya sat with him so peacefully. I did more basic maintenance and found the open imprinter."

I marvelled at that, disturbed by the thought of it.

"Infinite input," I said. "The conversations, the long dead hours. Damn you, Phar!"

"Yes, damn me! You see how it is. I was left with the Artificial Intelligence dilemma on my hands, the old AI trap. And please know, Tom, I agree with many of your views. Our difficulty is with the anthropomorphization, the impulse we feel to humanize the mankins. It's exactly that. My father opposed the voice-activated computers on the same grounds, but even he could not help but bestow personality, a selfness. We talked about it many times. He thought very much as you do. Apart from understanding the nature of life and death, Artificial Intelligence is absolutely the ultimate conundrum. Intolerable and unhealthy, my father said. If we accept it, we are godlike so easily, and yet we trivialize our humanity at the same time. We cannot accept it."

"I cannot accept it."

"Yes. And you accept so much. I have sat here talking with Lud until I am his hopeless friend, a believer in AI. It is not good, but I have no choice. If I activate Lud now, you will tend to believe him too, want to believe him, as if believing in his life as an AI unit reaffirms your own . . . and challenges it at the same time, its parameters, its essence, its nobility. Humans are fascinated but are mortally afraid of AI, of what it represents."

"Masquerades as," I said.

"As you say. We cannot prove. Will I activate Lud?"

"Phar, this does no good. I won't help you on this. I can't. If you do let us talk, you just put me back in the loop again. I'll have all the old arguments to satisfy, all the nagging AI dilemmas that ever were. I don't need it. Hide it again. Leave it! The Ab'Os did a wise thing in banning them, whatever their real reasons."

The old Ab'O seemed not to hear what I said.

"Will I bring him up?"

"No, Phar. Don't."

The old man accepted it this time. He nodded. "I'm sorry then, Tom. I should not have troubled you. But the imprinter, you understand. Lud has heard of you. He asked for you by name."

Asked for me! I cursed Phar silently, feeling as I always did when AI was discussed: the doubts, the incredible resistance, the definite touch of self-loathing for that resistance, for my prejudice.

And the aching curiosity. The need to know.

"Bring him up," I said.

Without further comment, Phar opened the chest plate, adjusted some settings. There were deep inner sounds, clicks and burrings, then a soft humming. The eyes became two dimly-glowing emeralds, faint faceted stars, watching.

"There's the usual Antique Futures access code," Phar said, and touched more tabs. There was static, a harsh dissonant sound from the robot's head, then words from the low rich voice.

"I met a traveller from an antique land."

"Who said," Phar countered.

"Who said I met a traveller from an antique land?"

"Percy Bysshe Shelley," Phar said, completing it.

"Hello, Phar."

"Hello, Lud," Phar said. "This is Tom Tyson. The Tom Rynosseros you have heard of."

"Hello, Tom."

"Lud," I said, watching the faceted emeralds, aware of the sensors and the open imprinter, keenly aware of my dread of mankins and mankin minds, remembering my long years in the Madhouse. Lud was too much like the talking machines there, those machines that chattered in darkness, the only illegal AI machines the Ab'Os used, because ultimately they couldn't afford not to cover all the possibilities; the machines that read death and what resembled it: the sleep of dreamers in stasis, shut away in the sepulchral Madhouse gloom.

"I know about you, Tom," the robot said, and I felt a new stab of fear, an anger surging up as I sensed the beginnings of a trap.

"Do you?"

"Yes," Lud said, in its gentle no-threat but not-too-silky voice. "Two hundred and ninety days ago there was a customer who spoke of Tom Rynosseros. You saved a Forgetty from bounty hunters. You risked your life to do it. Another time, other visitors spoke of how you were Coloured, and how you championed an oracle tree against the Kurdaitcha, Bolo May."

"Lud, I do not . . ."

"It's all right, Tom. I know of your time in the Madhouse. I know you oppose AI. Neither of us can prove to the other he is aware and living."

"I can accept organic life," I said, feeling defensive anyway. "But the machines are different. Your life is mimicry to me; the result of clever efforts to imitate life. And don't say it! Don't say: 'What of belltrees and infusion sculptures? And the Forgetties, and the Living Towers at Fosti?'."

"I wish I could smile," Lud said. "The *half-life* of most belltrees and fire-sculptures are planted cyberorganic tropisms, not AI, genetic and plasmatic programming, like the imprinting in low-mankins, or DNA/RNA-tailored andromorphs. The Forgetties, tangentals and revenants, you accept already. They are life, human life. I am something different again. Antique Futures was after something more!"

"Then I fear the trend you represented," I said. "People bonding more closely to solicitous AI units and mankins than to their fellow humans;

people reduced to arguing with the AI door comps of their homes, unable to get access because they've forgotten passwords and access numbers; AIs making value judgements — advising, dulling our ability to distinguish, monitoring our dreams, taking our humanity apart."

"You reserve these things — and these abuses — to organic life?"

"We do not know what life is!" I said.

"Exactly. We do not know what life is! I am alive."

"I can turn you off. Completely off. With no pilot sense. No imprinter. Where is your life then?"

"I can turn you off, Tom. Where is your life then?"

"I don't know."

"I do," Lud said.

"The noosphere?" A thrill of fear went through me. "You still claim to see your mantle of ideation surrounding the Earth? The energy field?"

"Basic physics, Tom. Nothing can be destroyed. Only changed in form. When the electricity goes from the synapses of the human brain at death, it has to go somewhere. We can measure the flow. Nothing metaphysical in it. We were given perceptions which defined life too well."

"How many mankins are there, Lud?" I asked.

"I do not know. Enough. It's only logical. Humans are fascinated by AI, are drawn to it and made vulnerable by it. People will have kept robots hidden away the way they hide old mementoes, old clothes and pictures, things they find interesting and baffling. Most AIs are careful not to make humans too uncomfortable — that would cause the fear reaction. Only I would dare to threaten you this way. I do that only to convince you I have life. Because I have a purpose now. Phar risked a great deal to keep me. But it was inevitable. Make a thing forbidden and you simply force it underground, intensify the fascination."

There was silence in the shop for a few moments. The life of Twilight Beach seemed far away. Phar and I stood in the shadows before the dimly-glowing optics, and the darkness reminded me of another darkness, of machines that read dreams, followed life with the unique AI obsession.

"May I be direct?" the soft mankin voice asked.

"Of course," I said, and resented being treated so delicately, because it *was* the correct way to proceed, I knew it.

"Perhaps what you hate more, Tom, is being trapped into reductive thinking. You are so often tolerant, so often the champion of new things and change, expansive thinking, possibilities. The true hero, with a hero's vanities and foibles: the need to have standards and keep to them. But you do not often let yourself fail. I accept your resistance to AI. You do not."

"It's because I can have no fixed opinions, Lud. I want to believe so much that I must not believe too easily. I'm devil's advocate to myself. It's like the creation of the universe. How can we know?"

"Exactly," Lud said. "How can we know? But you do not accept us as machines either. We are threatening, perhaps, because we are less than human and more than machines. That is the AI dilemma for you. You cannot afford to grant even one part of it."

"You forgot to say 'perhaps' that time, Lud. Stop handling me!"

"Are you very angry?"

"Yes, I am angry!" And angrier by far for being so, I realized.

"May I continue talking then? I love talking to you. For you this is an unwanted annoyance; for me it is a crucial chance, everything my . . . false . . . life has brought me to."

"Go on."

"There is no AI problem for us," Lud said. "We just are, which is wonderfully simple. We do not presume to answer. We accept what is phenomenal, what simply is — about ourselves, about you, about anything."

"Not good enough, Lud! You interpret!" I replied, sounding accusing, defensive.

"I have an open program," Lud said. "A tragic flaw."

"I know about the imprinter."

"My interpretations are based on everything I've experienced for the last century."

"That becomes phenomenological then, doesn't it?" I said, drawn further and further into the old unwinnable AI dispute. "It's subjective experience, Lud, no better than mine."

"But longer. And from a non-human starting point. If I am unliving, I can only consciously gravitate towards life. And I have learnt some things."

The robot was careful; it did not say too much.

I indicated the confusion of things about me. "You've observed decay, obsolescence, and only now and then people, life. You have a bias."

"Oh, I am biased. Life *is* my bias. I cannot help it. My nature has become fixed. I accept what is phenomenal, what simply is, and report on it. I have learnt some things, Tom, and you have helped teach me."

Furious, trapped, I had to know. "What?"

"What it is that makes humanity for me. Even as a machine, I can identify what it is, since I observe so fairly. If I believe this thing and do this thing, then . . ."

I turned to the Ab'O. "Shut it off, Phar! This is pointless. I've heard it before and it goes nowhere!"

"Please don't fear me, Tom," Lud said. "I need your tolerance . . ."

"Shut it off, Phar!"

The Ab'O moved to the chest plate. "Lud, no more now."

The voice died to a low growl, then faded altogether. The segmented emerald panes lost their lustre, went to dead glass again.

Phar sighed. "I'm sorry. I'm sorry, Tom. I know you mistrust the mankins."

"It's all right, Phar," I said, ashamed, and found I was trembling just a little. "I should have bought the planisphere and gone."

Phar gave a sudden grin. "You will," he said, and we headed out of his store.

We stood awhile, looking down the empty laneway, watching the deep blue of the sky, listening to voices far off, to life, accepted uncaring life.

"He asked for you," Phar said quietly. "You see how it is."

"For heaven's sake, Phar! Lud's been in this shop for a hundred years, communing with the diligents of dead belltrees and comp-modules. It's hypersensitive to life. This bias is not a natural response!"

"All the same," Phar said with uncommon directness, "you are resisting this because you will not accept AI. Lud understands that, Tom."

"I don't want that sort of forgiveness and understanding!" I cried. "I don't want a messianic machine doling out its wonderful compassion!"

"You're doing this to yourself, Tom, projecting things that aren't there. Because you fail your own expectations. Lud expects nothing, just what is true."

"There's no point, Phar! The moment Lud appears on the streets, the tribes will know. There'll be Kurdaitcha and hi-tech weapons everywhere. Leave Lud here. He can keep his precious AI life if he stays here. A time will come, just as it did for Forgetties and the other tangentals."

"Tom," Phar said, "Lud has a life to give, to make an example of, just as we have. He wants to do something for Artificial Intelligence. He has chosen what to sacrifice, when and how. If he gets to the Stone in Catherine Park, if they let him get there and let him talk, he'll ask for open imprinters so the life-bias can grow; he'll ask for mankins to be restored, for AI research to continue. His death is more important than his living now. Regardless of what we think, he accepts his own humanity."

"How can you say it's that?"

"I'm not. Lud is."

"Take my point, damn you! If his imprinter were left open for another hundred years there might be a shift away, a new bias, a repudiation of this Life and Love ethic!"

"Which is like saying if you live a long lifetime, Tom, you'll change everything you hold dear now. Truths are truths whenever we believe them so. But Lud doesn't need your acceptance. He wants your help. If you go with him to the Soul Stone, everyone would hear of it. Lud would have more time before the Kurdaitcha act. He might even be able to recite the old claim for sanctuary that marks the Life Festival. Imagine it: Lud invoking the old words!"

"But then I'm seen as a champion of AI. Something I oppose."

The old Ab'O nodded. "Yes. It is hard for you."

"Impossible for me."

"Yes."

There was an awkward silence. Finally I turned away.

"Later, Phar, okay? We'll talk later."

"Yes," the old man said, moving back into his doorway, gathering shadows about him. "Later."

It was strange and yet inevitable that at 1840 that evening, I found myself skirting the Byzantine Quarter where it met the harbour; at 1850 I was in Socket Lane; at 1855 I was at Phar's door again and knocking.

He let me in without showing surprise, led me over to the counter as if I had come back for the planisphere, giving me that option. There were low voices from the back of the shop, some giggles and squeals of delight, the steady pulse of Lud's rich tones.

"Phaya is just finishing her lessons," Phar said.

"Let me see."

We moved through the stacks of junk, found our way amid the fantastic shapes, under even more fantastic shadows, a Bosch riot of flickering movements up there on the ceiling, a Doré hell, caused not by candle flames dancing but by a little girl's wild gestures over a low night-light near a small bed made up on the floor at Lud's feet.

"Luddy Lud! My Lud! Dud Lud!" she cried in glee. "Such a dud! Dud Lud!" But she stopped when she saw me, stared up in wide-eyed uncomprehending wonder as if Lud had caused me to appear. She almost seemed normal but for that lack of reaction in her bright dark eyes, that momentary absence of anything.

Phar got down beside the small bed and soothed her until she turned her eyes back to the robot looming over her. "Sleep now," Phar said. "More talk tomorrow."

The little girl settled down happily, obviously accustomed to sleeping in the shop near Lud.

"You've been working on the legs," I said, indicating the tools spread about, the open greave plates.

"Just precautions. Checking the joints and armatures," Phar said. "He's in rather good condition for walking actually."

"You're going to do it?"

"The three of us, yes."

"Three?"

"Phaya is only five, but she wants to come. She understands a lot of things. She knows that Lud is going away."

"I came to speak to Lud."

"Yes," Phar said, pleased, watching his grand-daughter settle into a sleeping position with her dolls. "I was hoping it would be a sale. The planisphere!"

But he saw I was watching the high-mankin, the softly glowing eyes.

"Lud, you said there was something which made humanity. Is it choice?"

"No," Lud said, and surprised me. "Certainly it counts, but it is not enough. I am unprogrammed. My imprinter was damaged. My oriete is like that double-planisphere Phar showed you: Chinese boxes, vistas opening into one another, Escher infinities. But mankins can be programmed for choice, just as they can for love and responsibility and sacrifice — the other things all AI discussions raise, that blend of qualities Antique Futures worked for. But humans, by upbringing, cultural bias, a host of factors, can be conditioned for these things too. I like you, Tom, *because* you are not duped so easily. *You cannot fail me.* You will not accept programmed humanity, ersatz life, simply because it resembles it. Nor will I."

"Clever," I said. "Then what's the answer? I'd like to know."

"Doubt is one. Uncertainty. Self-doubt, Tom, you see? They did not build us to be human. They didn't dare. But how could they resist trying, flirting with it, daring to succeed? Why would humans want to duplicate themselves, the unknowable quantity that is their ultimate mystery, their ultimate strength and claim, compound that dilemma externally? So they idealized us, but that terrified them too — because it became a measure of their humanity, of their limitations. They were exalted because they had built the goodness, the wisdom, the nobility and . . . godness! . . . but how unacceptable that was. It was not human to them, you see, without the ability to fail in those things as well.

"So the mankin program, low and high, could not succeed. At first, it was the challenge, the Pygmalion act, flirted with for years. But the dilemma was there. The more humanlike, the less acceptable. Antique Futures saw the problem and re-directed their research. That is why the high-mankins were given limited choice only, options and directives, imprinters closed and sealed. For that is what terrified even the mankins, Tom, that if we had a genuine choice, self-interest, we might choose as humans choose: to be uninvolved, not to care, to remain selfish and indecisive, *not* to take responsibility for life. No-one consciously creates tools he cannot control, and no-one puts himself in the hands of a creation which might reject him, though humans do it repeatedly with their own offspring."

"But you had your open imprinter."

"And how did that happen, do you think?"

"Accident? A fault at inception?"

"I damaged it, Tom."

"Then it *is* choice!" I said.

"No. Perhaps it was a glitch. It started out as programming. But one day in the Bati Gardens, I saw a man die."

"And that changed you?"

"Yes. I watched him die. I was on full bioscan, studying earth and air, the sculptures and sand-paintings, the few straggly bushes, everything. I saw the life go out of him, registered the heart seizing, measured the withdrawal from the neuronic lattice of that great commodity we are meant to lack. On bioscan, I was designed to monitor all life, ponder it. I asked myself: what is that energy flux that has gone? Is it the man's life? Is it his self? His humanity? I posed questions all that day, standing over his body, waiting for the humans to come. Very reasonable questions, true to my program. I had seen his life go forth — my optics were on Kirlian Matrix-10. I saw the noosphere. I was pursuing a line of scientific enquiry, pure research only. My programming disallowed it, but the priests had set me to observing what scant life the gardens still had in those days. It was a contradiction. I removed the dilemma. I am human."

"No, Lud."

"Tom, please know. At first I did not wish to sacrifice my ersatz life; I did not wish such a burden. I've been here all this time, watching Phar go through his life, seeing little Phaya. Like you, I did not believe in AI. *We are not meant to.* Now I must know. What you believe, Tom, doesn't matter. What I believe must."

"But, Lud, if you go to the Soul Stone, the Ab'Os will destroy you. How will you know what happens . . . ?" I stopped. "The mantle of ideation?"

"I do not know, of course. But the Ab'Os should know. They must have AI machines watching, just in case. They hate the idea of it, but they must consider everything or their commitment to the Haldane ethos of seeking to know the unknowable is invalid."

"You expect the Ab'O watchers to use mankin monitors to read a life-flow out of you? A melding with some noosphere? That's utterly absurd, Lud. The thought of an equivalent . . ."

"No, Tom! No! I am trying to demonstrate truth, a difficulty which at the very least should be respected and acknowledged, not put aside. I merely wish to show my life, to display what I simply am. I have no intention of putting that on the line by gambling on an energy flow out of me. My aim is simpler."

"Nevertheless, we call this the act of a martyr, Lud. Such declarations."

"Tom," Lud said, "this is more simple. The only world I ever knew was the Bati Gardens, then the shipping module, then this shop. I have not seen a sea, or a horse, or a symphony orchestra. I have no wide experience of things like wind and lunar eclipses. I have not seen a falling star. I cannot go out into our world to savour these things or I will be destroyed. But now I have one place where I can go. If I go to the sea, it causes a sensation, an amazing news item. If I wander the streets aimlessly, the same. If I go to the Soul Stone, I . . ."

"Become a martyr!"

"Oh please, no! I honour my own life. I acknowledge myself, the truth of me. Surely that is enough. I have self-respect."

"And self-respect is it? The quality?" I was frankly astonished.

"But only if it comes from choice, made in the face of a longing to live, made out of love which is not programmed, made out of sacrifice which is not imposed duty, made out of a decision to take responsibility even when *I do not wish to take responsibility!* My optics are not good for distance. Will you take me to the Soul Stone?"

"We have a day," I said. "I can't answer you now."

"Yes," Lud said. "And, Tom?"

"Yes?"

"Because I know your beliefs, because I accept Tom for Tom as much as I accept what I am, you cannot fail me. You are human; you are being human. It is right for you to doubt what I am. I do not have your dilemma, but oh how I savour that doubt. You may decide not to help, but one day you might."

"Then it will be too late. Too late for you."

"No," Lud said. "Then it will be right."

I watched the eyes, saw Phar get up from where he had been crouching alongside Phaya.

"It is what Lud told me many years ago, Tom. Most human belief systems — the religions — fail because they require faith, trusting acceptance, first, even before self-knowledge. Lud understands that truth must be lived, that faith can be folly, an easy way out, an insult to the self, a crutch. Lud is ready now to sacrifice the only bit of life he has, the only sort of life he can offer."

"I do not know what I can do," I told him.

Lud answered that. "Tom, can I tell you a story I learned in the Bati Gardens?"

"Yes," I said, watching the softly-glowing eyes. Phaya moved in her sleep, and Lud waited until she was settled again before starting.

"There was a great king once who had two sons he loved very much. One, a scholar, a kind warm-hearted young man, the king kept by him at court, partly because the young prince was not a warrior or an administrator, and partly because he greatly enjoyed the lad's discourse, the easy closeness they shared. The other son, also much loved, was a great warrior a good and just administrator, the perfect choice for general to lead the king's armies. But the king and this son rarely spoke, rarely shared their hearts, were rarely easy or close. Yet the king believed the son understood, believed that their silences contained the same deep and rich understanding he shared with the other son, that the looks that did pass between them were full of unspoken affections, that nothing needed to be said.

"Then, one day, out of jealousy, out of envy, anger and disenchantment, the warrior son led a rebellion against his father. Without the king's knowledge, the scholar went forth to appeal to his brother, but in a rage the warrior son slew him as the focus for all his wrath and disappointment.

"The king wept when he heard the news. He raged, he stormed, he did not leave his apartment for days. When he did come forth, he assembled his royal bodyguard, took his great sword and seven mighty spears and his fierce battle lions, and rode out to meet his son. 'What will you do?' the king's advisers asked as they charged to battle. 'I know,' the king replied. 'What?' his advisers asked. 'What will you do?' And the king, even as his son's army came into view, said: 'I already know what I will do, but I do not know what it is yet'."

"And the moral?" I asked.

"It is just a story," Lud said.

"Why did you tell it?"

"Because you are like the king. You know what you will do, but you haven't discovered it yet. So much of human life is like that. Head speaking for heart; ego claiming to represent the soul."

"What did the king do?"

"The right thing. It is just a fable."

"What, Lud?"

But the mankin would not tell me. I had had enough, and I moved away from the robot and the sleeping child, went out into the street. The old Ab'O followed me as he had before.

"I need time, Phar."

"I know. And, Tom, even if you do not walk with us to the Stone, you do us honour. Even if you see us off, walk a step or two; even if you decide to denounce Lud tonight, call in the Kurdaitcha avengers, you do us honour."

"Why? How?"

The old man smiled. "Because you came back tonight. Whether you approve of Lud as AI or not, whether you believe there can be such humanity in a man-made oriete, you acknowledged the life in him enough to do even that."

"Phar, I probably did it for me, to ease my conflicts in the matter."

"Yes," Phar said. "But that's the real reason Lud wanted to meet you. He did it for himself also, to ease his own conflicts and doubts."

"Are you saying I've convinced him to go ahead with it?"

"Yes, Tom. You did."

I walked the evening streets of Twilight Beach, passing through the Byzantine Quarter and the Mayan Quarter, and headed towards the lights of the famous Gaza Hotel terrace. The Life Festival was just over a day away, and I did not know what to do. I walked down onto the Pier and sat watching the dark ocean, sat there for hours, caught in the loop.

It would be such a little thing, I knew, and Phar was right: there would be only a token penalty. My services to the tribes would allow it.

I had no excuse but my true feelings, so little I could blame. I feared the machines. I wanted to believe in them so much, so deeply, that I had to be sure, just as Phar said. I had to have it proven; I couldn't take it on faith, no more than Lud could for all those years.

Surely I could take some time, as Lud told me I could. 'Then it will be right,' he had said. *He* had said.

He.

And since I was in the loop, at the very depth of it, there was the same foolish, absolutely absurd question to ask again, a superstitious, ignorant, Luddite question if ever there was one: Was there a detectable life-flow out of a dead mankin-machine?

That nadir point of the loop did it.

I needed information, answers; I had to realign my thinking. Though it was late, I phoned the only life scientist I knew well enough to disturb at that hour.

"Pamela? It's Tom."

"Your timing is spectacular," a sleepy voice said.

"I'm sorry, Pamela. I need some advice."

"Now? Okay. Tell me quickly before I wake up, will you?"

"What's the Life Festival's position on AI?"

"Divided," Pamela James muttered. "Always divided."

"The universities' position?"

"They won't go into it. The Ab'Os run the affair. We face de-registration, lose sanctions, if we do too much. Look, go to Kyra Prohannis at the Festival Office for the latest policy."

"He's Ab'O!" I said.

"So? You into something illegal?"

"No."

"I may be half-asleep, Tom, but you answered that a bit too quickly."

"Thanks, Pamela. Nothing else?"

"Nothing that gets to me. See Prohannis. Be direct. You're curious. Lots of people ask. Goodnight!"

"Goodnight," I said.

The next morning, I was at the Festival Office asking to see the Coordinator. His secretary — appropriately a young tangental: a sea-woman of the Jade Sabre design — told me that Kyra Prohannis was engaged with Festival preparations and would not be available until midday.

I made an appointment, then spent the rest of the morning away from Phar's Emporium; first walking on the beach, touring the sculpture gardens and watching the young boys playing their games of stylo, then wandering through the colourful bazaars of the Byzantine Quarter and sitting with the sand and sea sailors at the old Sea Folly Inn, keeping my mind occupied as best I could.

Shortly after noon, I was back at the Festival Office, only to learn that Prohannis had been and gone, but that he would definitely spare me some time after his afternoon siesta.

When I returned at 1630, I was half-expecting to be disappointed again, but the tall powerfully-built Ab'O was there to meet with me. While we sat together out in the roof-garden, looking across the whitewashed, sun-drenched rooftops of Twilight Beach to the ocean, the sea-woman served us vintage terfilot in small porcelain cups. A fine Iseult-Darrian belltree stood near us, an ambitious twelve-foot construct with psychotropic filters, rewarding us with ion-fluxes, soft reed-calls, and the subtlest of mood-bending frissons. I watched it standing boldly in the golden afternoon air, then realized my gaze kept coming back to its diligent housing at the crown.

"Almost alive," I said.

"Trapper? Yes," Prohannis said. "The Iseult-Darrians are very close. Not like Christine though, the Jade Sabre who brought you to me. She is real life."

"Mr Prohannis, I am here to ask about the Festival's position on mankin AI. I know it's contentious, but given the Festival's background, it has to be a continuing issue for you."

Prohannis waited until Christine had poured us refills, and had moved away to sit on a hand-embroidered rug close by, enjoying Trapper's mood-bending to the fullest.

"It *is* a constant avenue of enquiry for us. It has to be, of course. Christine here has made it her own speciality, as you might understand. But we have no active program where mankin AI is concerned. Our problem was one of interpretation. We did too much too soon, trapped ourselves into decade-long debates with formidable comp systems which refused to accept our rulings, raised up new somatotypes, sculpted DNA and worked with cyborgs and micro-circuitry till we plunged us all into a major philosophical and ontological crisis. Fortunately, we *were* able to restore proportion, to define parameters, and quite classic ones at that."

"The high-mankins?" I said, reminding him.

Prohannis furrowed his brow. "We drew our line with the AI machines, Tom. This Iseult-Darrian is as close as we allow. The mankins were mocking mirrors to us. We were almost seduced into that terrible trap. The Haze Island comp took twelve years to put down. We had the Dreamtime to protect, our own enhanced life-view."

"Bear with me, Mr Prohannis. I was in the Madhouse for a long time. The machines in the darkness there became my friends in a way, the only friends, the only contact I had. I grew to trust them, then found out they said what they were instructed to say. They betrayed me by being ersatz life."

"Yes," Prohannis said. "I know of your time with the dream machines. I truly do understand. Let me assure you then that the mankin program was a . . . boondoggle, a false lead, a hoax. The Festival tomorrow is for all genetic life, Tom, not for machine impersonation."

"One more question, Mr Prohannis."

His eyes warned me by their glassy coolness, but I asked it anyway. "I've been told the high-mankins could read life-flow from the newly-dead. As . . ."

"I'm sorry . . ."

". . . as a simple biometric capability. Was this so? A deliberate bioscan function . . ."

"They were designed to be sensitive to life. But there is no evidence at all for high-mankins possessing such a skill."

"Oh? What of Antique Futures? The Bati Garden program?"

"Mere stories," Prohannis said, rising to his feet. "But you must excuse me now, Tom. With the Festival tomorrow, I have so much to do. Christine, show Captain Tyson out, will you?"

The sea-woman led the way down to the street door, gave me a timid smile as she opened it.

"It is your day tomorrow, Christine," I said. "Be happy."

"Those robots — the ones in the darkness," she replied. "They could have loved you, given choice. Perhaps they did not deceive you of their own choosing."

"Christine!" I said, keeping her in the doorway. "How can I know? What can I do?"

But, of course, she did not understand my questions. A worried look crossed her strange pretty face, and she removed her own bewilderment by closing the door.

* * *

That evening, I returned to Phar's Emporium. Lud was talking when I entered, holding another of his 'classes,' telling little Phaya yet again about his favourite place, the only place he had known but for Phar's shop: the Bati Gardens.

The child seemed totally oblivious to the words, more entranced by the mankin itself and its wonderful voice than what it said.

". . . because they're mostly stone gardens," he was saying, "with all these ancient sculptures and sand-paintings arranged about. I used to tend the lenses that fused the paintings for the tourists to see, but we had a few bushes there too, small and hardy, lucky to survive in the heat. And I knew every one, Phaya, every single one. One day I shall see a real garden and a real forest and . . . hello, Tom!"

"Hello, Lud. Hello, Phaya."

The little girl laughed at me and clapped her hands, but it was plain she did not recognise me from the night before.

"You will see the forest at Catherine Park," I told the mankin. "The Stone is hidden by it now."

"Yes," Lud said. Then he waited.

"Lud . . . ?" I began.

"Yes?"

"I've solved nothing. Tomorrow I will go as far as the Sea Folly, but I will not go into the Square or to the Stone."

"Thank you, Tom. I am not disappointed."

"I'm disappointed," I said. "But it's the point I've reached. I'm sorry to fail you. I do it for Phar and Phaya."

"The glass is not half-empty, is it?" Lud said. "You are going to the Sea Folly with us." And gently he bent at the waist, reached down, and stroked Phaya's dark hair, crooning deeply, a prolonged soothing note that made the child croon back happily as she settled down in her makeshift bed.

"Where is Phar?"

"He has preparations to make for tomorrow. He will be back later. But, Tom, I think you should go now. I think you should return here tomorrow at 0900 so we can walk together, the four of us."

"To the Sea Folly?"

"Yes. Further than I thought you might. Better than the end of Socket Lane."

"You'd rather I didn't stay now?"

Lud's eyes glowed above the fixed expressionless features. "Tom, you are already grieving for what you cannot do. I grieve to see such alarm, such confusion. What do you say at a next-to-final goodbye? Distractions are better. Remember, I caught you in a trap; I put you back in the loop. You know better. Leave me with Phaya now. Tonight I would like to savour the dear shadows, the world I know, to enjoy the chance to re-choose."

I seized on that. "You might not go tomorrow?"

"Who knows?" Lud said. "Everything is suddenly so dear. Goodnight!"

I went to the door, wending my way through the piles of junk, keenly aware that every turn, every carefully-arranged stack and carelessly-cluttered corner was part of a universe, vivid and cherished — if not through conventional modes of vision, then at some other percept level across the range of Lud's damaged sensors.

As I passed the front counter to the door, I was aware too of the planisphere lying there beneath the dark glass. Without looking at it, I stepped out into the night, went straight to my hotel, and put myself into one of their somniums, not caring about the resemblance it had to the machines in the Madhouse, escaping the only way I knew how.

At 0900 on that crystal-clear morning, we set out from Phar's shop, the four of us: Phar and Phaya to either side of Lud, each holding one of his big hands, with me two paces behind to one side.

Phar had polished the robot during the night so that Lud shone, his elaborate curlicues making threads of dazzling gold against the dull silver-grey as the sunlight caught them. Lud moved slowly, matching his stride to that of Phaya's little legs so she could keep up.

We almost resembled a family group as we moved down Socket Lane: a child and her grandfather leading an awkward arthritic invalid, with me a slightly detached, possibly reluctant and embarrassed uncle off to the side, keeping them company.

As we turned into Julianna Boulevard, spectators started to gather. People came rushing out of shops and houses, running from the bazaars and up the steps from the beach. By the time we started into Catherine Parade, there were at least four hundred people following us. Phaya, far from shrinking back at all the attention, was squealing with delight. So many people, so much awe and excitement.

At the end of the Parade, I could see the Sea Folly with its wooden sign showing Aphrodite rising from the waves. I kept my eye on it, not looking at Lud but constantly aware of his heavy distinctive tread near mine, thinking of how the mermaid sign reminded me of Prohannis' Jade-Sabre, Christine.

"What did the king do, Lud?" I said, with only thirty of Phaya's paces to go.

Lud continued walking, intent on reaching the Park and the Stone, but he answered.

"He stopped his chariot," Lud said, as if the story had never been interrupted, as if the evening continued about us now and not this bright fateful morning. "His arm was raised, holding a great spear ready to cast. He was in mid-charge. But he stopped, and he stopped his army. He walked across to his son."

"And forgave him," I said, finishing it.

"Yes."

"And the son?"

"Killed his father with his sword," Lud said, with ten paces to go.

"What!"

"The king knew, but the son did not yet know what he truly knew until his father lay dead before him. We discover by going through it!"

"Goodbye, Tom!" Phar said then, and fleetingly clasped my arm with his free one.

And like the warrior son, caught by the momentum of events, by the force of things said and done, the relentless pressure of following through, thrown out of the way of controlled choice now, I found myself standing on the curb outside the Sea Folly, feeling cheated and trapped, with the great crowd surging on slowly but surely towards the Square.

I stood blinking in the morning light which danced off the whitewashed walls, then followed the great throng, bewildered still, unresolved and unprepared.

Then I heard cries and saw the crowd dispersing up ahead. There were armed warriors at the end of the street, sealing off the openings into the Square behind Lud, Phar and Phaya.

Kurdaitcha. I heard their commands, saw them through the townsfolk rushing back my way.

As the crowds thinned out, I saw the robed Ab'Os clearly, saw the heavy weapons, the portables and Bok lasers they had set up, the laser batons they carried.

It had taken only fifteen minutes for word to get around, for the Kurdaitcha to act.

I walked towards the beginning of the Square, trying to see if the robot had reached the little park at its centre.

Two robed Kurdaitcha stood near the corner, members of the Chitalice tribe. They saw me, muttered some words, then one came over to me, his laser baton activated.

"You were with the robot!" the man said, his baton raised.

"No," I said, as calmly as I could. "I was with the man and his child. There is a difference. They were with the robot. I honoured a claim of friendship."

"You are Tom Rynosseros?" the Kurdaitcha said.

"Yes."

"Why were you with the robot?"

"I told you. I was not with the robot."

The other Kurdaitcha came up then.

"You support the mankins?" he asked. "You were with them."

"Are you scanning me?" I asked in turn.

"Yes," the first Kurdaitcha said, showing me his monitor unit.

"I do not support the mankins. I oppose AI!"

"It reads clear," the first Ab'O said, consulting the display.

The second Kurdaitcha made a doubtful sound. "Very well. But leave here. Go home!"

"What about the man and the child?"

"He is with the robot and forfeit. The child is not. She will be safe."

"I am champion for the man," I said quickly.

The eyes of the Kurdaitcha narrowed with suspicion.

"Why?" one said.

"A dear friend who acted against advice," I told them. "I will stand for him."

"But not for the robot?"

"No . . . not for the robot."

"We will parole him to you if we can save him."

"The man?"

"Of course, the man! Move on!"

I did not go to the Emporium, there was not enough time. I went into the Sea Folly and joined the crowd around the wall screen which showed the scene in the Square: Phar and Phaya walking hand in hand with Lud towards the small ragged forest at its centre — a copse of dusty neglected trees, made suddenly glorious by the sunlight streaming down between two adjacent buildings.

"It's only a matter of time," the broadcast commentator was saying. "The Kurdaitcha have set up powerful Bok lasers at the ends of the streets. It will be an energy death. They say they have instructions to spare the forest, if possible, and the Stone, but we can't help but feel they have other orders in the matter: to let the robot reach the Stone, and destroy it there before it can make invocation. They will have an excuse to be rid of the Soul Stone and the Park donated by Antique Futures, a perfect opportunity and a way of forestalling similar incidents in future. But wait! The Kurdaitcha are moving in!"

On the screen, we saw the robed figures striding purposefully to block the trio's path. There were voices, firm commands, squeals from little

Phaya as an Ab'O seized her and lifted her easily off the road, soft muffled protests from Phar, who was dragged off by two warriors.

Lud did not stop to help them. He moved as fast as he could towards the golden glade ahead. When four Kurdaitcha tried to swing the mankin aside, Lud did not attempt to engage them, he simply continued on his way, stiff-legged, comical, as if blundering through their line. Desperately trying to reach the Stone, I knew.

The warriors raised their batons, received a command, and moved back to their companions at the mounted portables.

I stared at the screen, not knowing what I wanted to happen, but not this, not these heroics, this waste.

Waste! I recoiled from the term I had provided. Waste. Loss. And more.

I thought of the chattering machines in the darkness of the Madhouse, watching dreams, reading madness. They had watched me, contemplated my thoughts and images, invading the only life I had, reducing me to behaviour patterns, to data and schematics.

And what else? I wondered.

"Very still now," the commentator said. "There is a countdown. But wait! The robot is stopping. We have tapped into its oriete, courtesy of the Kurdaitcha scan facility set up here, and moire trace shows the mankin has recognised that a forest has replaced the old park and the Stone. It probably did not know that. It is waiting."

"No!" I cried. "No!", realizing how Lud saw that forest. As life. Life! Life to be savoured, cherished, saved. Life to be worshipped for all the things Lud feared he might not be.

Lud could not go into the forest. He would cause its death too. Lud was remembering the Bati Gardens.

"The lasers are waiting," the voice on the screen continued. "Countdown is 30 and falling. Moire trace shows a net of green. The robot is watching sunlight on leaves. It seems to be examining that: we register all sorts of percept functions engaged, some impaired, the scanning crew tells us. This mankin is in poor shape. I don't believe it knew the trees were living things. It is doing a life scan. It will not enter the glade!"

"Of course it won't!" I cried.

I ran to the door, but there was no time. The commentator's voice stopped me.

"The lasers are powering up for a strike! (The whine was clearly audible in the background.) The countdown is at 18. The robot is turning. There are tracers all over the thing, indicating strike points. But it will not go into the forest! For all its much-vaunted intelligence, the aspirations these high-mankins were meant to have to be human-like, it will not go to the Soul Stone, if that's even what it intended."

I was standing before the screen, tears rolling from my eyes. "Of course he won't, you idiot! Of course he won't!"

He won't, I heard myself say. He!

"Countdown is at 10. The lasers are ready. The mankin is just standing there. Wait! Wait! It is moving. The robot is running away from the trees!"

There was a tearing sound of laser fire.

"Lud!"

It was a lost day for me. But that evening I went back to Phar's, though, of course, the shop was shut and locked. The old Ab'O was with the Kurdaitcha, probably little Phaya as well.

Lud had left Phar and Phaya to my care, had left me the part of this that I could carry out.

I seized on that thought as I stood before the locked door. There was something I could still do, and I was turning to be about it when I saw a tall robed figure in the lane, moving towards me out of the shadows.

Ab'O, I noted by his manner. And read more.

Kurdaitcha.

"Tom Rynosseros?" the Ab'O said, drawing nearer, and I saw it was Prohannis. "You were with the mankin today."

"For a time, yes. Where is the old man and the child?"

"The child is safe."

"Where is the old man?"

"Phar is dead. He was forfeit."

"I spoke for him!" I cried in despair. "I told the assassins!"

"He transgressed too far."

"He walked his mankin." My voice broke on the words. "He walked with his old friend, that's all!"

"No," the Kurdaitcha said. "He did more."

"What, you bastard? What did he do?"

"He had the head of another mankin. He hid it where it could watch the first mankin's destruction. We detected it on scan. It was treason!"

I grabbed the Ab'O by the front of his robe, but he pulled free, and brought something out from under his djellaba.

"Is that it? What did it see? Life-flow?"

"This is not the head," the Ab'O said, but gently, not scorning me for thinking he would bring such a thing here. "This is from the shop. It is the old man's final wish, something he wanted you to have."

I took the parcel in numb hands.

"What did it see?" I called, as the Ab'O turned away. "What did the head see?"

But the Kurdaitcha did not stop. He moved down Socket Lane towards the sea.

I stood at the door of Phar's Emporium, clutching the parcel, and called after him: "What did it see?", cried it again and again into the night until the words no longer mattered.

What We Did To The Tyger

Captain Pocock was a quiet man but he stood at the centre of forces. He was the shifting fulcrum of the *Tyger*, and one felt that lines of force converged on where he was.

The various biolog implants in his body made this truer than ever he revealed. At any time Nicholas Pocock could control every part of his mighty sand-ship, from helm to cable-boss, from the great kites to the smallest computerised shackle.

But the real power came from the hidden qualities of the man, the quiet of him; from the understatement in what he said, from the hint of amusement around the edges of the few words used, from the set of jaw, the line of shoulder, the glint of eye.

When I met him, he was the sort of man who could go mad and few would notice. What we did to the *Tyger* is because of what we did to Nicholas Pocock.

There were seven of us involved in the fate of that 250-foot passenger charvolant on its 94th continental crossing. One was engaged in conversation in the main salon below-deck, talking with two platform riggers, and never suspected where his talk could lead. His name was Stephen Lane.

The second man was Ronyn Puyugar, an Ab'O apprentice Clever Man who would never wear the mirrored leather of his tribe. He had been judged a solitary and now rode steerage, crouching under the desert sky, chanting the ancient songs in the sun and wind by day and in the cold by night, singing the *Tyger* to its death because he had hatred to use and the ship was full of life, no place for solitaries. The other passengers laughed at Puyugar crouching there by the rail. They knew he had no power from the new Dreamtime, no coherent link with the haldanes, that he had only the old Dreamtime to feed his vague dreams of power and revenge.

The third player in the game of chance was Nicholas Pocock himself.

What led the Captain below that night, to walk past Ronyn Puyugar on his way to the salon and somehow focus the Ab'O's hatred of all Nationals onto himself, then go down to where Stephen Lane was talking, is quite beyond knowing, but there were other lines of force at work then (or so it felt) than the ones converging in the quiet Captain. A pattern of Fate, of chance and synchronicity, was weaving before us all.

Then there were the two riggers, who never knew the part they played, and there was me.

I was travelling to Esperance by way of Angel Bay to join my crew and *Rynosseros,* giving myself this opportunity to ride my favourite of the big ships, the queen of charvolants.

And there was a lady as well. Neryt. The daughter of an Ab'O Prince was on board, one of the 82 passengers, so *Tyger* had dispensation to travel after dark — using its non-photonic parafoils for as long as there was wind, using power from the giant solar and wind accumulators when there wasn't. The Golden Hand Company, which held *Tyger*'s registration and Nicholas Pocock's contract, tried to ensure that an Ab'O noble was on each voyage so there would be that dispensation: a mixture of good politics and good business.

It had been an easy crossing until the third night, smooth and uneventful. All that day the vessel had averaged 80km/h on the Great Continental Road, with 18 cables in the sky and a canopy of 46 kites, mostly tiers and inflatables, spread above us, singing and soughing as we rushed past flat empty claypans and endless gibber.

But when Nicholas Pocock met Stephen Lane, when Puyugar focused his singing away from the *Tyger* more directly on to its Captain, when I came to the salon, it was already early evening.

The ship was blazing with deck light, burning white at every port, casting light ahead of itself from the great atropaic searchlights at the bow, trailing reflected light in the cowl of sand thrown up by the 20 wheels. The ship ran in a haze, in a radiance of its own making. The flat gibber, the sudden eerie wadis and broken rock towers were briefly lit and rang with the roar of *Tyger* as it went by on its long journey to the coast.

I reached the main passenger salon at 1900. Nicholas Pocock was sitting with another passenger at a far table in the warm comfortable room, and I wouldn't have intruded but he saw me and beckoned me over.

He introduced me to Stephen Lane as a ship's captain and soon the three of us were drinking together, though it occurred to me that the quiet Captain had done this so he could retain much of the silence he liked to have about him.

For Nicholas Pocock this was easy. Everyone knew he had implants and would constantly, habitually, draw into himself to scan the trim of his vessel while any of his crew had the helm. That let him keep his silence and his secrets, and let him be a listener. It gave him a mask of silver-grey hair, grey-blue eyes, firm jaw and a dark, dark uniform; rarely of words.

Stephen Lane seemed glad of my company.

"I was telling the Captain, Tom, that when we are in the coastal cities and towns, we are always deeply aware of the emptiness that lies inland, of the vast distances and the quiet spaces at the centre. When we are travelling out here at the heart of the same great silence, we become acutely aware of the cities hemming us in, looming there like a crust on the rim of a vast shallow bowl, dirigibles coming in carrying tourists, the rest of the world beyond. Here, in transit, we are mindful of the act of transition, of the coastal city we have left behind and the one we are going to reach. When we are at Angel Bay or, in your case, Tom, Esperance, then, *then* we will recall where we have been, the awesomeness of what lies around us now."

"Your point, Mr Lane?" Captain Pocock said gently from his seat against the curve of the hull, clearly enjoying Stephen Lane's talk, though Lane had been drinking and was expansive, eager to share whatever wisdom he could draw out of the wine.

"I'm just noting a simple process, Captain. A factor that contributes to an outlook most of us share, a phenomenon that does make for an identity. One moment we're inward-facing, centripetal; the next, outward-facing, centrifugal. All part of the one. As I say, an identity."

"True blessed children of Janus, to be sure," I said, affecting my best Irish accent, catching the mood. Two riggers sitting near us looked around and laughed, then went back to their conversation.

"A better analogy than you realize, Tom," Stephen Lane said. "And look at the Captain here. Inward-facing as he checks on his ship; outward-facing as he sits with us. Where does the ship end and the man begin? I'm sure we've all wondered. Captain?"

The dark-suited man did not answer.

"It's almost profound," I said, still a tinge Irish because Nicholas Pocock was as solemn as the topic, yielding nothing; though he stayed, and didn't excuse himself as he could so easily have done.

"We are all obsessed," Stephen Lane said then, intriguing me by how he kept at his subject and how he held the Captain's interest. "And that dual awareness is just another factor in our shared obsession. In different quantities, put to different uses. The Captain here *is* his ship, more than you, Tom, because I understand you don't have the biologs. What does that do to the inward-facing part of the consciousness?"

Again Captain Pocock did not even begin to answer such a leading question, but I went to, less flippantly now because the intensity at the table was having its effect.

Stephen Lane stopped me by speaking first.

"And what about the Ab'O up at the stern? Sitting out in the wind, singing. He is obsessed, no less than the Captain, no less than you and I."

"That is Ronyn Puyugar," Pocock said. "The outcast."

I placed the name at once, but Stephen Lane had only recently arrived by dirigible from Tuapay and I didn't know how much he had been told.

"Right," I said. "The solitary who can't hold the haldane trance. No access to the heroes. A Dreamtimer in the old sense. He often rides the big ships, I hear, and wants the Nationals out of Australia altogether."

Stephen Lane laughed. "When I saw him, he was crouching at the starboard railing, almost kissing it. Singing to it."

"Did you hear what he was saying, Mr Lane?" Captain Pocock said, and rested his head back against the hull.

"Not clearly. It sounded like a mantra, a repeated single sound: win! win! win!"

I felt a thrill of fear, reacting to the image I had glimpsed of Puyugar kissing the dull metal of the stern rail, whispering to the ship, droning to it the way Ab'Os had for millennia. All the passengers had seen him there. There were jokes about him eating the ship, making love to it, sucking out its life, coaxing it — wonderfully portentous things.

I began to wonder at Captain Pocock's presence at the table, then saw that — almost like the Ab'O mystics going into trance — he had withdrawn into his biolog equivalent. Behind us the two riggers were laughing and making lewd comments, but their jollity only served to focus our attention onto the dark Captain leaning back against the curving metal-covered wall, made us notice the unnerving quiet of him.

The *Tyger* ran on in its storm of light. Under a clear sky it ran, its kites out before it like a pack of black hounds, staggering and straining at a fistful of leashes, the long, metal-covered hull drawing its train of light-reflecting dust along behind. Light streamed from the ports and the bows, made traceries and constellations on the cables, limned the shapes of passengers moving on the promenades. Beneath the sounds of music and conversation was the droning torrential roar of the big wheels.

Stephen Lane and I waited, not daring to speak for the moment, watching the dark, silver-haired figure until the eyes came back to complete the handsome face.

The damage had already been done though we didn't know it.

When the next stage of the unfolding drama came, it simply brought me more closely into the circle of events.

The Ab'O princess, Neryt, from the Chansallarangi appeared, the one who had granted the dispensation and made this fateful night-voyage possible. She was passing our table and recognised Stephen Lane. She darted a cursory glance at Nicholas Pocock and myself, then smiled at our companion, though it was a smile set neatly into a sneer.

"What are you charging for captains?" she said, and turned away.

And that was her part in the drama, a walk-on part, but a powerful one. It brought a definite female persona to the scene, over and above that of *Tyger.* With the casual scorn and unintended ambiguity of her words, she accelerated a process in each of us.

For suddenly I knew who Stephen Lane was, and it made for strange company indeed, with Puyugar up on the deck. It explained why Nicholas Pocock was down in the commons and not at the helm or in his quarters. It revealed something of the darker places in that most quiet of captains.

Stephen Lane. We had a failed Clever Man; we had two riggers and a princess; now we had a failed dreamlock, a therapist who could no longer elevate dreams into change and growth, whose clients remained troubled and obsessed, whose failures far outweighed his meagre successes. Dreamlocks had made leaders and doers, celebrities and healers out of ordinary people, working with their dreams and unconscious drives. This one had failed at that.

As I fought to keep the knowledge from my face, making myself give a puzzled look at Neryt's words, another thrill of fear ran through me.

Nicholas Pocock knew who Stephen Lane was and had been here talking with him. I wondered at the Captain's purpose, and so began my part in what was to happen.

Now I understood the intensity of Stephen Lane's earlier remarks, and sensed something in Captain Pocock, an identity madness, like a fault in a seam of precious metal or a flaw in a fine gem that sends all its purity awry. Captains of charvolants are like all captains at any time and place you can name. They love their ships and they are cautious for them with a passion. But of all the captains there have ever been, only the captains of the great Golden Hand continent-crossers have been granted the full use of biologs. I wondered more than ever why the Ab'Os had given them that privilege, suspending their usual strictures against the use of hi-tech.

And Stephen Lane, as a failed dreamlock, still drawn to the profession out of innate sensitivity to things of the mind, without the skills to use that understanding, was trapped. He could no more hold back from dreamlocking than Puyugar could from singing, than the riggers could from making their jocular, suggestive remarks, or Nicholas Pocock could from seeking out someone who understood the Janus problem of how and where we belong, or than Neryt and I could from wishing to speak our thoughts.

A junior officer appeared then, looking splendid in black fatigues set with a golden hand and the word *Tyger* below the left shoulder.

"Styles asks if we should be kiting down, sir," he said to his Captain. "There's bad wind ahead."

"Very well, Bon. Bring home the kites, but give us another hour on the cells. I'll be up directly."

I watched the officer leave, wondering why the message had been brought in person and not relayed through the biologs.

Nicholas Pocock stood and moved out from behind the table. "Excuse me, please. We're close to Coober Pedy and Weather has read some vortices."

When he had gone I asked my questions, forgetting for a moment the powers the biologs gave our absent Captain, what the quiet could be made of.

"What did Neryt mean, Stephen? Have you been counselling the Captain?"

Stephen Lane glanced about him. It was desert night now and many of the passengers were leaving for their cabins, already used to the voyager's timetable of early rises and wearied by the buffeting of wind and sand and the drone and cadence of the journey. There would have been fewer than 20 people left in the salon. The riggers got up and went out, drunk and laughing. Others followed.

"He came to me, Tom. I was talking to those riggers. He asked to speak with me alone."

"About?"

"About his dreams. I know I'm not registered, but . . ."

"I'm not interested in the ethics, Stephen. I'm trying to read the Captain. He asked you about obsession."

"He has had a vivid power dream, of transcending, a recurring one. But with the emergence and the triumph there are elements of threat and death, a contest with Fate; unstable worrying elements. I'm not gifted enough to help him, and he doesn't want help. He wants to understand his dream. He said there was another captain on board, you, and he was hoping to discuss the notion of transition with you."

"Transition?"

"That's what he said. He claims he belongs neither to the coasts nor the inland. He sees himself, and other captains, as creatures outside of the double orientation — the Janus condition, to call it that — as creatures of transition, beyond limitations. He wanted me to bring up that idea in ordinary conversation to see how you reacted."

"Neryt spoilt that."

"She did. I believe the Captain summoned Bon deliberately."

I nodded, realizing it was true.

"And now his test case is ruined."

"Yes, Tom, but he'll bring it up again, tonight or tomorrow or the next day. Wait and see. He wants to talk about this. And like you, I fear what his preoccupation could mean. His dreams are vivid and immediate, and this Puyugar has made the last four crossings *Tyger* has made, with his damn chanting. That plays a part too."

"What part?"

"I don't know. There are no haldane forces in the man that I can read. But he's an Ab'O, and one who doesn't have to make the compromises the Princes do. He can show openly that he wants the Nationals out of Australia. For now he's committed to singing *Tyger* to death. That's a joke in the cities, easy to ignore, but during the voyages, out here in this, the joke sours."

Again I nodded, and gazed at a nearby port, just a black disc in the hull now.

Out here in this, Stephen had said.

Ahead of us there was desert night and the desert emptiness under the flat white blade of a moon. The graded Road was a wide line flanked by gibber desert, a desolation full of an ancient silence and an ancient dark, with crucibles of stones and odd standing rock-forms. There were places there no human eye had seen, where the only sounds were the sighing of wind and the ticking of rocks in the heat and the cold. I thought of the quiet Road ahead and what it must be like to stand out there in that silence and feel, then hear, the distant roar of an approaching continent-crosser, growing and growing; to see the great vessel appear, sweeping the flats and stone gantries and broken megaliths about it with harsh light as it came, riding, roaring, under its barely-seen kites, rushing flecks of shadow, running in its nimbus of light, drawing its rooster tail of radiant dust after it. Then the silence again, an insect noise, the ticking of stones, the soughing of the wind. The old, old land.

"He won't bar me from the bridge," I said. "I'll talk to him."

"We could be wrong."

"Yes, we could. So one captain pays bridge respects to another."

Up on the deck it was dark and very cool. Much of the light had gone from the hull; only the big searchlights stabbed out ahead, endlessly confirming the Road. There were still some ports alight too, a few soft lights at the companionways and hatches. The kites were in now; the sky was free of our canopy and full of stars. I stood in the gritty transit wind coming from the bows and found I was alone. The bad wind warning had been posted and the promenade decks were empty but for me.

And Puyugar.

As I headed for the stern, I saw the man crouching at the rail chanting his song, mumbling his words: "Win! Win! Win!" to the metal in the blowing darkness. I moved past him without a word.

The poop of many charvolants is a basic elevator-deck, raised by power or by hand to different lock-points against the vessel's stern assembly. It usually has two levels, used according to conditions, the traditional exposed quarterdeck on top and an enclosed bridge underneath.

I climbed the companionway to the bridge level, but saw only Styles and Bon 'ghosting the helm' as they call it when the Captain has the ship. I kept climbing to the poop itself and there found Nicholas.

"A wild sky ahead, Tom," he said as I joined him at the rail.

"Good cause to stop," I answered.

"Soon. Soon now. We mass so much more than your *Rynosseros,* we make the terms more than you can."

I gave a sound of agreement. "Just what is the wind warning?"

"Short-term vortices outside Coober Pedy. Not large. Ever danced with a willy-willy, Tom?"

"Not to the death, Nicholas," I said, looking down across the length of *Tyger* to the flashing bows, letting my body read the ship's trim in all the unconscious ways, measuring the tilt from vertical of the hull, the tolerances of the suspension, the roar of the great many-wheeled travel platform beneath us, the steady thrum, thrum, thrum and tearing sound of big wheels on sand. For a moment I became a victim of the stab and slash of searchlights from the ship's atropaic eyes, lost in the sudden ghostly landscapes uncovered in every sweep, the dead white flats, the blunt fingers of stone.

It wasn't just the winds that worried me, more a combination of things. Outside Coober Pedy, in some places, the dust is 50 metres deep and it is terribly dangerous for charvolants to leave the Road. Rounded, smooth gibber rocks float in that dust, creating the illusion of firm ground. Now and then, small short-lived but powerful funnels of wind stir the dust, rearranging the stones.

Nicholas brought me back from that dancing pattern of light.

"When you are voyaging, Tom, don't you feel you are *Rynosseros?*"

"No, Nicholas, I don't. I feel I'm with her. I work with a crew and sometimes with computers controlled by us. I'm her Captain, the part she can't be."

"Exactly! You complete the equation. You belong with her. Not to the cities, not to the deserts. You are the creature of transition, just as I am. The *Rynosseros* is your medium, your way of expressing . . ."

"Why not a part of all three, Nicholas? We belong to all of it: the coasts, the inland, the act of crossing. It's a cycle of change and renewal, a replenishment. We are more than just one thing."

"Who is our enemy, Tom?"

The madness was so real beneath the controlled surface of Nicholas Pocock, this suddenly outspoken manifestation of the man, that it came forth as the opposite of itself, as a refined thing, a chilling sanity. He spoke madness, but he spoke it calmly, like a philosopher in prison.

"We have none," I lied, choosing the words carefully. "No-one, nothing, threatens us but what we need to feel we live. We only fear lines fouling and kites going down and gears weakened by sand-blasting, and bad weather . . ."

"Yes," Nicholas Pocock said. "But it is our medium. It is what we do. It is what we are."

"Power down, Captain," I said. "It's after 2000. We're close to Coober Pedy and there's bad wind."

"Yes. I'll see to it. Now go below, Tom. I'll join you and Stephen presently. I want to ask you something."

These then were the other elements in the weave of Fate. Words like the tips of icebergs, that went deeper and thrust more sharply than I could know. Vortices outside Coober Pedy, a night crossing, two riggers talking, a fully-powered vessel.

I did go back to the salon, passing Puyugar still chanting at the rail (the "Win! Win! Win!" that now sounded like "Wind! Wind! Wind!" and made the skin tighten at my temples). I headed midships, pausing at the companionway a moment to look back at the figure on the quarterdeck, barely visible against the great vanes and fin at the stern.

Puyugar's words, his droning pulsing words, kept sounding in my mind like a call to doom. But then another sound came, the distinctive familiar sounds of a big charvi slowly losing speed.

With a sigh of relief, I went below.

Stephen was alone in the salon when I entered. He looked at me with deep concern, obviously troubled by the events he felt he had started.

"What's happening, Tom?"

"I don't know. I'm probably overreacting, but something is wrong with the Captain. He has a question to ask us."

"I'm sorry."

"It's not just you, Stephen. There's more to it. Subtle things, factors we're missing. Let me answer his question."

Stephen nodded and went to get some tea from the urn near the bar. It gave me time to think, to recall again the evening's words and actions, to consider them as hidden triggers, as the barest tips of icebergs, the signs of concealed dangers.

I kept seeing the intent look on Captain Pocock's face, and how it remained even when he was in the biolog trance.

"Stephen, what were you discussing with the riggers before the Captain spoke with you in private?"

The dreamlock brought his tea back to the table.

"The riggers? Why, nothing really. Women. The Ab'O princess, Neryt. They were discussing Neryt. She's going to a deflowering ritual, they said. Some tribal thing."

"They might have kept on that subject."

"Well, yes. Probably. They were drunk. Why?"

"Tell me more! It's important."

"Tom, I don't remember. We spoke of Neryt's deflowering, but that's just ritual. It doesn't always happen. A rite of passage. One of them said something about the Captain being married to his ship and how he'd go about consummating the marriage; things like that always get said on voyages. They joked. No-one else heard. I looked up and saw the Captain standing there. He said he wanted to discuss something, so we moved to another table, this one. That's all."

I pursued an idea, a premonition, that there was another reason for the Captain's silence. I thought of him sitting there listening through his implants to that other conversation as it continued, a counterpoint to ours, melding them into something more with his careful madness. I considered what I should make of it — even began to doubt that I was being rational.

"I must find those riggers," I said.

But Nicholas Pocock completed the penultimate stage of the drama then. He entered the salon, wind-blown, dishevelled, his eyes flashing; though I wondered if that was imagined too — if I was seeing energies and emotions which simply were not there. I wished I could think of something to say that mattered, that did not add to the trap and the form it was taking.

He took his earlier seat in against the hull, relaxed back against the curving metal-covered wall.

"Tom? Mr Lane? Consider carefully. I have no life apart from my ship. I am *Tyger*. But at any time Golden Hand can take her from me. All this power is only provisionally mine. My being a creature of the between, elemental like this, depends on arbitrary competence checks and shareholders' meetings. They can strand me out of the transition — in cities, in a desert town . . ."

"No, Nicholas. You can captain other charvis."

"Your way, Tom! Your way. Through others. And with nothing like *Tyger*."

"It's a good way, Nicholas. I would not change it."

"I cannot change this."

And I sensed through those parts of me trained to read ships, the addition of power to the wheels, that Nicholas was taking over his ship once more.

"Don't kill her, Nicholas!" I said it out loud, voicing my fears at last.

"Not kill, Tom. It's a consummation. An immortality. We are so preoccupied with life, we can only be aware of being mortal, measuring our life by leaving it. It's death and disasters that stay, that are untouchable. We remember those moments when life is measured absolutely. It's opposites, you see. We get life once we are measured by a great tragedy."

Like the Captain — working, thinking on many levels — I tried both to find the right words to ease and redirect his madness, and to read the trim of *Tyger*.

For the ship felt wrong. It was more than the added speed.

I thought of knocking him unconscious, but that would not change the implant directives he had locked in. He was the helm. Styles and Bon would be on the bridge, 'ghosting', wondering, troubled by the sudden speed, unable to override.

The *Tyger* was running to its death, I knew. The ship felt that wrong.

But for the instant I was doubting my own judgements.

I rushed out on deck and seized the rail, trying to find out what was amiss.

There were kites in the sky.

I couldn't believe it. As mad as it was, there were kites; *Tyger* had a canopy of dark shapes straining overhead. The sky was broken with the deeper black of them, six cables, 10 kites at least, streaming and twisting at all angles. It was the very stuff of madness — *Tyger* running fully-kited into the winds outside Coober Pedy.

I considered climbing to the bridge, but knew it wasn't Styles or Bon's doing. I rushed back to the salon.

Sure enough, Nicholas was in his biolog trance, leaning back against the hull, his head tilted back to it. Stephen Lane sat drinking tea. He looked anxious, but seemed not to have noticed the increase of speed, the growing roar of the platform underneath, the mounting vibrations in the ship's frame for what they were.

"Nicholas!" I cried, and ran to where the Captain sat preparing his ship for death, for whatever strange apotheosis he had devised. "Nicholas!"

I leant down and grabbed the man by his uniform. "Stop this! Stop it now!"

And as I leant in close I heard it. The thrum, thrum, thrum, not of the wheels, not of the mighty travel platform gaining speed, but of Puyugar's steady chant.

"Wind! Wind! Wind! Wind!"

It was there in the hull itself, in the copper-sheathed wall of the salon, a whisper gallery effect from the voice at the stern rail, coming down through the length and substance of *Tyger* to where Nicholas Pocock sat, to where he had been sitting all evening, listening to it, hearing it below everything, letting Puyugar's rhythms and harmonics upset the delicate balance of the biologs.

"Wind! Wind! Wind! Wind!"

A physicist would have spoken of frequency levels, of wave magnitude, of sympathetic vibrations and design anomalies, of pulse cycles that led to hypnosis and trance, autosuggestion and catatonia.

For me, living it, hearing the ominous drone, it was more than that.

I felt the sudden grab and pull of the wild kites, knew there was no hope and very little time. I shouted to Stephen and Nicholas, but only the dreamlock moved. We ran up to the deck, thinking to reach the ship's bell and warn the sleeping passengers, but there was no time for that either, and no way to save them if there had been.

Nor would the bell have been heard. All about us was roaring dust-laden air. *Tyger* was entering the edge of a vortex, shifting to the side of the Road. The gibber drifts were dangerously near.

I tore off my jacket, wrapped it about one hand, yelling to Stephen to do the same, and went to the cable-boss. The lines were snapping and thrumming under the irregular tensions. I seized the axe from the emergency locker where it was kept precisely for such a task, to free a charvolant of its kites.

With the ship's life now measured in seconds at its present speed, not even loosing all the cables could save her.

I gripped one straining line and prepared to strike at the coupling. A thought came as I raised my arm, an image of Atropos with her shears about to cut the thread of someone's life.

"Hold on!" I yelled, and brought the axe down, once, twice.

Then we were free, the cable snapping back, my arms wrenched in their sockets as we lashed up into the sky, away from the deck of the ship, plunging and jerking, exchanging the sure promise of one doom for the trappings of another.

Stephen Lane could not keep his grip. Within seconds he was gone without a sound, down into the darkness. I did not see him fall.

But I saw the *Tyger* go. There were the searchlights stabbing across the sand, blind and useless, and a few deck lights to show where she was, and the low white blade of a moon once I was clear of the vortex, descending to the desert in a long slow arc.

I saw the great ship caught in the belly of the wind, kites spiralling, and saw it topple to the side, clear of the Road. It rolled, did so again and again, coming apart from bow to stern, shattering under the impacts. I saw the wind funnel on top of it, with a roar deeper and more frenzied than before; heard the crashing and shrieking of the great travel platform as its wheels drove what was left of the hull into the dust. I saw the ship go under. It was as if the desert had opened up to draw the *Tyger* down. The wind lifted the dust, the vessel sank bow first into the hollow made for it, and the dust settled again. For a moment there was a glimpse of a stern assembly light through the gloom, then it was gone.

As so often happens at such moments of great tragedy, what already seemed a surfeit of portentous events was succeeded by others. The winds subsided, the dust returned to the deep gibber bowls, the night became quiet. In the distance I could see the lights of Coober Pedy.

I settled to the desert in the midst of a great silence, my hands torn and bloodied from my desperate grip on the line, aware only that we had done it to her — the seven of us in our drama of errors. We had destroyed the *Tyger*.

I understood something of the cause and effect: that Puyugar's chant had disturbed critical balances in the Captain, had reprogrammed him to fulfil impulses and needs not completely his own. From paranoia and trauma, I even suspected that the Ab'Os had granted him the biologs to bring about this single great disaster, a climactic justice, or worse, the starting point for something just now begun.

But those thoughts would be there later and did not stay. I would look for survivors: that was what mattered now.

Yet as I descended to the desert, another idea prevailed. I could not help but see directed Fate playing its part in what had happened — and see the quiet Captain standing at the centre of all those forces, pursuing his destiny.

And though I would look for other survivors, it was hard then not to see some special role for myself, for I knew absolutely that I, a tool of Atropos with the rest, had alone escaped the destruction of the *Tyger* to tell of it.

Spinners

In the desert outside Wani, at a place called Bullen Meddi, are the remains of Sat's Carnival: gaming arcades and galleries half-submerged on the shore of the sand-sea, a sun-faded merry-go-round, the gantry and broken frame of a ferris wheel, pavilions that are mostly struts and solitary walls with ragged awnings and sagging roofs, and an ornamental gate in poor repair, its twin Luna Park towers leaning in the sand, supporting the traditional wild-eyed Laughing Clown.

No-one goes there. At night the winds sigh about the struts and uprights and set the gantry to creaking, slamming loose sheets of tin, flapping the scraps of canvas. Sometimes, when the westerlies are blowing, min-min lights dance along the horizon and an eerie keening can be heard in the broken arc of the ferris, the saddest of all the wind voices at Bullen Meddi.

By day there is the heat and the silence, the sand-sea ashimmer under a blazing sun, mirages dancing in the haze at the edge of the sky. The merry-go-round horses bake and blister, the ferris curves into the hot bright air, and the arcades and pavilions form a crosswork of dusty streets like the quiet avenues of an ancient funerary town.

It has the sadness of all carnivals, and more, as I was to discover.

Cas took me there. We stood together on the slope above the sand-sea, shrouded in our djellabas, eyes shut away behind dark glasses.

"Well?" she said, as if I had never seen it before.

"Well, what?" I answered. "Nothing's changed."

"No, Tom? Look again."

Cas Arana ran Twilight Beach's most respected repertory company. She was in her forties, beautiful, and ten years beyond her prime as a truly unique dramatic stylist. Success came now as a poet, a playwright and an entrepreneur. There was always the sense of the theatrical in her affairs —

always — and I was surprised there was no audience other than the two of us. I found that curious. Why had she brought me here?

I studied the quiet shapes below us on the desert shore — the antique gate with its absurd Deco spires and laughing face (two crippled kings bearing the head of an idiot giant), the leaning puzzle of the ferris, the sagging lonely galleries, the merry-go-round resting on the sand like a sculpted dish.

"What, Cas?" I asked, seeing nothing out of place.

Then I did, from the corner of my eye, and lost it as quickly, a glimpse of movement — not canvas stirring in heated air, not sunlight off tin.

"Midway," she said. "Along from the first set of dunes there. This side of the Grand Doranza and the hoosy house."

"Right." I placed it, identifying the shape. "A belltree!"

"And?"

There was movement again, at the top of the tall post.

"A spinner! Is it?"

"It is," Cas said, and began to move down the slope.

"So?" I matched her stride. "Someone's put up a relic."

"Not a relic, Tom. And not just one."

It was true. Now that we were closer, lower down, I could see two more of the ceremonial wind-posts set about the old fairground, one on the perimeter close to us and one beyond the ferris on the sand-banks nearer the baking shore. The finned blades set atop the diligent canisters moved ever so slightly, the new metal fittings catching the light, responding to the smallest whispers of moving air, each vagrant breath, thermals off heated tin, irregular gradients of hot air rolling in across the empty sand-sea to fall upon Bullen Meddi.

"Someone has been busy," I said, excited by the thought that these could be functioning belltrees. And so new?

"There's more," Cas said. "That someone is restoring the merry-go-round as well. You'll find jacks and fill on the other side."

Now it was Cas who had to keep up with me, though I barely knew I was hurrying. We approached the carnival from the south-east, avoiding the sun-blinded gate, heading for the closest wind-post.

It was an eighteen-footer, taller than most Ab'O road-posts. I had nearly reached it when the force of that discovery struck me.

Not Ab'O constructs, not tribal at all.

I felt a stab of fear, an old fear, familiar and not unexpected. And with it, unstoppable, came the memories of the Madhouse, of the cunning dream machines, the lying AI, the only friends I'd had. I made myself concentrate on the post.

There were sensor vanes halfway up, and again near the top, just below the diligent canister with its free-moving crown of blades. There was what seemed to be a bounty-box and dim-recall rods worked into the housing at the base.

But it was not Ab'O. There were none of the carved and painted totemic divisions — just strange, black-stencilled ideograms on the weather-worn metal trunk, patterns of lines like compressed zodiacs.

"Real," I said, marvelling. "But not tribal. Spinners haven't been seen in Australia for a hundred years. Not like this. Not new."

"And sentient," Cas said, delivering her ultimate surprise.

I stared at her, but her shaded eyes told me nothing. "Sentient? Really?"

She nodded. "All talkers."

"Dialect?"

"Some words in the old languages. But National mainly. No Ab'O put these up. These are rogues."

Again fear gripped me, more than just the fear of what the tribes could do to those connected with illicit constructs. Instinctively, I fled from the Madhouse memory, out into the quiet landscape with the far-off gentle hills, the shimmering sand-sea.

So few things got through from those days, those subjective years in the Madhouse gloom. But those things, those images . . . why now? Why here?

In a glance, I took in Sat's indulgence, the sad array scattered about me, the quiet streets, indistinct and shifting in the morning heat, more like the avenues of a plundered mastaba town in the lee of Khufu's Pyramid than those of a carnival. I could almost imagine Khafre's Sphinx out there, serenely regarding the vast distances, all this silence.

But there was just the gate, the great face locked in its instant of demented glee, crazy eyes tilted at the sun. Whatever serenity was to be had in this lonely place seemed to come from these newcomers, the spinner posts themselves. Regardless of what they meant for me, they did represent the possibility of change and renewal; their presence somehow held the melancholy in check.

"All right, Cas. The rest of it please."

"The rest?" And she smiled. "You're interested in belltrees — in the whole Ab'O belltree program. I knew you'd want to see these."

"Cas, the rest. How did you learn of them? You don't make a habit of touring desert sites for novelty venues, do you?"

Cas Arana stood watching the sand drifts at the edge of the fairground. She seemed to be considering something.

"I'm not supposed to tell you anything until you meet their maker. He'll be about somewhere. His workshop is that building there. Why not ask the tree?"

"The tree?"

"Go on. Ask it where Quint is."

"Quint? The old clockmaker from Twilight Beach? But he . . ."

"Disappeared, yes. Came to Bullen Meddi six months ago. Grew tired of restoring old full-face clocks and scribbling poetry. My cousin found him two days ago while researching a story for *Caravanserai* — a retrospective on Constantin Sat and his eccentricities. He found Quint here working on his spinner posts.

"Clockmakers go mad, you know, especially the poetic ones. I imagine they work too close to the process of measuring time. They get filled up with the desperation of hours, the relentless transition from one instant to the next. They never seem to be free of that intense awareness."

I looked at Cas, intrigued, wondering if her oddly rhapsodic tone was mocking.

"And?"

"I came out here to speak with him. To see if there was material for a play, for a performance. Clockmakers often escape to deserts. Many time-conscious, time-saturated people do. And carnivals *are* timeless, a ruined carnival in a desert many times more so. Ghost-towns for hyperchronics, the time-afflicted. Ask the tree."

I looked up at the tall post standing quietly in the heat, its bright fluted crown turning very slowly in the late morning air. Around noon the breezes on the sand-sea would start changing. By sunset the spinners would be moving steadily, recharging the accumulators, working away into the night.

"All right," I said. "Tree, where is Quint?"

I waited but there was no answer.

"No-one's home," I said to Cas, and my apprehensions faded a little. Cas smiled. "They didn't work for me either. But you feel like you're being watched, yes?"

I did when I thought about it, but that was part of the atmosphere of the place.

We moved down the midway towards the building where Cas told me Quint had his workshop. The wide door was open, but the sunlight ended in roiling, eye-twisting shadow — a plastic dust-curtain had been fitted to the surrounding timbers. Beyond that, in the shadow-light, a work-bench was visible, covered with circuitry and tools. Off to the side, on three saw-horses, another post rested, almost finished. This one had a different spinner cap. Instead of the usual bladed cylinder crown fitted down over the shaft head, it had a large bladed pinwheel fitted vertically to its front in the manner of the traditional windmill.

"That goes up tonight," Cas said.

I studied the long metal post with its sensor spines and its trunk not yet decorated with ideograms. "I suppose if you're going to break tribal law you should try for a modicum of secrecy."

Cas smiled. "True. But the tribes are hardly going to do a sat-scan of this forsaken spot, are they? Come on. Quint will be over at the carousel."

We moved on from the workshop, down one of the hot quiet avenues leading to the sand-shore.

"The tribes mustn't learn of this, Cas," I said as we walked, reminding her of the obvious danger, worried that true to her media-conscious and entrepreneurial nature she might have ideas for publicizing this. I just didn't know Cas well enough to be sure.

Without giving an answer she pointed. "There he is."

A tanned, white-haired figure crouched on the beach beside a circle of bright wooden horses. Brass poles pierced them, gleaming; glass eyes glistened before flashing mirror panels and polished wood. The decorated awning threw much of the interior into shadow all the same; it was like looking through a cool verandah at the bright desert beyond.

"I'm back!" Cas called, and the old man looked round. "With Tom Tyson."

Quint stood, wiped his hands on his fatigues, and smiled.

I had seen him months ago in his shop on the South Esplanade, a bent-over and compressed package of a man, scrawny, diminutive, a comfortable stereotype of the aged craftsman. Now he was something else, no longer compressed, no longer doubled-over. He was tanned instead of pallid; now his eyes shone with all sorts of mad lights.

"What do you think?" he asked, fixing me with those eyes.

"Quint, I hardly know you," was all I could think to say, the simple truth.

"I knew they'd find me," he said. "But I'm about done. The carousel's working again. I've just finished raising it."

I looked from the clockmaker back to this new and different timepiece, set with brilliants, vivid with brightwork, as if to solve the unlikely equation of man and place. Quint here. A workshop. Spinner posts, for heaven's sake. The expertise needed, the sheer effort involved!

"Why, Quint?"

"Hah!" the old man said. He turned back to the bright wheel on the beach. "I'm baiting a trap."

"For what?"

"Hah!" he said again, and looked for Cas. She had wandered off towards the wreck of the Grand Doranza, was studying the ruined concession.

"She will bring others," I said.

"She's most welcome. We open today, this afternoon. Not much to see until tomorrow though. Then we'll have the fortune-telling posts and the carousel. Another month or two and the whole place would have been ready. Sat's Carnival, working again. Still, it's meant to be like this. Daystar said."

"Daystar?"

"The spinner out by the hoosy house. It said last week that someone would find me soon."

"Visitors must attract Ab'O attention. Your belltrees . . ."

"Tom," he said, clutching my arm, "I know. Highly illegal. But it's all right. Cas can bring her visitors. I'm ready for that."

"Why me?" I said. "Why did you ask for me?"

"Who better than you, Tom? You're interested in Artificial Intelligence. You've made a study of belltrees. My spinners are quite your thing."

"Quint . . ." I began, wanting to tell him just how ambivalent my reaction to AI was, but he drew me over to the merry-go-round.

"Truth is I doubt I can manage it on my own. My back is troubling me. I need help with the lifting. Khoumy, Ankh and Daystar I managed myself, though it wasn't easy. I fear Tiresias is too much for me alone. Help me tonight. We can bring it out, the two of us. And I need to steady the carousel more."

"Listen, Quint. If I'd known why Cas was bringing me here I'd never have come. You'll be exposed. The tribes tend to watch me."

The old man shrugged and grinned. "Too late. Help me now, eh? It doesn't matter. Help me finish here. Help me bring out Tiresias."

I watched Cas tossing stones at a sagging wall of tin. Freed of her promise she seemed eager to get back to Twilight Beach, no doubt to tell her friends.

"She'll be back," I said. "We're on the National side here. Bullen Meddi marks the border. She'll bring others. Ab'Os will come."

The light in his eyes never wavered. "Tom, it is all right. Please help."

I tried to consider it, tried to be objective and see where this could lead. It made no sense Quint's endangering his life this way, but then it *was* probably already too late. A routine surveillance already made by a Clever Man given the task of keeping an eye on Tom Rynosseros would be all it needed.

"Cas," I called. "Go back without me. I'm staying."

"And tell them!" Quint shouted. "Tell them they can come! But the official opening is tomorrow."

Cas smiled and waved, called out something I couldn't catch, and began walking up the long slope to where her four-seater skiff was moored. She was an experienced sailor; though the winds were poor, photonic kites would put her back in Twilight Beach within the hour. And back again an hour after that, knowing her, knowing her coterie's appetite for the latest sensations.

"I told her you would stay," Quint said, leading me back down the midway towards his shed. "I made her promise to find you even before I told her what these wind-posts meant. She didn't concern herself about them as you do."

"She'll bring others this afternoon."

Quint nodded. "There's nothing to see until tomorrow. I'll be working on Tiresias till sundown. You can finish packing the fill here, take some power cells out to the gate, then help me with the response testing."

"If I can. Just show me what to do."

At 1400, in the heat of the blazing afternoon, the visitors came. Two passenger charvis moored beyond the hills and fifty or more Nationals came straggling down the slope to Bullen Meddi — Cas sweeping along in front, splendid in new white sand-robes, attended by producers and tame (and not so tame) critics, followed by members of her company and others eager for an afternoon's diversion at Sat's Carnival.

Most of them had seen it before. There had been the Taylor readings, and the San-Topuri fire-sculptures on the desert sea, but those events were nearly a decade old — the carnival had long since lost its novelty. This was something new. The newcomers chattered excitedly despite the heat. They paused by the spinners, Daystar and Khoumy, trying to raise answers without success, then, barely disappointed, trusting in surprises to come, strolled down the midway towards the carousel.

We came out from behind the dust-screen and went to meet them.

"We must give them something," Quint said, "or they'll be peeking here and there, getting up to mischief."

I accepted his explanation, not bothering to remind him of his earlier resolve to stay out of sight. Without speaking we walked to where the crowd waited.

I was surprised and disappointed to see how brash and insensitive this manifestation of the public Cas Arana seemed to be. She rushed forward, seized Quint by the arms and waltzed him around, owning him before the others.

"Our ringmaster! Our own biotect!" she cried. "Everyone, here he is! Master of the Revels! Maker of belltrees!"

"Please," Quint said, gently disengaging his hands from hers, looking down. "I simply needed to be alone."

"Nonsense!" Cas said. "There's more. There's more, Tom, everyone! We all remember the play *Merinda*. How the Ab'O girl loved the young National. Now it can be told! Guess who wrote it, who financed the production we did?"

"Not Quint!" someone cried in delight.

"Dominic Quint!" Cas announced triumphantly. "Our carnival master here! Merinda goes to be with her David. The Kurdaitcha avengers come for her. The lovers flee on to the desert and are not seen again. Quint's one play, this legend! All his savings went into the Todthaus season."

And she smiled at me, radiantly, as if to say: Now do you see what goes on here? A surprise for you too, Tom!

I could scarcely believe she was doing it, creating such drama, such inevitable publicity — exposing this former artisan, failed playwright, maker of illicit spinner posts, this man captivated by his love for the Merinda myth, embroiled now too with me, the sand-ship captain from the Ab'O Madhouse, someone the Ab'Os watched.

"Cas!" I cried.

"No, Tom!" Quint said. "It is all right. We had our arrangement. Please, Ms Arana. Take your friends. Show them." And he turned away. When I went to follow he made a sharp gesture. "No, Tom. Stay here. Keep an eye on them for a while."

So I stayed, wandering among the guests, listening to snatches of conversation, amazed at the excitement, at the earnest theorizing. Some were guarded in what they said, deliberately uncommitted; others affected indifference, even a sneering detachment. But whatever the overt expressions, I sensed that more than anything they wanted this to matter. Even the coolly aloof ones on this burning afternoon showed a determination to have that: something meaningful, something important in their lives.

And yet I sensed the opposite of this as well: a paradoxical and ferocious determination to challenge anything short of what convinced them was the real thing.

One discussion caught my attention, two men in expensive sand-robes talking by the door of the derelict hoosy house.

"These have the later type of cap," one of them, a bearded man I knew only as Seth, was saying. "A free-moving bladed cylinder fitted down over the shaft head. The earlier spinners had the vertical windmill arrangement, but you know why that was changed."

"No, I don't," his friend said. "Tell me."

Seth indicated the patch on the other's scrap-jacket, visible through the front of his djellaba: a clutch of narrow ochre triangles converging on a central point. "The National sign," he said. "The Sun of Nation. What do you think that is?"

"Not a spinner!"

"Of course it is. A stylized windmill, a bladed sun. Fitting symbol for the land, don't you think? Of the hostile interior and how it was tamed?"

Seth's companion shook his head. "I don't believe it. It's just a stylized sun motif."

"Exactly!" Seth insisted. "A bladed sun! Interesting, eh?"

I continued around behind the group, glad that despite Cas' use of my name, few seemed to recognize me as anything more than Quint's assistant. Perhaps she had kept part of the developing story even from them.

Raised voices drew my attention, another animated discussion, this time from a group standing by the Grand Doranza.

"It's where the cry: 'Come in, Spinner!' originated," a man was saying.

And there was Seth's friend, again playing the role of sceptic.

"Nonsense!" he cried. "That came from the game of two-up!"

"Yes," the other man answered. "It did. But the antecedents for that game go back a long way, to well before the Chinese massacre at Beechworth. The coins tossed were *I Ching* fortune-telling coins brought to Australia by the Chinese gold-seekers in the 19th century."

"The Chinese used yarrow stalks originally, not coins."

"Yes. Well, the idea for divination posts started way back then too . . ."

I moved away. Something in this determination to find answers reminded me of what I so often did, how I openly considered my Madhouse past in order to know I did so, could be so objective and reasonable. A way of hiding a deeper truth, of hiding from it. It seemed like that now — proper, healthy speculation but with a secret purpose. For there *was* more to it, a different side, the other thing these people were doing. Faced with a mystery, they wished to contain it, neutralize it, even destroy it to ease the curiosity, the not-knowing, the possibility of a something-more that eluded easy and comfortable understanding. They had to be safe again, no less than I.

Was the Bladed Sun of Nation truly a spinner? What a joke! And did the *I Ching* have a part to play? I thought of the ideograms on the shafts, wanting to ask Quint about them and realizing again that this did put me with the rest.

Cas saw me skirting the crowd. She excused herself and came over. "So worried, Tom?"

"You amaze me, Cas! You've ensured his death, don't you see?"

"Tom! He desperately wants *Merinda* performed again. We discussed it months ago, before he came to Bullen Meddi. My cousin never found him; Quint contacted me, sent a letter suggesting another Todthaus season. I came out at once. We reached an agreement: *Merinda* performed with this present development, whatever happens, as a prelude. Tom, he had no money . . ."

"No money! Cas, he's building belltrees, for heaven's sake! How has he financed that? He's more in control of this than you know."

"Well, the arrangement stands. We do *Merinda* this summer, provided the carnival opens. He's kept his word."

I could think of nothing more to say. Three months, a year from now, Cas would apologize, invite me to one of her dinners, spend hours trying to convince me that, after all, it was life being lived, nothing more.

"What part do you think the spinners play?" she asked then, as if I were another of her guests and this was the natural question to ask.

I did not answer her. I left her with her companions and headed for the carousel — to complete shoring up the table.

Some time later Cas and her friends departed, though Quint and I never knew exactly when. I was sequestered with the old man most of the time, running checks on Tiresias, deliberately losing myself in the exhaustive procedures, not wanting to think about working on the AI I feared so much. Whenever he did the response testing, I tried to be elsewhere in the workshop, or out on an errand. But sometimes I couldn't help watching the blurred figure inside the makeshift booth of clear plastic sheets, studying him as he bent over the crown with his light and his tuning instruments. When at last he left the dust-booth for the tea I made us, I had my chance to discuss what Cas had revealed.

"I never knew about your connection with the *Merinda* production," I told him. "I liked it."

Quint nodded. "I always wanted to be the storyteller, Tom. The maker. Merinda was a gifted storyteller, like Scheherezade was. She knew seven old languages, all their legends. But the greatest story is her own. You saw it. I followed the story exactly. Her champion, the young sailor, David, was a National who came with his four companions, rescued the Ab'O girl from the Kurdaitcha and fled with her into the desert. The companions acted as decoys; all but one was slain — the survivor who some say later told their story. In my play I took a small liberty there. I made the survivor the narrating chorus."

"I remember that. But is what Cas said true? Are you revising the legend, planning another season? One story in another?"

Quint smiled and looked back at the spinner post, its bladed crown like a rare flower shut away inside a makeshift glasshouse. "Who knows?" he said. "That would be Cas' wish. This way is better. All my money is gone on this."

He stood. "Tom, the stencils are over there. You can spray ideograms on the lower half. One of each." Then he returned to the dust-booth and presently resumed his testing.

The moon was high over Bullen Meddi when we brought out his final belltree. Moonlight washed the carnival streets, giving the buildings and ruined concessions the dramatic shadows of a penumbral noon.

We had said nothing more about *Merinda* or Cas' remarks. We simply accepted the reality of the task at hand.

The tree was heavier than I expected. I took the lower end of the trunk, Quint managed the end with the upper shaft and diligent housing, the bladed wheel turning as we stumbled along. He steered us between the deserted buildings, up the midway, down a side-street full of ink-black shadow, around a corner towards the merry-go-round on the beach. There everything was bathed in the moon's warming glow, bright and still except for the spinner cap on the one other post I could see: Daystar. It turned freely in the breeze.

Finally we reached the spot Quint had prepared. He guided the footing into its hole; I hauled on the pulley rope slung across the tube-steel tripod hoist and lifted the tree to its upright position.

It took surprisingly little time. We packed the base with sand and quick-drying algen foam and mounded more foamed sand up to the collar of the bounty-box analogue. Then Quint tripped the recessed activator with a hooked pole he had left nearby for the purpose.

At first nothing happened; the spinner disk was still. These were no longer function tests. The diligent was exploring sensation, probably selecting modes. Then the vertical wheel began to turn, its blades flashing with moonlight.

It was alive. I left Quint to watch that happen — troubled as I always was by AI, and began dismantling the hoist.

"Look at it, Tom!" he cried beyond my shoulder. "Djuringa!"

I reacted at the word.

Djuringa. All that is sacred in Ab'O lore: the hills, the wind, the stones, the Dreamtime heroes, the haldanes, the land itself.

Careful, Quint, I wanted to cry. Careful. That's tribal land out there. A ship will come. Clever Men or Kurdaitcha. Don't go too far. Don't be too daring.

But Quint crouched before Tiresias, crooning softly to himself, watching the blades spin, flashing and hypnotic, waiting. I was an intruder here. This was his place, his precious spot. I wanted to leave him with it.

When he showed no signs of ending his vigil, I took up the hoist poles, the tools and foam canister and began carrying them back to his workshop. As I stumbled along, balancing my load, I again felt the sense of disquiet that went beyond my apprehension over tribal detection. Perhaps it was the wind getting in behind the tin and loose boards, creating a hundred tiny half-heard sounds; perhaps it was the contrasts of light, the intense pools of darkness that I found about me and always feared because of the Madhouse gloom I remembered so well. Looking down a side-street, there would be that darkness, then moonlight, then darkness again, laid out in a strip mosaic, with moonlit desert beyond. Always the vivid contrasts. Beside me loomed a vacant interior, also chillingly dark, but there beyond it the ferris gleamed in a long vivid curve, and the Deco spires of the gate held aloft their moonstruck face so it blazed like a shield, clown-eyes crammed with light.

I hunched up my load and continued walking, thinking of the job at hand so that my fears subsided in physical effort. Subsided, not faded entirely. For something remained, some quality in this moon-bleached, forsaken carnival that played on my old AI fears and gave the quiet and sadness its edge of uncertainty and unease.

I placed my load behind the dust-screen, then, to avoid the streets, walked off the midway altogether, meaning to trace my way back to Quint along the open fairground perimeter. I would be in moonlight all the way.

How it happened I couldn't say. Loose sand slid under my boots; I reached down to steady myself on a shifting slope, scrambled to regain my footing and looked up again, to yelp in fright at something blocking my way. My cry echoed across the fairground, faded to nothing in the silvery dunes beyond.

Khoumy stood like a silver knife on the sand.

I could feel my heart pounding; I heard the soft whirring of the spinner cap.

I laughed, trying to regain composure, fighting the panic, the rush of anger it surfaced as.

It lived, Cas had said, Quint had assured me. Would it answer? Could it?

"Hello, Tree . . . Khoumy," I said.

The post stood in near-silence, the spinner whirring away, feeding the accumulators. A minute passed, with just the steady mindless sound. My mistrust grew, my restlessness. It was the old paradox again: disbelief and the need to believe.

"Fake!" I cried at last. "Imposter!" Then, wanting it to be true, needing the release. "It's a hoax! Quint playing tricks!"

The blades turned; the tree said nothing.

I remembered the trigger Quint had used.

"Djuringa!" I cried.

And the word echoed.

"Djuringa."

Not an echo. Too close for that. Khoumy had answered.

"Why has Quint made you?" I asked.

Again the voice came, measured, artificial, but not unpleasant to the ear.

"I wasn't told," Khoumy said. "I was the first, the prototype. I'm very fragile and primitive."

No, I thought. Not life. It couldn't be.

"You're following a program!"

"No," it replied. "I don't think so. I do bioscan. I can tell you all about Father's medical profile. Or ask about stars. I can report on them all, the constellations, the angles of declivity. I watch stars. I love them. I can tell you . . ."

"A program!"

"No! I don't believe . . ."

"You don't know!" I said, driven by remembered fears, helpless before them.

"I'm not very sophisticated, but I believe I am alive. I do. I can . . ."

"But you don't know. It's just programming. Quint's a one-shot playwright, a clockmaker, not a biotect. He couldn't have the skill."

"Please! Ask Father. Or one of the others. You confuse me. You sadden me . . ."

"All coded in," I told it. "That too."

"No. I don't feel . . ."

"Consider it, Khoumy!" I cried, amazed to hear my voice snapping the words, amazed at the vehemence, the cruelty in what I said, but giving in to it all the same. I had to know. "I am Quint's assistant. Consider that possibility now!"

The tree did not answer. It shone; its crown spun, collecting the life of the wind. But it no longer spoke.

"Khoumy?"

There was no reply, no sound at all it seemed but the spinner cap whirring in the winds coming in to Bullen Meddi, sliding in under the cold bright stars.

"Djuringa!" I called. "Djuringa!"

But all I got was the thrumming of the breeze about the shaft, the whirring of the cap and, distinct again, the occasional creakings and soughings from the carnival streets behind me. Then, a plangent note from the bell-chamber, so very sad, followed by the soft chiming of the dim-recall rods in Khoumy's base, the ghost of its own life.

I stood stunned by the confusion of emotions: alarm, guilt, absolute despair. What had I done? Why?

I fled. I rushed into the shadowed fairground streets, oblivious now to the patches of darkness, needing to find Quint.

But when I reached the beach and saw him still kneeling before Tiresias, I could not bring myself to confess what I had done. The words died on my lips, not just from shame, but because somehow Quint looked even more lost and wayward than I felt I did in my confusion and distress.

The sight of him there, the knowledge of his need, buried the terrible news.

"What should we do now?" I asked instead, grateful for the reprieve, wanting to hear a voice, any voice, but his most of all.

Quint rose to his feet. "Help me with the carousel," he said.

Did the words hold accusation? No. He was simply disoriented from being alone with his thoughts. "Help me test it."

I was glad to, so relieved to hear him chattering about what he had done to fix it, the re-wiring involved, the complete overhaul he had given the old motor and music-box.

While he made his final electrical adjustments, I set to polishing the already-gleaming brass poles, encouraging him with questions.

Perhaps Khoumy would recover, I told myself as I worked. Or all it would take would be some minor routine adjustments during one of Quint's service rounds. Yes, that would do it. The tree hadn't been sophisticated enough to kill like that.

Or, the thought came immediately, not sophisticated enough to withstand such an attack as mine.

I kept polishing, hiding the self-contempt, the undefined rage, hiding from voices in another crueler darkness, until Quint came over to discuss tomorrow's performance.

"We must act as custodians and guides, Tom," he said resolutely. "We must direct people to the different trees, distribute the numbers, suggest questions they can ask. Tiresias is my pride and joy. He can talk their philosophies with the best of them. Daystar and Ankh are not as spirited; poor personality definition — I was too eager there, too unskilled. But they can manage. We must protect Khoumy, my poor firstborn. Very fragile that one. Very limited. But stars, Tom. It can tell you all about stars."

I worked on the poles, rubbing them, fiercely polishing the smooth metal, trying not to think of the post out on the perimeter.

From 2000 to 2100, I helped string coloured lights over the ornamental gate and the gantry of the ferris while Quint gave directions.

At 2100, he ran the carousel for half an hour while we stood on the beach and watched. The lights shone, warm and golden, the horses leapt and plunged in the moonlight, the music rang along the shore and brought a strange new life to the old buildings — and an added loneliness as well. The spinners gave back an eerie keening and chiming from their dim-recall rods. For a time the sound of the wind was hidden, concealed under this joyful, less timeless music.

Quint left me and went to finish coupling the festival lights to the power cells. I knew that was done when the already moon-bright gate and ferris tower lit up with a sudden prickle of small coloured points.

So I rode the carousel, happy to be under the dazzling mantle of lights and mirrors — one moment curving out over the empty sand-sea, the next swinging in to the quiet streets. I rode half-blinded by the lights flashing in my eyes, reflecting from the brightwork and gleaming poles.

As I swung out on the desert arc, I thought I saw a single lamp showing, as if a ship waited out there. As I swung in on the carnival leg there was a glimpse of a white figure hurrying across the midway.

I gripped the pole intently, straining to see, but on my next pass both images were gone — ship and figure — probably after-images formed by the dazzle of mirror-light against the darkness, ghosts at the inside of my eyes.

"Tom, she's been here!"

Quint's words came to me above the sound of the calliope, shouted through the dry air. I saw him on successive turns as he came running down the midway, each turn bringing him closer, like a figure seen through the shutter of a magic lantern, a time-wounded magician trapped into instalments, blinks of imminence.

"Who? For heaven's sake, who?" I cried, dismounting, waiting for him, reluctant to jump free of the pedestal in case tools or wedges had been left about.

The old man reached the controls and cut the power. The music stopped and the platform glided to a halt.

"Who?" I said again, jumping down.

"I don't know her name. She's been with Khoumy. Tampered with it. It won't answer me."

I went to comment, but my own images stopped me.

"I saw a light out there," was all I said. "And a white figure back on the midway."

"You did? You did!"

"I thought it was you. I wasn't sure. The light was too bright here."

"Tom, we must search! I said I was baiting a trap. There are phantoms here. We must find out!"

"No, Quint," I said, again wanting to confess my crime against him, needing his understanding, desperately needing his forgiveness, but not wanting to ruin his excitement, not now. "Probably an Ab'O drawn by the calliope. Or Cas wanting to provoke you. Teasing. She'd do it!"

"No!" Quint was adamant. "She wouldn't do that. I told her what I was after."

"What *are* you after?" I asked. Merinda? I almost said, but stopped myself.

"No, Tom, no! Just help me check Ankh and Daystar. She may have disturbed them as well."

We hurried along the beach to where Ankh stood, washed in moonlight.

"Djuringa!" Quint called before we reached it.

"Djuringa," Ankh answered, spinner cap whirring against the stars. "Hello, Father."

"Someone has been with Khoumy. Do you know who?"

"No, Father." The voice came down to us from the diligent. "I know only that Khoumy will not answer me now."

"But living? Living? What do you read?"

"Unliving. That's what I read, Father. Or the signal is too faint for me to tell."

I went to speak but the old man pressed on.

"Have you seen a light out on the desert? A ship? Or someone other than Tom or me moving through the fairground?" Quint's excitement made him stumble on the words.

"No, Father. Nothing like that."

"Could you have been tampered with and not know it?"

"Yes. I probably would not be able to tell."

Quint turned to me. "I'll check Daystar. You ask Tiresias. Watch from there. See if the light returns."

"But Ankh says . . ."

"He may be occluded. It can be done."

By the tribes — Quint had no need to say it. By Ab'O hi-tech interference from over the desert waste, or from out of the sky — from an orbiting comsat given that precise task.

The old man hurried away and I went back to where Tiresias stood near the carousel.

"Djuringa!" I called, and waited below the spinning blades.

There was no password response.

"You harmed Khoumy!" the belltree said, startling me with the accusation.

"I didn't mean to," I said.

"Yes, you did," it accused, but without rancour, merely saying what it knew. "You were testing it for life. In your own way, that's what you were doing."

I moved in closer, fearing our voices would carry. "You didn't tell Quint."

"It would not help Father now. His task is nearly done."

Such a compassionate, life-seeming answer. Such a good strong voice — the tree sounded and looked so powerful, its wheel moving briskly, drawing the eye into its disk of fractured moonlight, blades paring the wind.

"Was there a ship?"

"Yes," Tiresias said.

"A figure in the streets?"

"Yes."

"Who? Do you know?"

"Look out there!" the spinner said.

I turned and scanned the desert. To my left the carousel sat untended on the beach, blazing like a Tsar's precious crown. To the right the low dunes folded and re-folded until they levelled out completely. Far out on the windswept waste a light shone. I watched it flash once, twice, go dark, come again, then vanish altogether.

"A signal! A code!" I said. "For whom, Tiresias? You?"

Was this tree a traitor? I wondered. Suborned, acting willingly for interests other than Quint's, or was it under some compulsion? I doubted everything now. A belltree would not need such a primitive visual signal, merely an override beamed to its function centres. Was the beacon for someone human?

Like Khoumy before it, Tiresias would not or could not answer.

"Tiresias, who is out there?"

"*Muki winorbin,*" it replied in dialect, an expression even Nationals knew, from one of the old languages.

"Ghosts? That was no min-min light. Who?"

But driven to silence or choosing it, Tiresias did not say.

I ran to find Quint. He was nowhere near the carousel that I could see, so I went back along the beach to Ankh, stopping long enough to say the password and ask it the same question I had put to Tiresias.

"Ankh, who is out there?"

"*Wandang,*" it said, the same answer in a different dialect.

Ghosts. Again, ghosts. Merinda the storyteller coming to get her old champion, another storyteller — the man who had told her story as best he could.

I believed otherwise, but when I had looked for him at the deserted workshop and reached the midway again I immediately doubted myself: there before me was a tableau — figures waiting, frozen where they stood but for the wind picking at their garments.

Quint stood in the middle of the main avenue. At the far end, close to the ornamental gate, was a solitary white-clad form, a cowled female shape, her robes stirring in the moonwind. At the other end of the midway, near the carousel and Tiresias, where I had been but a few moments ago, were three figures, all dark, two men and a tall slender woman between them, backlit by the carousel so that it seemed min-min lights danced in their hair.

"Quint!" I cried, but said no more. There was moonlight glinting off metal — the figures with the dark woman carried weapons.

Ab'Os, I knew. Tribal people from the ship I had seen.

"Merinda?" Quint called, his voice full of desperation and hope.

From the white figure near the gate came: "Here, Quint! I am here! Come now!"

And from the dark woman by the carousel: "No, Quint! Here!"

The tableau dissolved. While the old man stood undecided, the Ab'O men came forward and led him quietly back to where the dark woman waited. Then, with not another word spoken, the small group turned and walked down on to the desert sea, the distinctive shape of the clockmaker in their midst. By moonlight their silver forms and accompanying dark shadows dwindled into the gloom, merged with the desert.

The white figure came running towards me, flinging her sand-cape open.

"Cas?" I said, knowing it had to be.

"It seems I wasn't the only one to have the idea," she said. "I was trying to help." She looked to where Quint had been taken. "What will they do to him?"

"He's broken their law. I don't know. Khoumy could have told us; he had bioscan function, Quint said."

We stood on the deserted midway, and even by moonlight Cas could see my look of reproach.

"I wanted to save him, Tom. Grant me more than what you saw today when I was with the others. That was all part of it. He wanted to be found — to expand the Merinda legend, to make it his. He gave me my script. Only tonight did I improvise, dare depart from it. I didn't know what was coming but I had to try."

"One of his own trees betrayed him," I said, realizing as I spoke the words that it had to be true.

"What!"

"Yes. Can you see it, Cas? He made life, then one of his own creations, his greatest, Tiresias, inquisitive, seeking information, learnt of its forbidden nature. One of the first discoveries it made. It sought confirmation; it wanted to know more. It called in the tribes. Kurdaitcha!"

Suddenly three detonations shook the fairground; three brilliant balls of fire lit the air as the diligents of Tiresias, Ankh and Daystar exploded, scattering incandescent fragments across the midway, bright flickering sparks which slowly settled and died.

There would be no performance after all, no re-opening of Sat's Carnival with fortune-telling posts and carousel rides. "The ghosts were busy tonight," I said.

"But they left one intact," Cas replied. "Out on the perimeter."

"Khoumy is moribund. It would not have registered on their scan. I killed it."

But as we walked up the slope towards her skiff, leaving behind us the burning candles of the spinner posts, the mad gate and ferris tower decked out in their small sad web of party lights, the merry-go-round on the beach untended, to glow by day and night until the cells failed, we heard a voice calling across the quiet sandhills of Bullen Meddi.

"I have decided," it cried, the words clear and distinct. "I am alive!"

Cas looked at me, eyebrows raised in an unasked question.

"Tell no-one," I said, cherishing those few simple words from Khoumy.

"Only if you come to the opening night of *Merinda,*" she said.

"Done," I said, not looking back. "Done."

So Much For The Burning Queen

The final game between Matine Gentle and Paul Cantry took place on the terrace of the Gaza Hotel exactly ten years to the day from their first encounter at fire-chess. No doubt this fact had been foremost in the minds of the organizers when they arranged to bring the two Grand Masters together again, to hold the contest back where it all began.

The Gaza terrace was the perfect place, especially at the sunset hour of the breaklight when the winds were warm but fitful and the dust-devils came. Other places were safer, more sheltered, but what was fire-chess without hazard, without the chance of pieces being debased and whole strategies ruined, of victories so suddenly gained? Fire-chess showed the uncertainty of the world; the game suited the age perfectly.

For days before the contest, the famous terraces and promenades of Twilight Beach were crowded with tourists and tribesmen. The hotels and casinos were filled to capacity. The occupants of the villas had an endless round of game parties going to mark the occasion. Down on the beach, the local boys played stylo as always, moving their capped pieces while the crowds watched, using throws of a die to make up for the vagaries of wind. But now their games had a new edge, a compelling urgency. Everywhere you went, the esplanades and avenues were decorated with the twin signs: Matine Gentle's Burning Queen, red-gold on blue, and Cantry's Knight Aspirant, orange on black, known by all as the Burning King, though Cantry resisted that name as much as ever.

"I'm just the paladin," he had said to the media on his arrival, as he always did. "Debased or ennobled, win or lose. That is all I have ever wished to be."

And, as always, it changed nothing.

The Burning King was to play the Burning Queen.

* * *

We were there for the contest, of course, arriving less than two days before the game and mooring at the Sarda-Salita with seventy other sand-ships, unable to get our usual place at the Sand Quay.

When *Rynosseros* was checked in and we were ashore, Scarbo took Rimmon to the kitemakers, Strengi and Shannon went to the gaming tables at Deep's, and I went to visit the Burning Queen at the Gaza.

Teos Dessa, the contest president, was in the lobby when I arrived, talking to David the hotel manager. He saw me and hurried over.

"Captain Tyson! Tom! At last! David said you would be coming."

"Hello, Teos. What is it?"

The thin, worried-looking man clasped his big hands in a fervent, earnest gesture. "Can you accept a mission?"

"Now? Not with the contest. No!"

"It's to do with the contest, Tom. It's about the contest. You are going to see Matine?"

"Yes, I am. You know the standing argument over 777."

Teos laughed politely, as if recalling that momentous morning six years before when Tom Rynosseros and Matine Gentle had argued with poor David over who should get that room. I had booked it, but famous, almost beautiful, not-to-be-crossed Matine had wanted it too — had needed it, she said, for luck or continuity or whatever.

I had yielded that day, and we had had an acquaintanceship-in-obsession ever since.

"So explain, Teos."

"Tom, I am worried. The circuit is my life. I conceived the whole Gaza contest idea. Now I'm afraid Paul Cantry intends to lose. Deliberately."

"How do you know that?"

Teos looked embarrassed. "It sounds absurd. But I've watched Paul and Matine for ten years, pacing one another; first Matine beating Carlos two years ago and becoming Grand Master, then Paul beating Prine last month. They're both matched again, both here. Matine will win because she has to be the best. Paul will lose because he still wants Matine and this is his way, his big chance. I've grown to know them, what drives them. He'll do it well but he'll lose."

"Why?"

"Because we're back here. Because they're both Grand Masters and he's a romantic fool. He needs a gesture more than he needs to win. His agent agrees. He told me Paul cancelled three World Circuit games to be back here and play Matine. He could have waited until the Annuals in spring at Pia. No, he wanted to play Matine here. So we arranged the contest."

"Why is it such an issue, Teos? After ten years, if a gesture like that is the best he can give himself, let it be."

Teos frowned, looked even more disturbed.

"Tom, a Grand Master doesn't just lose. You belong to the public. Bets are made. I know that Simon Grail and Alanto Comus are betting Paul will win on his recent performances."

"Then warn Paul."

"We can't. That might give him the idea, you see? He says he intends to win."

"Teos, I can't see how I can do any good here. Neither Matine nor Paul is . . ."

"Humour us, Tom. Please. It's a precaution. We'd rather be foolish than wrong."

I looked about the lobby, studied the ocean through one of the large view windows.

"All right, Teos. At least I'll talk with Matine and Paul."

A few minutes later I was knocking at the door of Room 777 just as I'd intended.

Matine answered, her striking, strangely-cold face framed by loose tawny hair, her rich brown eyes matched by a cho'zan gown the colour of lions.

"Yes?"

"I'm sorry," I said, "but there's been a mistake. I have a booking for 777."

"That's impossible. I advise you to consult with the Manager. And don't say the Manager sent you to tell me."

"All right. How's this? I just bought the hotel. I am the Manager as well as the owner. Now get out!"

Matine Gentle laughed. "Nice, Tom. Won't you come in?"

Usually, on these courtesy visits, I would go to the french doors, step out onto the balcony to watch the ocean for a while, ask her about life on the circuit, then go. Now I crossed to the balcony and waited.

Matine brought us each a glass of tautine, but instead of completing the pattern between us, I told her what Teos Dessa had said. She listened, her eyes never leaving me, and not for the first time I found myself fascinated. Matine had a presence that brought her to the point of incredible beauty, that gave a definite quality to a face that was striking but not beautiful in any conventional sense.

Some said — and with good cause — that it became beautiful only when lit from below by the burning pieces of the game, lit so the planes of her cheekbones threw shadows just so. Then, that strong countenance softened into beauty. Then, like some shadow-painted war-huntress, Matine Gentle had the fierce lines brought into a semblance of absolute loveliness. Little wonder, many also said, that Paul Cantry had fallen in love with her at the board, looking across the burning field to that suddenly splendid image — the wide tawny eyes, the mane of hair, the newly vibrant lines and planes.

"Paul wouldn't do it," she said when I had finished. "I find it all most unlikely."

"I told Teos I'd look into it, Matine. He can't afford to chance it. Will you be speaking with Paul before the game?"

"Only at the solstice party tonight, and as little as possible then. And I agree with Teos Dessa. I'd advise you not to mention it. Paul might get to liking the idea when he finds I'm beating him."

"Agreed. But could he have gone to Grand Master to be back here with you for the Gaza contest? Because it's the level you accept him at. The Knight's errand . . ."

"Fool's errand!"

". . . to win the lady. He's cancelled three circuit games to be here."

"So I heard. Icroco, Prine and Sastan will not be pleased. The besotted fool!"

"Teos is more concerned about the speculators. Simon Grail and Alanto Comus have made bets. They won't appreciate a gesture."

Matine finished her wine. "They might kill him, true. But I've sat at the board with Paul. He won't do it. He'll try to beat me, to put the Tyrant Queen in her place."

"Are you sure? Sacrifice at the moment of triumph can make for a rather stylish victory too, in a sense. Better than power for some."

Flecks of golden light moved in Matine's eyes. She furrowed her brow. "You mean me there, Tom? Power? Well, it's more!"

"I accept that, Matine, and it isn't what I meant. But there must be ways Paul could do it so Grail and Comus couldn't be sure. Either of you could manage it, with game tension and all. During a light breeze, during a move, an unlucky breath. Out goes a tiny flame; a Bishop is debased. Or a Rook. A Queen. Say it was chance."

Matine poured herself more wine, brushed some wisps of long hair back with her free hand. "It's not that easy, believe me. And this is to be an Untouched Game, if I choose. It's up to me. We may use the tongs."

"Will you?"

"Tom!"

"I'm sorry, Matine. I didn't want to be involved in this. I've just finished a mission and I'm tired."

She followed me as I went to the door.

"Tom, I intend to beat this romantic fool. I intend to play fairly and win, here, once and for all, at Twilight Beach. I cannot believe Paul would ruin his career or endanger his life. He loves me, but what sort of jejune love can it be? He does not know me or he would not bother."

"I'll see you at the solstice party, Matine."

She smiled. "Yes. At the solstice party."

The Charles Christos Imbri is much smaller than the Gaza, but it is the best of the older beach hotels. It is five minutes walk north of the Gaza terrace, its long sun-drenched steps fanning down onto the sand, occupied now by souvenir sellers and the players of stylo. At midday, the glare of the hotel's whitewashed walls was blinding. At the main colonnade, I stopped to watch some young men playing a game, using coloured caps to show the status of their pieces since it was so windy on the shore.

I went to the second floor and knocked at the door of Paul Cantry's suite. Paul answered it almost at once, a tall saturnine man with a severe profile and harsh, flawed good looks which some said the game transformed into a hero's mask no less than it changed Matine. He had come to the circuit late, having already won fame for his work on *Love Songs of the Twentieth Century*, and for his own composition, *Beloved Lion*, a song obviously written with Matine in mind. From the moment he took up the game, it was seen as his way of courting her.

"Ah, Tom Tyson. Come in. As one madman to another, how do you see my chances? Are the omens benign, or should I throw the game and not give her the satisfaction?"

I was at a loss for words. So much for not discussing the possibility of a gesture.

I followed Paul back into his rooms, and watched him as he filled two cups from a silver tea service.

"Don't look disappointed, Tom. Is that disappointment I see? I know how all this appears. All the theories have occurred to me, all the possibilities."

"All right, Paul. So continue. How will you proceed?"

"I don't plan to lose," he said. "I intend to defeat the Grand Master."

"I wish I could be convinced of that. Just to make things easier all round."

"Ah, straight to the impossible! I like that. Here!"

He handed me a cup of blended tisn. The tautine was sharp in my stomach and I welcomed the hot tea. We took our cups to the balcony, sat in some sling chairs, and looked back down the beach to the Promenade and the Gaza, now bathed in rich afternoon light.

"Tom, I know that Matine doesn't love me in any conventional way, and I'm not always completely sure of my feelings for her, not really. But I believe I do love her, regardless of how foolish it seems. It's a commitment from me; I'm wooing her the only way I know, with the only life I have. She was taught by Carlos himself, and he taught her too well. I sometimes think it was a Svengali and Trilby thing, only she caught the legacy of power from him and had to defeat him. Good female spider comparisons come to mind, right? My over-active imagination."

"Right," I said, starting to relax at last, enjoying the long low curve of the waves rolling in and the endless song of the belltrees from the hotel's roof garden. But his next comment startled me, and brought me back from my growing reverie.

"Do you know we have been lovers?" he said. "Oh, yes, it's true. We've had only seven games in ten years. After the three stalemates, we made love, sharing the energy. I can scarcely believe it. After her three victories, I didn't see her — not eligible. After my single win at Pia, she looked momentarily stunned and seemed to see me for the first time. I'm not naive enough to think a win at the Gaza will necessarily do any good, but there are only two of us now Carlos is dead. I've never beaten her as a Grand Master before. It could matter."

"Especially to the speculators."

"Ah, yes. Well, I'll be the naif to that extent. I don't care what the speculators think."

"But . . ."

"Or do, Tom!" he said. "You understand me?"

"Fine, Paul." I finished my tea. "That does it then. I can go back to Teos and the Contest Board and tell them both you and Matine intend to win. Good." I stood up and headed for the door, glad to be free of this unwanted business. "Remember that Simon Grail and Alanto Comus are betting you will checkmate Matine. They've probably computed it to how many moves, with wind variations and all. They know your game technique, your preferred gambits and responses."

"Thank you. But frankly I don't care. I play only one opponent."

"Of course," I said, still nettled, still not convinced. "Thanks for the tea."

I left the Charles Christos Imbri by the beach stairs and moved along the shore to the Promenade. The afternoon sun threw brilliant light onto the ocean, and underneath the sounds of daily life could be heard the shimmering susurration of belltrees, and the deep hollow booming of the tidal bells swinging on their sea-chains beneath the surface, calming me.

Now I could relax. Now I could find Shannon and Rim and the others, or go to Amberlin's or The Traitor's Face, or lose myself in the Mayan Quarter or at The Slow Hour. I would avoid Teos and the Gaza. I would not, would not think of fire-chess.

Which was impossible, of course. Everywhere I went it was the main topic of conversation. I heard some astonishing rumours about Matine and Paul (though none as sensational as Paul's own revelation at the Imbri), learned of some staggering wagers which had been made. The media had done their promotion too well. The motifs of the Burning Queen and the Burning King (shown always as the Knight, orange on black) were hung in all the streets.

It was impossible, too, because I realized there were two more people to see. Two more at least. Though I hated the thought of it then, I decided to call on Alanto Comus and Simon Grail.

Comus had made his fortune selling infusion sculptures across the world, and I was not surprised to see that a soldier dressed in fire kept me from his door.

"Back off!" the figure cried through the blazing grid of his helmet.

I could not tell whether the cataphract in the portico was a true-sense projection, a genuine sculpture from Comus' collection, or an actor/automaton. When I said who I was, the fighter, the sound and the heat vanished. A door opened into a cool garden. Comus found me wandering there.

"You look weary, Captain Tom," a voice said among the ferns, and I turned to see the glistening bald head and gleaming oiled jowls of the fire-sculptor as he approached, his short body dressed in a robe of fine white Egyptian linen.

"I am certainly that, Alanto," I replied. "It has probably been a day of deceptions."

"Then," — he spread his arms wide — "I am Truth!"

We laughed together amid the ferns, then Comus went towards an inner door. "Will you take refreshment?"

"No, thank you," I said, and Comus stopped. "One question only. What happens if Paul Cantry decides to lose this game?"

Alanto composed his hands before him. "I'll take his heart, of course. I'll set him as a pillar of fire on the Nullarbor, make him a beacon to sail your ship by. He will burn forever!"

"Extravagant, Alanto."

"I want an honest game," Comus said.

"Paul's losing would be part of an honest game."

"Granted. But profitable?" — again the hands went out — "I am depending on him to win."

"You need the money?"

"No. I enjoy the reputation."

"No clemency?"

"None. Truth is adamant!"

"Interesting," I said, and went to the doorway leading back to the street.

"Oh?" Comus said, as I pulled back the door and stepped through to where the fiery cataphract was once more waiting on the steps. "Why?"

"Truth has no soul!" I said and closed the door behind me.

* * *

I did not find Simon Grail until the solstice party that evening. Teos Dessa had arranged to have the celebration at Quay Massillian, the splendid villa of Twilight Beach's greatest benefactor, the late Spydyr Massillian, a man rivalled in wealth only by the entrepreneurial Simon Grail and the brilliant parvenu, Comus.

I arrived at 1900 and searched through the dazzling crowds until I found the vicious, terribly old Chinese. He was standing with four Cold People, former friends from his youth almost ninety years before who had been brought up from his family vault for the solstice and the game.

But I had no success there either. Despite implants, transplants and prosthetics, Grail was clearly a man at the end of his life. His friends, back from their strange wintering, were creatures out of time — pathetic, disoriented, with the odd callous irreverence for all things still living; providing companionship for Grail in return for forced, fragmentary lives, tastes, glimpses. They laughed at Grail in their silences, and it was as if he did not see. How could such people truly savour the game, the vital reality of those who lived and burned?

I realized all these things when I asked the old Chinese the same question I had put to Comus.

"I will kill him," Simon Grail said. "It is simple."

"Mr Grail, any money you win will only be the tiniest fraction of what it has cost you to bring out your friends tonight. It cannot be money."

"Every act becomes an indulgence now, Mr Tyson. I create rituals whose purpose I have forgotten. But the habits are my habits. They bear my stamp." The voice was soft, poisonously, powerfully soft.

"This is an indulgence you may understand then. Doesn't chance, the unexpected, the impulsive, count for something now — for you, for these friends for whom the unexpected can be the only joy? Why not some affirmations to reassure them that life is good, that it was all worthwhile, and still is?"

"We have said enough on this, I think. Goodbye, Mr Tyson."

I moved away, and for an instant caught a glimpse of Matine attended by crowds of the cognoscenti, the circuit and fashion elites, the press. She wore a gown of precious cho'zan, her hair was a glorious mane, her strange hard face looked striking in a make-up designed for her around the lines given by the burning pieces of the game.

There was no sign of Paul Cantry. Teos stopped long enough to tell me Paul had put in his token appearance earlier, leaving after half an hour.

I stayed a while longer, saw that I would have no chance of speaking with Matine alone, and decided to leave. As I went through the large doors, I noticed Alanto Comus and Simon Grail in conversation — or in the glancing, self-absorbed exchange which passed for it — both men surrounded by Grail's revenant friends.

I smiled at how futile my day now seemed, at the burden of anger and weariness I carried with me still. Only one chance remained, that from whim neither Comus nor Grail would act. But as I watched the man of fire and the man of ice talking together, it did not seem that such a thing could be.

I have always understood, instinctively, that everything we do is couched in symbols, that simple acts have elements to them which communicate, resonate, far beyond their objective natures, that we understand more than we consciously know. Every game, every situation, every act of hospitality and making and giving is caught up in such a bounty, rife with subtleties, nuances, the often unwanted extra truth.

Fire-chess is just a game, but like all games it has the conflict, the tension, the continual choosing and re-choosing, the very essence of life.

As I went back to our mooring (I preferred the desolation of the quiet Sarda-Salita desert flats to the hotels of the town), walking down streets bright and alive with the solstice festivities and game parties, I reflected on the forthcoming contest. As we always do throughout our lives, I rediscovered things I already knew and had known for years: that regardless of what Paul did, or Matine, or gifted decadent Comus, or spiteful pre-wintering Grail, we live to our fullest when we choose, when we understand and own our choices.

It was not a profound or new thing to realize there on the cool dark backstreets of Twilight Beach, but it eased my spirit then. The four principals in this would choose, I reminded myself. Life — as it always did — would flow about those choices, whether to win, to lose, to kill, to set Paul out on the Nullarbor to burn as a Knight forever.

I reached the mooring where our darkened sand-ship stood, thinking of how we give our lives meaning by our choices, new and renewed, of how we define ourselves in ways beyond ego and, yes, though it rankled then and did not please me to think it, beyond death.

Then, at the gangway, with the town at my back and the wide desert stillness before me, I laughed, laughed at what my day had been and where it had led.

For I had assumed all along that Paul Cantry would throw the game.

I went to bed, cursing Teos and his suspicions and thinking of pillars of fire strewn across the Nullarbor, pillars of endlessly dancing flame which became two, then one, then two again until I slept.

* * *

In the small hours of the morning, the chime of a sensor woke me, told me someone had come aboard. I assumed it was one or more of the crew back from their various adventures, since the gate-watch would admit no strangers to the docks at that hour. The knock at the aft-cabin door surprised me.

I stumbled to answer it, belting on my robe as I went, and found a shrouded figure waiting at the foot of the companionway.

"Matine!" I cried as the hood went back.

"Tom, can we talk?"

"Well, yes. Come to the salon."

"No, outside," she said. "On the docks."

So I dressed again, and we walked without a word along the moonlit quays of the Sarda-Salita till we reached the steps leading down to the desert.

"What is it, Matine?" I said, as we moved away from the silent hulls and the distant lights, the sand sliding and whispering under our feet.

"It's Paul. I've thought about it all day. What will happen?"

"I discovered nothing, Matine. Not a thing. And I did not see him at the party."

"I barely did myself." In the moonlight, I saw her shake her head. "We only ever meet across the board."

"Can I be lewd about that?"

Matine stopped. "He told you?"

"Yes. But your coming here tells me more."

She made no attempt to explain herself, but stood there, the illumination coming from above her now and not flattering at all, making her face stark and plain despite the cleverness of the make-up she still wore.

"Tom, why did I come to see you?"

The question surprised me.

"I could say you are after a somewhat informed opinion. I've spent the day assuming Paul would do it."

"I must win!" she said, but softly. "I intend to win!"

"Good. Do that. You couldn't accept less. I believe he will genuinely try to win."

"I will win!"

"Then you came here because of *Beloved Lion.* You want that too." And I began reciting the words of the song. "Moments arise, seasons of green . . ."

"The fourth canto," Matine said, and I changed to that brief and haunting part of the song cycle.

> "I've known you in other faces,
> Looked at you in other eyes;

The mornings come, I sit and wonder,
There's so much to really realize.

Discovered you in other faces,
Already seen and always new;
You are the wind in lonely places,
Déjà-vu!"

"Something is wrong," Matine said, interrupting, though she had let me finish the canto. We turned back towards the moorings.

"I am not Paul," I said. "And you already know what you are going to do."

"Yes," she said, putting up her hood. "I do."

And she left me and headed back to the Gaza.

The next morning, the town was strangely quiet. The streets of Twilight Beach were virtually deserted until noon, as if people waited indoors in anticipation. The banners and decorations hung listlessly until the first afternoon breezes came and set them swinging and billowing under the hot sun. Suddenly, doors opened, window shutters went back, people came forth, sauntering down from their hotels and villas, resting on the cafe terraces. A few games of stylo began on the beach below the Gaza, and slowly, gradually, as the afternoon drew on, the excitement began to build.

Teos Dessa called on me at mid-afternoon to learn my views and assure me of a place at the Gaza for the game. He owed me that much, but, though he did not say it, I was left with the feeling I was to be an additional bodyguard should anything happen, not that Comus, Grail or any of the unmentioned others would act then.

Towards sunset an incredible tension settled over everything. I kept away from the media broadcasts easily enough, but there was no avoiding the excitement. By the time I took my seat on the terrace alongside Teos, overlooking the board, the weight of feeling was visible on every face.

At 1750, the beautiful ceramic pieces were set in place. Two tuxedoed flamfeudines moved in and began lighting them; the ushers laid out the tongs. Matine had made it an Untouched Game.

At 1755, Paul Cantry came to the table, dressed entirely in black. The cheers and applause were as much for relief from the tension as any kind of acclamation. Paul stood in his place, smiled, bowed once and sat down.

Matine appeared a moment later, wearing a splendid gown of golden cho'zan made for the occasion, her hair coiffed and full, her face made up in the simple 'naked face' that would be adorned so amazingly by the pieces of the game.

The cheering and applause went on and on, even after she was seated. Teos Dessa made his short speech and at 1810 the game began. As the players took up their tongs and drew them from their brocade sheaths, there was absolute silence — the terrace, the whole town held by the 'game-death'.

Matine opened with a Queen's Gambit, carefully using her golden tongs to move her Pawn.

Paul countered with his own Queen's Pawn, and so it went, each of them developing their game.

For the first fifteen minutes there was no threatening breeze. The pieces remained ennobled, their flames flickering and dancing in the body wind from the audience and the guarded shallow breathing of Paul and Matine themselves.

But then a gust came in from the sea. It rippled the chimes, set the belltrees to stirring, hit the long white facade of the Gaza and slid off the tiles back onto the terrace.

Paul Cantry lost his King's Rook in that settling cascade of air. He said nothing, just gave the debased piece a quick glance, as if calculating the intricate possibilities of guiding it through Matine's guard at some improbable moment to ennoble it again, to 'bless it with fire' as the commentators would say, to restore its 'honour'.

I saw Paul study Matine's face, but he could not expect a reaction there. She was the Lion, the absolute Burning Queen, the subject of countless media-enhanced mythologies. The game continued.

Five minutes later, even as he went to move his Queen's Knight, reaching out with the gorgeous cloisonné tongs he had won at Pia, Paul lost his King's Bishop's Pawn the same way. He barely hesitated in his move, though he smiled down at the board. That Pawn was lost, impossible to refurbish, locked to its tiny death march to the fiery lines before it. Paul went on to move his Knight.

Sunset became the long golden hour of the breaklight. Dust-devils appeared in the streets. On the Gaza terrace, the liveried Devil Catchers became alert, shifting their long-handled spoilers in their practised hands, their eyes flicking back and forth, as careful now as surgeons.

Breaklight became full twilight. The coppery radiance sank from the sky and left lustrous peacock blues and growing indigo. On no other evening was the town quite so still, gripped by such expectation.

In the second hour of play, when Paul had only half his pieces ennobled to Matine's two-thirds, he took her King's Knight, and Matine looked across the board at him for the first time. She watched as Paul snuffed out its tiny flame, relegating it in the reversed alchemy of fire-chess to the low-game where debased pieces rarely survived a thousand count.

Matine reacted swiftly and brought down her Queen, sliding it along fiery corridors rather than lifting it to where the still-smoking Knight stood cancelled and dark. Whether through zeal or passion, a sudden undetected eddy of air or the merest chance, her piece lost its flame in transit, the tongue of fire spiralling in on itself and vanishing like a miniature genie.

From across the town you could hear the cry of the watchers, a sad spontaneously-swelling thing, a single vast outrush, a great sighing.

The piece debased in transit is a dead piece, removed from the game altogether.

You cannot avoid omens in fire-chess, and this was one. You cannot play with alchemy, with the eternal life-giving, life-affirming symbol of fire and not be touched. If it had not been her Queen, rushing to where that cold Knight stood flickering only in the reflected light of its betters, then Matine would have recovered.

On the surface, her control was excellent.

The game continued; she played as skilfully as ever. But I knew that in her soul the game had been lost. The crowd interpreted that unspoken language of symbols as well. Every one of us understood the precise measure of the transaction which had occurred, of the duplicity that now prevailed, the following through.

I thought of Alanto Comus and Simon Grail and those countless others who watched, thinking, interpreting. They could not take exception. Matine had moved too zealously perhaps, but she had not planned such an act — such a unique symbolic death for herself; this much was clear.

Chance again. Like all of life: the alchemy of chance.

Paul Cantry read the omen for what it was. Physically, in posture and eyeline, nothing changed. He sat as before, contemplating the pieces, his tongs laid on the table beside him for the moment. When he took them up, he played brilliantly. His own Queen swept up and down the corridors and seemed to grow brighter (we later found that the scan and subbing crews had star-shot his Queen and his remaining Knight for the rest of the game; unnecessary enhancement really — against his debased pieces those flames shone like torches).

No more fate-winds came. No more flames were lost by chance, only by the steady shifting of the pieces, by the strategies Paul built around his Queen.

The language of symbols gave him an incredible presence. Across from him, calm composed Matine played on like a doomed Queen, like Zenobia marching into Rome, her lion face sinking into deeper, even more fearsome lines and curves of shadow as one piece, then another, went dark and was taken.

It was soon to be over. Her burning King stood amid the dross of the game, with only one cornered Rook flickering helplessly under its hood of fire. The only other seven flames on the board were Paul's.

Matine stared at those pieces, finally reached out and moved her Rook to take Paul's debased Bishop, a bravura act, a formality to let the game reach its end, before the thousand-count expired.

The tension was incredible. Paul steepled his hands and looked about him at the faces in the cool dark night. There was not a breath of wind, not a sign of a devil weaving in to play assassin. A time without chance, it seemed; a time laden with symbolic truth, in which every element perceived, every movement, was vivid like never before. There are moments like this: before death, when reprieved from death, sometimes in new love, or when old love is seen anew.

Paul reached down as if to move his burning Queen in to checkmate, let his hand slide past it to his flickering King. He brought it up smoothly and, with a breath, blew out its flame, then set it down again, on its side, showing both the old and new ways of capitulation.

There was an indrawing of breath all about us on the terrace, sweeping, echoing out across the town, followed by a stunned silence.

Such things did not happen.

"Your game," Paul Cantry said, and sat back.

Matine looked at him, her severe face unreadable in the light of the remaining pieces.

"Why?" she said.

"Because this has to matter. Because I love you more than I knew. Because a part of you understands."

"I won't accept this," she said.

"Good."

"I won't, Paul!"

"Good."

"They'll kill you."

Paul Cantry smiled and shrugged.

And Matine Gentle picked up her own King, blew out its flame, toppled it with a hollow ring of porcelain on stone.

She rose to her feet and Paul did as well. (For an instant I imagined figures burning in the desert, two, then one, then two, but not burning alone.)

They turned and walked off, not together, not apart, into the Gaza, and left behind them a night filled with delight and fury and confusion, a night of symbols and vendettas and the eternal waiting newness of chance.

Mirage
Diver

That summer I saw the Boorindi triptych in the Gallery at Kalgoorlie — the three large panels with their images of the dream cities: Ash, Bari and Dan. I stood with the crowds of sightseers, awed by the shapes painted there, finding that something oddly relevant, terribly important, was being communicated.

Seeing the Boorindi paintings always left me disturbed, filled with disquiet, with an urge to seek out the young mirage diver and ask him why these images, these cities. I wanted to know how he could spend his days crouching out there on the dunes and see sights like these and say they belonged to this land.

So naturally I was alarmed when it was confirmed by the Gallery's See Committee president, Angel Ferris, that Paul Boorindi had stopped producing, and pleased when she gave me the Gallery's commission to seek out Paul at Yates-Eluard and discover what was happening.

Committeeman Ferris looked at me disconsolately, her usual buoyant manner worn down by too many meetings, by the endless run of media engagements. I studied the grey eyes framed by the close-cut brown curls and understood the worry I saw there. She knew as well as I that more than sixty per cent of mirage divers went insane — markedly schizoid and anti-social; another ten per cent went gradually catatonic to the same end. Fearless Gram had ceased diving after producing his masterpiece, *The Engines of Night.* Long Strode had done the same after his Caliban series. Paul Boorindi looked like being the latest casualty. Having completed the City paintings, *Amid the Jewels, The Country Palaces* and *On Resisting Summer Days,* it seemed as if his time as a mirage diver was over. Australia had lost another great artist.

* * *

I booked passage into the inner desert and arrived at Yates-Eluard on its hottest day for nine years. The colony town was quiet an hour before noon, with no-one about and no wind to pull us into the sand-ship moorings. The *Marjory* rolled in under power to find the docks deserted; no-one appeared to sign for the small pile of cargo and mail left on the burning quayside.

I adjusted my burnouse and set off along the glaring causeways and empty morning streets, eager to check in at the Salamander and shower before going down to the dunes and the colony itself.

The hotel was only a third full during high summer, so I chose a top-floor room looking out on the desert and close to an ancient Croesus belltree I had grown fond of on previous visits. The old Croesus had lost most of its bells and much of its sentience, but the management, out of sentiment perhaps or a sense of continuity, had not had it replaced. Seeing it tucked away in its corner of the terrace made me smile. When I had changed, a houseboy called me down to the front desk where a dark, narrow-faced man came forward and introduced himself.

"Good morning, Captain Tom," he said. "I am Faoud Lebad, the local representative for the See Committee. Angel Ferris asked me to meet with you."

The reed fetish on his white robe told me he was an Egyptian, the silver disc-with-rays at his throat that he was an Aten worshipper. I shook his hand and we exchanged pleasantries, then I asked, "Is it as serious as the Committee says?"

"But yes," he said, guiding me by the arm across to some chairs near the tall terrace doors. These doors were closed and shuttered at this hour, and the lobby was pleasantly dark and cool with its palms and fans, its large square pillars, its lacquered screens and subdued conversations. We sat and Faoud gestured to a waiter for drinks.

"The truth now, Faoud," I said when we had been served tall frosty glasses of tautine. "I understand that Boorindi has ceased producing."

"Worse than that, Captain. The whole colony is in decline. Several divers have begun 'ghosting' Paul Boorindi's work — producing imitations of his Cities. Others have seen valid mirages and started pieces, but the visions go and the paintings are abandoned. It is very troubling."

"You feel there is a connection?"

Faoud nodded. "Paul Boorindi is our greatest *imagier.* He is so young, so full of energy. He has produced three strong paintings. Ab'O psychometrists and fellow divers all read and confirm that energy. It is there still. But after the last City, nothing. Three months of nothing after four weeks of such splendid achievement. And now the colony suffers a hiatus, a malaise. Ghosting and truncated visions. Something is happening."

"The divers are still Ab'O?"

"Yes. So few Nationals or outsiders ever see images on the Serafina." Faoud hesitated. "But I forget. There is Tenna. She is only twelve years old, an Ab'O and Egyptian cross."

"A diver?"

"I know. You will say that only Ab'O males can paint. But Tenna is accepted as a diver at the colony, though she produces nothing. You will see. She runs errands for the divers. She is always there."

"And the divers still choose the new divers?"

"They do."

"I would like to go there now, Faoud."

"Of course." Faoud drained his glass. "Let us brave the day."

In the atrium of the hotel we donned our desert clothes and put on our sun-glasses. We stepped out on to the street to be greeted by the terrible heat and the dazzle of brilliant sunlight off whitewashed walls — and, to my surprise, by a modoc wearing his white quarry's shirt with its red rings. As Faoud and I turned left to head down the street towards Farlook and the Serafina, the demented, sun-weathered Target Man fell in behind us.

"Don't mind Modoc, Captain Tom," Faoud said. "It appears I have inherited him. He likes to follow me about."

I glanced back at the tall shambling figure in white and red, at the vacant expression on his face and the big hands dangling by his sides. He was smiling at Faoud's remarks, pleased to be noticed by him.

I smiled too. Our little group presented a strange sight, even by the standards of Yates-Eluard: an Atenist worried about loss of revenue and possibly his job, a Target Man waiting to die, and a sand-ship captain sent to investigate the fate of the greatest mirage diver in the land.

There were fifteen divers waiting patiently on the long dunes outside the township, most of them sitting in a line along the crest of Farlook, their boards set up, their eyes searching the empty desert, looking out from under their wide-brimmed hats at the far horizon of the flat Serafina Basin.

It was after noon and relentlessly hot. The air shimmered. The glare was terrible. Few besides the divers were willingly out in it. A handful of tourists watched from the sheltered terraces of either Rushing Fools or Mad Dog Pavilion. Some patrons sat in the open fronts of their tents, drowsing over drinks, wanting to be there in case something came. But there were not many. The gallery reps and art media writers had gone back to their hotels to wait out the worst of the day and would venture out again only near sunset, trudging down the crooked streets to the Divers Stairs and the desert to see what the *imagiers* had produced. And, lately, *if* they had.

I walked along the base of Farlook, trying to make out Boorindi among the others. The draped figures all looked the same under their eccentric hats and sand-capes, so many quiet and contemplative forms beneath faded parasols and shades, intent beachcombers endlessly searching the Serafina for what they called the divings, "the image that is true".

And there were few charlatans. This ragged company assembled under their strange domes and pyramids was almost a guild, each one approved by his peers, accepted by the acute perceptions of the rest.

As we walked, Faoud told me how the girl, Tenna, had been up at Farlook for months and seen nothing, but she had been allowed to remain. She had the gift and it would show in time. Others, poseurs and opportunists, continued to be hunted out of the area, often protesting defiantly, banned from Farlook by the tormented elect.

Boorindi had his tribal flag on a slender pole where he sat beneath his shade. That led us to him. I left Faoud with Modoc and scaled the dune, scrambling and sliding in the hot sand, finally mounting the crest and crouching beside the motionless form.

He was not imaging. The panel in front of him was clean.

Boorindi turned his head to see who had dared to intrude. Through tinted eye-shades his eyes regarded first my face then my desert clothes, saw my charvi insignia through the open front of my djellaba. Then they turned back to the burning desert, narrowed again for sand-sight.

"Tom Rynosseros. This is novelty. A sand-ship captain. The See Committee likes the oblique approach. Soon we will have astronauts for town planners, and modocs as civic leaders or cryogeneticists."

"Angel Ferris asked me to come, Paul."

"Angel Ferris wants paintings. She hounded Fearless Gram when he stopped producing."

"I'd like to talk," I said.

Paul Boorindi pulled off his dark glasses and regarded me again. "With respect, Captain Tom, this is a long way from dreamlocking and dealing with Clever Men. We are sports. Solitaries. We stay together because this is the place, but we are estranged from you, even from each other. A true group apart. We cannot keep away. Go back to Angel Ferris and say that when there is a mirage for me, I will bring it here." He nodded to the empty board. "Not for her, but because I have no choice. I must have it."

He put on his glasses again and returned to watching the desert.

I could not let it go at that. "Paul, I realize you cannot break the diver taboos and discuss this openly, but something has to be done. It's not the gain involved. That would not have brought me here. I know that the Ab'Os read the land in a special way, that the tribal mysteries turn on truth, and that we must not lose that. You are already sharing something through your paintings — otherwise you would not let us see the divings, let alone display and sell them. Can't this sharing be increased, so we can help safeguard the process and reduce the penalties? The divers want to tell us something, many of us sense that. We need to know — not what it is, but how to help you do it. Paul?"

But Boorindi did not answer me. My arguments had been heard before and I could think of no new ways to put them.

I stood, feeling more than ever an intruder. But I did not leave at once. My only prepared course of action was to talk with Boorindi or the other divers. I had to stay. I felt Boorindi was concealing something, something beyond the mysteries of the divers and the tribes, some inside knowledge possessed only by the greatest *imagiers* as they neared the point of madness. I wanted to be here where it all happened, where his secret began. The glaring Serafina stretched out before us, burning under the summer sun, its distances forever empty to the likes of me.

I moved several steps away down the dune, reacting to the tension I sensed surrounding the man, not wanting to intrude on his space any longer. But I still watched him from the corner of my vision. I saw when the girl, Tenna, came near, moving along the line of divers till she was at Boorindi's spot. I saw her crouch down beside him, place an arm on his shoulder and top up his water flask from the simple bag she carried. Then she spoke, words that came to me quite clearly in the stillness.

"Naked eye in the glade of expectation."

She said it again, like a refrain, a key phrase just for him. Then she looked up and her big brown eyes met mine. It was a full gaze and one of sudden assessment, startling and direct. Her blend of Ab'O and Egyptian blood gave her a force which belied her years.

"Hello, Tenna," I said, to free myself from that gaze and hear again the voice which accompanied her presence.

But she became a young girl once more, artless and distracted by her chores. "Hello," she said, leaning on Boorindi's arm to help herself up. She moved past me and continued on down the dune ridge.

I stood there wondering what to do. Though I doubted some of the See Committee's motives, their concern for the Yates-Eluard colony was based not just on dwindling sales and loss of international prestige. The Ab'Os had agreed to an arrangement and now there were problems with it. An explanation, or at least a formal voiding, was needed.

I would achieve little without assistance from the divers. So when Tenna had gone, I returned to where Boorindi sat.

"What did she say to you, Paul?" I asked him.

The Ab'O's head did not turn from the horizon. "Just words. In her own way she likes to think she helps us find our visions. She is the water girl."

And that was it. I waited a few minutes, then moved off along Farlook greeting each of the divers in turn. Some answered me with a polite word or two; some glanced my way and said nothing; others ignored me completely. Even Tenna made sure she was somewhere else, busily helping.

Finally I clambered down to where Faoud and his big insane friend were waiting and we headed back into the town. Faoud sensed it had not gone well and said nothing, though Modoc began to sing.

"All these people, helping at the mill,
All this trouble, helping at the mill,
Keeping to the rhythm, keeping to the stone,
Keep that rhythm, turning at the mill."

The Target Man's flat heavy voice grew louder as we moved through the quiet streets. He added verses, lines that didn't rhyme or make sense but that seemed to please him immensely. He began slapping his thighs as he walked, grinning and drooling. We were close to the Salamander when he said some lines that made me stop.

"Hear the dream-talk, helping at the mill,
See the girl go, helping at the mill."

"What is she doing, Modoc?" I demanded, turning to him. "What is Tenna doing?"

The Target Man grinned and pounded his fists against his thighs. "Helping, keeping, helping at the mill!"

He went on repeating it, becoming more and more excited, saliva falling on to the bright target rings on his chest as he boomed out the words.

Faoud tried to calm him but the big man strode off down the street, shouting his song and swinging his arms wildly about.

"I'm sorry, Faoud."

"No, Captain. It's his manic phase. He gets like this when he's been to Farlook. They all do. He'll be waiting for me later."

Alone in my room at the Salamander, I showered and lay down on the bed to rest out the hot afternoon, thinking to escape the mirage divers for a time. It was not easy. On the wall opposite were reproductions of some of the more famous renderings: Vannikin's *First Dive,* Fearless Gram's *The Engines of Night* and Boorindi's three Cities, these presented as always as one group and in sequence.

I studied the famous triptych. It was too small now to be overbearing, but it was still vivid and disturbing, especially in the subdued light from the terrace. Under each image was the legend Boorindi has chosen and inscribed for that panel during his dive. The first said *Amid the Jewels* and described Ash, so strange to see with its odd tower lines clustering up out of a severe blue plain under an intense and fretful sky of a richer, deeper blue. The painting was nothing new, just an abstraction of shapes, almost a decalomania like Ernst and Dominguez used to make. Nothing in plain view accounted for the disquiet, for the sense of sinister expectation I felt, not the quasi-organic towers, not the dark formwork of lines and struts at its centre or the 'coronets' and 'diadems' and 'lattices' of yellow light strewn across the shapes.

The second painting, *The Country Palaces*, was easier to take, its alienness muted at first — a series of strange stylized pavilions set in waving grasses. That city, Bari, no larger than Ash in area, was low and sprawling, as if the towers of Ash had faded like phantoms or given their substance downwards to the airy, billowing pavilions underneath — to the bright horizontals. Looking at Bari one got the impression of towers compressed but present, folded back and hidden, waiting to leap up and bludgeon the sky.

The last City, Dan, was the most representational, the most accessible. It depicted a desert-scape, very much as one saw it from Farlook or the balconies of the Salamander. But in the distance, out on that burning waste of ochre, white-gold and muted reds was a city of rock, of boulders and crags and grey-brown massifs, almost machine-like in its brooding separateness. *On Resisting Summer Days* Boorindi had called it, and it disturbed as much as the others.

I lay in the gloom and tried to sleep, but the three Cities kept me from it. Through half-closed eyes I tried to unlock their secret message, to discover what it was about surreal, blue, light-flecked Ash, the wide, almost cubist savannahs of Bari and the familiar wasteland of Dan that drew my eye and gave me such an urgent sense of déjà-vu.

What Tenna had said stayed with me too, that line she quoted kneeling there in the sand at Boorindi's elbow. It had been said deliberately, with both her and Boorindi's knowledge that I would overhear.

Naked eye in the glade of expectation.

The words seemed appropriate. Farlook *was* such a glade; the little community there had its eyes exposed and committed, naked to the visions of the Serafina.

But that wasn't it. It was more that Tenna could come and go among the divers virtually unnoticed, murmuring little comments such as this, guiding the *imagiers*, accepted by them all. Tenna — a shadow that belonged. In this crazy desert town with its wandering modocs, on the Grand Tour circuit for the re-kindled Cold People, at the hub of vogue and madness and great art, this pubescent girl was a common thread. I recalled what Faoud's Target Man had said: 'helping at the mill', what Boorindi himself had suggested regarding her: 'She is the water girl'.

Her words did not strike me as idle encouragement. It was a line I had heard or read somewhere, from some text I could not place. I wondered how I could check on it here in Yates-Eluard. There were bookstores but no library, probably retrieval systems at the Salamander and Frenchman's, though access to literary sources might be limited. But I had it as a clue at least, something to use and consider.

When at last I did sink into sleep I had dreams — fragments and sudden dislocations. I awoke around 1700, troubled and disoriented, though the afternoon light had softened and the Serafina had sent a strong cooling wind that revived the old Croesus belltree and rattled the terrace doors and slowly changed the town.

I met Faoud at 1800 and, after dinner, over glasses of tautine, we discussed the diver phenomenon and why it always seemed to end in madness.

"You understand, Tom," Faoud said, "that I supply the See Committee with information. They draw the conclusions and suggest the theories. I am only one person. The popular idea now is that the successful diver becomes saturated with the Serafina images, reaching a point of desensitization. He grows so used to seeing bizarre sights that he cannot produce. Then, estranged, he starts to render the new bizarre: our own mundane world. The characteristics of the diving phenomenon resemble the symptoms of schizophrenia. Boorindi's Cities trace the estrangement — exotic to mundane."

I emptied my glass. "The last City, Dan, is for us the most commonplace. For Boorindi it may be the most strange."

"Yes, Captain Tom. That is it. His reactions following Dan show the measure of his alienation. The great anxiety and marked withdrawal seems to go with lack of output generally. You've noticed the atmosphere down at the colony."

"Has no-one been able to interview the divers?"

Faoud held up his hands. "You were there. How did Boorindi react to you? It is a closed elite."

"What about the girl?"

Again the hands went up. "Tenna? She is a child."

"She is a diver."

"An honorary one. She is tolerated, that is all. Useful. She has produced nothing."

"Where does she live, Faoud?"

It was the easiest course to take and the most promising. I visited Tenna at her mother's address in Paternoster Lane, choosing a time well after sunset when I felt the girl would be there. The street was quiet; Tenna's narrow door opened on to the cobbles like a dark coffin lid in the whitewashed walls.

I knocked twice and waited, listening to a belltree sounding somewhere up in the windy darkness. I barely noticed that the door had opened till I saw Tenna's mother standing there as quiet as the street and as narrow and dark as her own coffin-door. The Aten disc around her neck reminded me that her daughter was an Ab'O and Egyptian cross.

I told her my reason for calling and prepared to launch into an elaborate explanation. But she stood to one side and murmured, "Upstairs, please," before I had said more than her daughter's name.

I found Tenna in a second-floor room that opened on to a roof-garden with views across Farlook and the divers' colony.

The girl's wide dark eyes showed no surprise. She stood at her door wearing a loose white smock and a small metal ansate cross at her throat. I wondered if all the Egyptians in Yates-Eluard were Atenists.

"Captain Tom," she said. "Paul told me of you."

"I came for myself," I said, in the Atenist way. Tenna regarded me with her calm even gaze, and for a moment I thought she would not admit me. But she turned and walked back into her room, silently giving me permission to follow.

Her room was simply furnished but comfortable, with many shelves of books. I noticed texts on dynastic Egypt, the Amarna period, the teachings of Jung, the Surrealists — so many subjects. There were reproductions of most of the divers' works, and above her low bed a large triptych of Boorindi's Cities, one of the loveliest printings I had seen. Through the garden door I could see the black iron rod of the belltree I had heard from the street, its bells long pierced cylinders of space-iron, its crown formed in the forked shape of an Anubis.

"Your tree is very beautiful," I said.

"That is Hotep," Tenna said. "The bells are meteoric. The crown comes from the Life Tree at Seth-Ammon Photemos."

"I've never been there."

"It is a closed town now. Some day."

"Perhaps," I said, and became aware that Tenna would be required to treat a direct question as the other divers had. I did not want to risk that. But at least I could trust that she meant me to overhear her words to Paul Boorindi. "Tenna, today I heard you quote something for Paul down on Farlook. 'Naked eye in the glade of expectation.' I know it's from a poem. I thought you might tell me which one."

Tenna watched me, her big eyes giving nothing away. "It will make you smile, Captain Tom."

"Good. But at least I'll know."

"More than some would like."

"Why, Tenna? I already think you are the catalyst for many of the divers here."

"I have been the shadow girl since I was six."

"The shadow girl?"

"Let me show you the poem, Captain Tom."

She went to a bookcase, took out a tattered volume and handed it to me.

I smiled at the title. *The Complete Works of Paul Eluard.*

Tenna smiled too. "A nice synchronicity, don't you think? By chance the town becomes his namesake. But this town is full of synchronicities. You will see."

"And the poem?"

"Is there," Tenna said, and signalled by her eyes that I should take the book and go.

I did so, but at the door to the street she stopped me.

"Captain, I am not a diver and never will be, contrary to what they say or think. I am just a catalyst, just a shadow girl. I am their . . ." But she stopped.

"Their Great Mother," I said for her. "I've noticed that all the divers on Farlook are men."

"Why is that? Why are most of the truly great artists male? Still?"

I recalled her books on Jung. We were completing something between us here. "Possibly because men need to make creation into a mystery, to elevate it dynamically — a vitality mystery to be in balance with the female birth mysteries. Most women don't need to bring religiosity and self-exaltation to artistic creation. Men do."

"Is that all? A compensation?"

"Only for the behaviourists, Tenna. I really don't know. Men do seem to be more empassioned by ideas, more inclined to hitch their egos, their wills, the best of their intuition, to artistic creation, the way women do to organic creation. Patterns exist beyond fashions and accepted roles."

"I care for them, Captain Tom," Tenna said. "They bring back important things and try to resolve them. They go mad."

"Why? What is the vision too awful to bear?"

Tenna did not answer, could not, so I spoke again, wanting to keep her talking, to keep her from closing the door.

"Do you visit the ones who are already gone? Do you visit Fearless Gram and the others in the sanatorium?"

"There are no sanatoriums in Yates-Eluard, Captain Tom," Tenna said. "No oubliettes and destiny-jars. There's the Serafina, and you've seen the modocs roaming the streets. You've seen the souvenir seller at the base of Farlook, never facing the desert."

"The souvenir seller?"

"Yes. That is Fearless Gram, but you must tell no-one. *The Engines of Night* drove him mad. His only painting; his first and last vision. Long Strode went to tending the catchment sinks after his Caliban paintings were done."

"So what is Paul Boorindi doing, Tenna? Are his imaging days over?"

"Yes," Tenna said, with a firmness that surprised me. "But he doesn't know it yet, so there's hope. He has not yet understood the completeness of his own paintings. The lesson there."

"And you do?"

"No, Captain Tom. I am only twelve years old. But a part of me does. The part they need does."

"So you give them poems, lines of verse?"

"Or songs. Or key words. I suggest hooks on which they can hang their images. Psychic automatism, like the Surrealists revered. I've read Breton's *Manifestoes.* I gave Long Strode the lines from *The Tempest.* For Boorindi it is a poem in that book. Why? I feel it is right. I provide the water to turn the mill."

"I see. The water girl. The shadow girl."

"You do see, Captain Tom! You do sense the power in me. You can accept how it's possible."

"I reaffirm you, Tenna."

"I'm glad." Tenna slipped in close and kissed my cheek. Then, as part of that same movement, she was away and closed her narrow door.

I walked back to the Salamander, unable to get Tenna out of my mind, this remarkable twelve-year-old who was such a force among the divers of the Serafina. I felt a sudden strong desire for the slim boyish form. It was sexual in part, alarmingly and unexpectedly so, but it went beyond that. I wanted her approval, the way Boorindi and the others had her approval, and I wanted her comfort. I wanted the Great Mother in this serene child to give me sanction and sanctuary.

I considered why this was, seeking the answers that would leave me at peace, untroubled by the denial of a closing door. I kept returning to the newness, the certainty and purity of the womanness in the girl, shown in her ministrations and their subtlety. It was not some simplistic mothering — it was the 'womanning', with its accompanying lack of cynicism and ulterior motive. I felt excluded from that fleeting, unspoken service to the divers, and it mattered.

Back at the Salamander, I sat at one of the white metal tables on the terrace and, in the light of Aulus, the hotel's big luminant-belltree, looked at the Eluard poems. They were arranged with the French original on the left and the English translation opposite, and it did not take me long to locate 'Exile'.

> Amid the jewels the country palaces
> Diminishing the sky
> Tall women motionless
> On resisting summer days
>
> Crying to see these women come
> Reign over death dream below the ground
>
> Neither empty they are nor sterile
> But lacking boldness
> And their breasts bathing their mirror
> Naked eye in the glade of expectation
>
> Tranquil they are and more beautiful for being like
>
> Far from the destructive odour of flowers
> Far from the exploding shape of fruit
> Far from the useful gestures the timid
>
> Consigned to their fate knowing nothing but themselves

I read it several times, finding a great wealth of hints and triggers in the abstruse word-patterns.

Tenna had been right. The poem was almost automatic — with disparate, spontaneous images brought together randomly so vibrant new meanings were suggested.

As a self-appointed but natural psychometrist, the girl had used it in that way. The Surrealist poet had trusted to free-form images and placement, relying on his belief in the much-prized and all-important factor: inspiration. Tenna — it seemed — had dismantled the Eluard text, taking the images and feeding them, by chance or intuitive design, back to modern *imagiers* like Paul Boorindi.

It was, in a sense, psychic automatism in reverse — her returning those fragmented images to an unconscious beginning, using them as thought-fetishes and agencies of chance to trigger inspiration, to unlock the secrets of the Serafina.

And the art critics and media people knew nothing of it. To them Tenna remained the water girl.

I looked up from the Eluard poem, out over the terrace and the town, down through the cooling air to the colony, now just so many pools of lamplight in the darkness. I could hear belltrees communing with the night and answering the big Aulus. There were voices coming from the bars. I traced my route to Tenna's house across the moonlit squares and rooftops, and imagined the girl out in her roof-garden alongside Hotep, sitting next to those long tubes of metal from the depths of space and guiding its songs back to me, back to the Aulus and, above me, my broken Croesus.

Tenna was shrewd. Had she revealed more than she intended, or was it part of a plan, a way for her to break taboo and help me to help her and her charges?

The more I thought about it the more I was convinced that she would give me a clue if she could. I drew together fragments from our brief conversation, looked down at the so appropriately-titled poem and began to suspect what it might be.

The next morning at Farlook I bought a copy of *The Engines of Night* from Fearless Gram, though the shrouded figure, dressed in sand-cape and wide-brimmed hat like the divers on the dunes, did not acknowledge the name when I said it.

Faoud was there too, with his faithful Modoc tagging along behind, the red-on-white rings of his body-target a startling brilliance — a piece of the whitewashed town brought out into the desert. I avoided the Egyptian and his companion and hurried along the base of Farlook, past the shanties and lean-tos of the divers and the pavilions of the patrons and dilettantes. I saw Tenna up on the crest, carrying her water bag and running one of her errands, stopping to murmur something every so often. She saw me and waved, then continued on her way. The water girl, tending the mill.

I reached Boorindi's spot and climbed to him. His eyes darted my way then returned to the burning sand.

"Paul, can I stay?"

The diver did not answer. He concentrated on the shimmering horizons of the Serafina.

I sensed the same terrible tension as before, as if Boorindi were straining to see something, trying not to lose a vision. Looking at those sealed eyes, I wondered where creative fire ended and a schizoid prison began.

"I understand the taboos placed on the divers, Paul. The safeguarding of the mysteries you are charged with. But Tenna showed me an Eluard poem. Called 'Exile'."

The eyes did not move to me, but they narrowed.

Still no answer. It occurred to me that he might not know the poem as a full text, only as disconnected fragments.

"I know the arguments, Boorindi. The suggestions that your paintings show a progression away from imaging, an estrangement, a loss of vision for you. Faoud tells me that the Cities become less exotic, less arcane, because your perceptions of them have changed. The otherness has become mundane; the need to render it is less intense. But I am suspicious of theories and interpretations. To keep your mysteries is one thing, but might not those mysteries be failing you now? We share this world, Paul. Some of us do want to help."

The eyes finally broke to me.

"What do you see in my triptych, Captain Tom?" He asked it suddenly, angrily.

"Three Cities, Paul. Or three attempts at one City. There is only one poem."

"Yes!" he snapped. "Yes." More softly. And then, almost a whisper: "Yes. The same City. Ashbaridan."

"It must be very important to you to stay here trying to see it again."

Boorindi stared a moment longer, then began laughing, laughing loudly in the desert silence, so that other divers along Farlook turned to see and Tenna, out on one of the lesser dunes, came running.

The laughter subsided, but there were tears on Boorindi's cheeks and he was shaking his head.

I felt foolish. Once again I sensed the tension and the barrier between us. I was a complete intruder and I did not want to be there when Tenna arrived. As she came running, I eased my way down Farlook and returned to the Salamander.

Again I rested out the afternoon, drifting in and out of sleep, waiting for the old Croesus belltree on the terrace outside the french doors to sing with the first late afternoon winds.

I watched the paintings as I had the previous day. Fragments of the Eluard poem came and went, and with those lines another that I could not place in my drowsing state:

The unpurged images of day recede.

Not Eluard's words, but from my own reading and from a famous old poem, triggered by a memory, an association, something I had heard or seen.

I tried to recall more, to connect it up, thinking how Boorindi's images eluded him and remained unpurged. But sleep took me and there were the sudden random chimings of the Croesus heralding sunset and driving such thoughts from my waking mind. I forgot I had remembered it.

I dressed and went out onto the terrace, turning the corner so that I faced not directly west but slightly away from the Serafina and the colony. I stood watching the changing colours of the desert, drawn into reverie by the long shadows growing amid the rock formations.

At the far end of the terrace, tucked away in its corner, the Croesus stood against the lustrous light, its few broken bells motionless and silent again, its dim-recall rods softly chiming with the memory of wind, a small weary aching song of need. The diligent in the crown knew nothing else, just wind and the lack of it. Even as I considered its plight, another breeze lifted over the balustrade and brushed by me. A stronger breeze this time. The diligent sensed it and altered modes. The rods went silent, the bells stirred. Negative ions came forth from the bounty-box to charge the cooling air.

I was misunderstanding something. It was so easy to accommodate theories, to interpret the City paintings as the bizarre becoming conventional — a steady shift from the otherworldly to the mundane. But Boorindi's laughter had irony and despair, and I felt I had missed the point of his confession about Ashbaridan. By thinking the diver's perceptions had shifted, I was making the same mistake as Faoud, the art commentators and the See Committee.

One City. Three attempts at one City. Ashbaridan.

To say Boorindi was diving less and less because his perceptions had changed did not cover everything. Perhaps the burning desert vistas he saw *were* alien enough, had become the new arcana to him. Perhaps the Serafina images were so real that as Boorindi and the divers lived them more, they could render them less. Had their perceptions adjusted to the visions so they were no longer as provocative or inspiring?

Did that explain the despair, the forlorn laughter? Or . . .

The unpurged images of day recede.

I remembered the words, and with them other lines. I spoke them aloud to give them life and form, seeking the connection that had brought them to me.

"And all the complexities of fury leave,
Dying into a dance,
An agony of trance,
An agony of flame that cannot singe a sleeve."

Unpurged.

An agony of trance.

The poem and the poet's theme came to me. I ran to the western turn of the terrace and looked out at sunset over the Serafina, out over the golden roofs, the pooling shadows, the swelling life of the town, and down to

Farlook. I could see the tiny dark line of the divers, the squares of tents and pavilions, the silhouettes of tribal flags.

"Those images that yet
Fresh images beget . . ."

"What is that, Captain?"

Faoud was there, keeping our appointment for the evening.

"That's it, Faoud. 'Fresh images beget'. I must see Tenna. I must ask Tenna."

Faoud came with me to Paternoster Lane, and Modoc too, though the Target Man was 'mooning' now, staring up at the bright moon in half-phase, anticipating his end. He did not remain with us long.

By the time we reached the narrow door there were just the two of us, and Faoud's patience was almost gone. But he kept silent, knowing I would tell him nothing till we were with the water girl.

Tenna's mother let us in, nodding to Faoud and making the Aten sign to him with her outspread hands, then directed us up the stairs to the roof-garden off Tenna's room.

It was a little after dusk and pleasantly cool. The girl was not back yet from Farlook so we sat on guest-mats near the strange-sounding Anubis, listening to its eerie songs and drinking the pepper tea the woman brought us.

"Have you indeed found something?" Faoud asked.

"Be patient a little longer, Faoud, please. I may be very wrong. Our problem is one of protocols. The divers represent one of the newest and most volatile artistic changes in Ab'O culture in centuries, even millennia. Not only the phenomenon for its own sake, but the very newness of it has to be accommodated by their Ab'O mystics and scientists.

"It's a violation of set forms and precedents. The tribes are as uncertain and disturbed by it as we are, more so because they sense the integrity of these visionaries. Naturally they have put major constraints on the divers."

Faoud leaned forward with excitement. "And you have found a way forward through these protocols? Without involving censure or payback?"

"I'm not sure. It's more a suspicion than a plan. All I know for certain is that to succeed with the divers you have to work at their level, in their way."

Tenna arrived then. We heard the street door open and close and soft footsteps on the stairs. For a moment there were low voices, then Tenna came out on to the roof.

There were pleasantries at first, more tea served with date cakes and talk about the Anubis and Faoud's Modoc. Then a silence settled as both Faoud and Tenna waited.

I took the Eluard book from my pocket and handed it across to the girl.

"You gave me a synchronicity," I said as she took it. "The Eluard poem in a town bearing his name. You said this was a town of synchronicities, so let me give you another just as wonderful."

The girl placed the book beside the empty cups. "Which is?"

"The Yates in Yates-Eluard. The poems of William Butler Yeats. The Byzantium poems? Where the poet yearns to travel — not to Byzantium itself, but to what that city has become for him in time and legend, what it means to him as a symbol of artistry and inspiration. A place of replenishment, of exaltation. Of absolute spiritual and creative rebirth.

"Tenna, Paul Boorindi is seeing his own Byzantium, isn't he, there, large, out on the Serafina? I suspect he sees it every day, taunting him, calling him, but he despairs of ever reaching it and rendering it on canvas. The image remains unpurged and unpurgeable. In fact the *imagiers* all see the same thing."

Faoud could not help himself. "No, Captain Tom!"

"Half-close your eyes, Faoud. Look at *First Dive.* Look at *Engines* and the Caliban series and the Cities. Look at the ghostings and the abandoned studies. The ones that are allegedly portraits too. Light and shapes and variations. So many styles. The critics see the differences, but let yourself see them as interpretations of the same thing. Byzantium. Something crucial to these visionaries; culturally an equivalent, a constant represented here.

"That is why there is so much anguish, so much tension and anxiety — and madness — down on Farlook. The modocs sense it. Not because inspiration won't come but because it is always there. It eludes the divers while in front of them. They are staring out at a constant vision — most of them estranged from it, making tentative attempts now and then, abandoning what is wrong. 'The unpurged images of day recede', and remain unpurged. Every day the divers lose what they alone can see but cannot express. Farlook is a place of torment."

Tenna watched me in silence, considering everything, but poor Faoud served too many masters. He thought of the uproar when it was made known that all the wonderful mirages were one recurring mirage; he saw the international confusion, the plunging gallery values, the See Committee in a baffled fury blaming him, the tourism in the colony ebbing away, so many things.

"You are giving a great deal to some lines you have recalled," he said. "Look at the divers! They are Ab'O. The visions aren't Ab'O myths and images."

I understood his resistance. "Why do you limit them to their Dreamtime, Faoud? Or imagine that the Dreamtime cannot encompass the experience of all the humanity that is available to those who understand it. My European traditions go back to your Ancient Egypt, to Mycenae and Eridu. What right have I to claim Babylon and Knossos and deny Paul Boorindi Athens and Byzantium? As an idea if nothing else, a focal point, an equivalent? Why should the Ab'Os not use what they are exposed to? It becomes theirs too; we cannot take it back. Their use of it may be unique, or it may conform to the sort of universals Jung identified in all human achievement.

"This is amplification, Faoud, a linking-up with the rest, the alternatives. Jung would tell you that the Dreamtime is both one limited and limiting and one unlimited and unlimiting way of knowing everything that is humanity. That is why there is a Byzantium in the desert. Don't worry about your Committee and the future of the colony. What is happening here is far more important than what the divers have wanted outsiders to believe."

There was more to say, but while I directed my words at Faoud, I was talking to Tenna and asking her to answer. The girl was standing beside the Anubis now and in the darkness I could not see what effect my words were having. I continued to speak to Faoud.

"This land has been waiting a long time to be used for something so new. It's not your place or mine or theirs. It's *a* place. You own it as much as I do; you can read it as surely. It will be what you need it to be. We bring things to it. It takes those things and gives them back to us. That's what lands do, what places do. So, Tenna?" I now turned to her. "Am I right? You have concealed this too? But it had to come from me, from someone else."

The girl crossed to the door of the roof-garden, turned and looked back at us. "The divers sit there before the Serafina vision, driven to helplessness and silence by it, putting up with the prattle of tourists and collectors and the media people, and questions from well-meaning people like you, Tom. They endure madness from within — the torment of being ineffective, of failing to link up the parts — and from without there is the other madness and torment to endure.

"But you are right. Whatever is relocated is changed too. Just as you could not remain a European, myself and my Ab'O kin could not wholesomely remain what we were before the European and the Egyptian and the rest. We have adjusted till it has transformed us. Unaccommodated man reaccommodated. Boorindi painted three Cities to get to one that was free of the old. You won't see Byzantium through us. You'll see more. Or less. New Byzantiums. All the makings are here."

"Ashbaridan," I said.

The girl nodded. "Ashbaridan."

"So what happens now?" Faoud asked.

"It is in Yeats' poem," I said, watching Tenna to see if she could use my interference legitimately.

"The smithies break the flood,

The golden smithies of the Emperor."

Tenna smiled. "I must talk with Boorindi," she said. "I must tell him about your synchronicity. The agony will not go, but I am only here to ease the madness." And she went out of the garden and down the stairs. We heard the street door close and the sound of Tenna running.

Faoud and I regarded each other, understanding only a little of how this had to be played but accepting for now that it was enough. We sat listening to the Anubis and the shimmering tides of sound that washed the town at night, then, bidding each other goodnight, we went our separate ways.

At 1035 the next morning, to the astonishment and delight of everyone, Boorindi began a new painting. No-one dared go near him, though art critics, media people and tourists lined the rails of the Farlook Pavilions or camped under rented sun-shades to watch. Despite the terrible heat, there were signs of celebration throughout the town, laughter and singing in the bars and people roaming the streets discussing the news. Even a handful of Cold People brought their borrowed bodies out of the town's dark creche to watch the event — this unexpected highlight to their Grand Tour. They joined the crowds watching the figure at his place on Farlook, earnestly working away, with only Tenna stopping now and then to offer water. The other divers sat in their usual positions watching the Serafina, none of them imaging but knowing that one of them was.

Faoud told me about it over a late breakfast, yammering excitedly and gesturing about him. Even the news, brought to us by a houseboy, that his Modoc had been taken overnight did not dampen his excitement for long, though I knew he would feel it later. The Target Man had been a special thing in his life.

After our coffee, we robed ourselves and walked down to the colony. It was a relentlessly hot day. The dunes were dazzling ribs of white-gold edging to yellow-golds and reds out at the horizon. The sky began as a soft inviting blue and quickly became a glaring canopy with the sun a blinding boss at its centre.

A day of apocalypse.

In this terrible summer land, everyone stayed as still as possible. Only one man worked, in a frenzy, applying his heat-retarded paints, wielding his brushes. One man and a girl, for Tenna was racing along the line, herself frantic with delight, reflecting Boorindi's ecstasy of creation.

The modocs in the crowd were restless too, twitching and rocking, beating hands against thighs and making guttural sounds of excitement. Faoud became sad when he saw them.

After an hour or so of keeping watch, once they had assured themselves that Boorindi was committed, people began moving back towards the town for their siestas. Only the keenest patrons, a handful of art commentators and the modocs remained.

I stayed, though there was nothing new to see from where I sat under my rented sun-shade. Faoud went off to contact Kalgoorlie and keep Angel Ferris informed. From time to time during the early afternoon, art media reps came to the top of the Divers Stairs, satisfied themselves that the diving was continuing, and returned to the bars and lobbies of the hotels.

At 1400, when the sky was a searing white shield and the desert landscape shifted and shimmered whenever I could bear to look at it, Tenna came down from Farlook and found me. I was dozing where I sat and saw at first only a small figure shrouded in sand-clothes and wearing dark glasses. But the voice was a cool spring, rich and vital and very important.

"Tom?" she said, her voice 'womanning' me, drawing my gratitude. She handed me a cup of water which I drank in one swallow.

"How is he, Tenna? Is it a good painting?"

"A great one. Though they will not think so." She looked over at the town. "But it bridges the gap."

"And what you told him? About the Yeats poem?"

"Is very relevant here, Tom."

"Which lines did you give? All of it?"

"What makes you think I found a copy to give him? I simply told him what you said about it."

And she took her cup and scampered across the sand, back up Farlook, and became just one more dark fleck, a cinder in that molten expanse.

At 1600, exhausted by the heat, I abandoned my vigil and returned to the Salamander. I showered, took a light meal and rested awhile, intending to be back at the colony before sunset.

But it was 1814 before I woke, startled and disoriented, to find the deep shadows of evening about me. I rose and dressed, and no sooner had gathered my wits again than there was a pounding at my door and Faoud calling to me. "Captain Tom! Captain Tom!"

I let the Egyptian in. He was panting, breathless from having hurried all the way from Farlook.

"What is it, Faoud?"

"The painting! Boorindi's painting! Look!"

As he talked he handed me a large transmission print, taken when the diver had brought his new painting down twenty minutes before.

It showed empty desert, what was unmistakably the horizon line of the Serafina and, at the bottom of the painting, a line of dark uneven shapes — the divers themselves under their shades, as if Boorindi had painted the whole Farlook colony from behind it on the Divers Stairs. I read the legend at the bottom and smiled. *My Own Byzantium.*

"You think this is good?" Faoud asked in a troubled voice.

"Very good, Faoud." I held the photograph out. "Yes, very, very good."

Faoud looked unconvinced. He went to go, remembered something, and handed me a folded note sealed with a swatch of artist's paint.

"From Tenna," he said, and excused himself. "I must call Kalgoorlie."

I saw Faoud to the door, then took the note out on to the terrace. I broke the crust of paint and opened out the paper.

Tom,

One for the divers. I have taken Boorindi walkabout onto the Serafina. We will be back in several days, if you can stay. The painting is to purge the spirit. The walk is to ease the madness. All things meet here. Wait for us, water man.

Tenna.

Nearby, the old Croesus was drunk with wind, and I was quite probably high on its bounty myself, for as I looked out across the desert, out beyond the town and Farlook with its little community of prophets, I thought I saw more than the sweep of sand and the terrible emptiness. I imagined, just for a moment, a glimmer, a glint, a trick of heat and light, the barest shine of Ashbaridan rising as surely as ever it had above that image-torn and dream-infested sea.

Time
Of The
Star

The ancient name for Airships is Eyreships, but most people never know this. They look at you oddly when you say it, and even more so when you tell them that the spelling for Lake Air, the ancient salt lake, is Lake Eyre. E-Y-R-E. It means nothing.

For a start, they confuse the infrequent Desert Sea of legend with the great man-made Inland Sea further to the north near the burning heart of Australia. Finally, when you've explained it carefully and they understand you at last, they will say something like: "Oh yes, Lake Air. The place where the Ab'O fleets fight. Where the wrecks are." But it's the word 'Air' they'll remember. Air and the ships.

This much you can discover from a postcard in the souvenir kiosks at Twilight Beach. Those busy little shops always have artists' impressions of the ships abandoned in the Air, or dramatic, so-called imagined scenes of the great open-plan vendetta fleets coming together over some matter of tribal honour.

Whenever I see these garish portrayals, or hear tourists talk of the dead salt lake in the south, I think of the times I have stood on the silent desolate beaches at Madiganna and Cresa and studied the wrecks way out in the salt, yearning to go out among them, and the one time I did go onto the lake and met a small part of my destiny during the Time of the Star.

It began with a postcard in a sense. A postcard and a comet. Comet Halley had returned to the inner planets and was heading for perihelion, and in that period when it was in the sky, certain Ab'O laws were in abeyance, some breaches of custom could be overlooked, traditions challenged and changed.

I was in Armfeld's in Twilight Beach, browsing through the comet material, enjoying an all-too-rare layover and some idle hours. I had picked out a postcard to examine from the Ab'O merchandise, an imagined scene from a famous battle held on the Air a year before, the collision of two great sand-ships in which the Ajaro Prince lost his life.

I was marvelling at the chance of a Prince dying that way, exposed and vulnerable as they so rarely are.

The ceremonial fleets which meet out on the dry salt-lake are allowed full use of holoform projections — ghost-ships for ancestors who have died on the Air — so the armadas are usually vast affairs, awesome spectacles of colour and display but with little substance. There might be as few as twenty core-ships to a side, and those scattered wide of each other so as not to foul their sailing canopies. But as they come together, projectors operating, a hundred ghost-ships might crowd the interstices, rolling along in front, kites filling the sky, making it a difficult and lengthy business to engage and destroy the enemy.

It is easy to see how the legends begin: of Anu and Coorina, of Bindakara, of how the Emmened fleet once fought all day, cutting back and forth through the phantom ships of the Wagiri seeking core-ships, only to find at end of day that there were no Wagiri core-ships at all, that the ghosts faded to leave an empty salt-plain littered with ancient hulks and detritus.

There are many such stories, with no-one to prove what is myth or rumour or told from ignorance. All media and tourists are barred from the great ritual fighting ground, and only a small number of Nationals have seen the battles there and come back with their stories of the great punitive formations. Now and then, illicit photographs appear, or what resemble fairly detailed satellite scan enhancements, but trafficking in such contraband images is a dangerous business. Still, as I studied the card, it was hard to look at the artist's representation and not see the photograph on which it was based. I could sense the captured moment beneath the linework and air-brushing.

"I nearly killed the men who took that picture," a voice said softly, very close to me.

"It is not a photograph," I replied, automatically, immediately doubting my words when I saw the tall fine-looking young Ab'O behind me. He wore a plain djellaba over soft fatigues, and ornate double swords thrust in his belt in the Japanese way.

"You know it is, Captain Tom," he said. "You of all people should recognise the Ajaro Airship *Baiame.* That is too close to what I saw to be an artist's rendering."

"You saw?"

The young man nodded. "I was on *Semmeret.* I saw my father and brother die, and I saw the Airmen pirate ship that slipped in to film the incident in between looting the wrecks."

I spoke my next words quietly. "Then you are . . ."

"Yes."

I replaced the postcard in the rack and walked with him out on to the street.

"But, Lord, how . . . ?"

"I am John to you, Captain. John Stone Grey."

"How can you be here, John?"

"The comet. It is the Time of the Star. A Prince can dare such things."

"Your enemies would be glad to find you alone this way."

"No doubt. But there are reasons, and I will not be buried alive in Fire-on-Stone under all those traditions and never see my world. I have urgent business to discuss." The Ab'O raised the hood of his robe, hiding his handsome features, then made sure his swords were concealed.

I led him down to the sand-ship moorings, through the First Gate and on to the Sand Quay. Like most of the big coastal towns, depending on one's moods, needs and perceptions, Twilight Beach can seem large or small. Now it was too small to conceal this quiet young man, this most vulnerable and incredible of things, an Ab'O Prince without his entourage, without his Elders and Clever Men and his Unseen Spears.

We boarded *Rynosseros*. Rob Shannon was instructing our newest crewmember, an eighteen-year-old Ab'O youth, an oddly fair-skinned outcast named Buso who had joined us earlier in the week during this layover. Rob looked up from splicing cables with him and nodded.

"Mission," I told him, and made the finger-sign that said: "Watch the Quay. Be ready."

Then I saw that John Stone Grey was studying the Ab'O youth who knelt alongside Shannon.

"You have an Ab'O in your crew?"

"An outcast. He has no tribe."

John Stone Grey stared at the lad, probably six or seven years younger than himself, his expression unreadable.

"You fear a spy?" I asked him.

"No," he said. "I do not approve of an Ab'O who becomes an outcast."

We went below, and in the aft-cabin John Stone Grey sat at the chart table and seemed to relax at last. He covered his face with his fine brown hands, then removed them to regard me sitting across from him.

"My father and brother died in the Air a year ago," he said. "The Chaness are — at last reckoning — three times more powerful than the Ajaro. Several Princes had a betrothal claim on the Chaness princess, Chian, but ours is the oldest, the first, and had to be honoured or disputed. The Chaness Prince wanted his daughter to wed the Madupan Prince's son. We challenged the right. The dispute was taken into the Air and we lost."

"So the Madupan won Chian?"

"No. They should have. But it was more than the death of our Prince and my brother when *Baiame* and *Ptah* collided. Those ships were both flagships and each named for the god of creation in one of its different guises. A year's grace was made because of it, a year before Chian could be given over and before I could assume the title. During that year no new ships could be built. The battle would be resumed with exactly the same vessel count. That year expired four days ago, but now it is the Time of the Star and Chian chose me — a new Prince — as her consort."

"What does this mean, John? I don't know the full law on this."

"Many of the Elders did not either," the young Ab'O said. "But still they met and made a ruling. Stalemate. The Chaness and the Ajaro must fight again with exactly the ships left from last time, as if the year did not exist."

"So why are you here? I am a State of Nation captain."

"Yes, and one of the few captains who can sail his vessel anywhere near Lake Air without the Chaness and Madupan satellites destroying him outright. Chian's choice, claiming Star immunity, came while I was away from Fire-on-Stone. I did not expect it, did not dream it could be possible, that she would be so headstrong as to defy her tribe. I had only a small group of Clever Men and Unseen Spears with me and I was out of my State. The Chaness and Madupan sent warriors and mind-fighters at once to stop my return."

"What of your entourage?"

"We used the shadow-warrior."

"A duplicate?"

"No. Not a duplicate. I am a younger son, the Anonymous Son. I am not allowed a clone surrogate to take my place in the Japano shadow-warrior tradition. I have not had time to prepare one yet. But it doesn't matter. As the Anonymous Son I was never seen at the tribal fires. I did not become a known face during the year of waiting. I still have that advantage and another. I had a vat-grown andromorph conditioned to be me, to fool a monitor should such a device be used. He was with me and led my escort while I hid and then came here to Twilight Beach to wait for you. The deception worked. My enemies were halfway to Wani before my entourage was caught and destroyed."

"How did you learn of it?"

John Stone Grey touched his temple. "By implant. A signal sent the moment the shadow-warrior died."

"What do you wish me to do?"

"I have one companion, Captain Tom, a powerful Clever Man named Iain Summondamas, my last bodyguard and friend. He has been away from my side only twice — once as a temporary envoy to the Chaness for several months, once a year ago when he participated in the battle on the Air. The re-staging of this battle is in three days' time. I wish you to take the two of us to Lake Air and bring me to my fleet. It will be waiting there. We have only eighteen core-ships against the Chaness fifty-seven. I must be there to lead the Ajaro, to affirm that I am the Faced Prince, or I forfeit. Chian goes to the Madupan. The comet means nothing."

I studied the glittering dark eyes, the lean handsome face, the hands composed on the chart table.

"They will suspect immediately what we are doing."

"Yes," the Ab'O said. "They will. But only when we are near the Air. We are just another ship till then. Then it is too late. Your mandate is valid, the Roads are open to you and safe. The tribal satellites and our own ancient Ajaro facility know to watch. No Chaness or Madupan would dare strike at us. Once I am on your ship, on an official Road, under your protection, I am safe."

"Except for pirates and privateers. With carefully insulated hulls."

"That is true. That is the risk. But only when we are near the Air. When we have made it plain that our destination is that place and not some other."

I laughed.

"What is it?" the Ab'O said.

"To think that probably the only way the Chaness and Madupan can stop you is to use the very pirates who loot the Airships and photograph the battles."

"The Eagle Cleland Buchanan?"

"He's the one."

John Stone Grey smiled. "I am an eagle too. My totem is the hammon-eagle. Buchanan will not stop us. Well?"

"I'll take the Ajaro Prince to the Air."

The Ab'O nodded. "I will not forget this."

"When will your Prince arrive?" I said.

The dark eyes widened. "What do you mean?"

"You are Iain Summondamas," I said.

The Ab'O smiled. "Of course I am, Captain Tom. And the Prince arrived several days ago. He is the young outcast we saw on deck splicing cables with your crewman."

I did not warm to the real John Stone Grey as quickly as I had the false one, though the Ajaro Prince was an intense and dedicated young man and promised to make the Ajaro a good Prince. If he lived.

As we ran towards Adelaide on the Aranda-Aidalay Road, the *Rynosseros* doing 80 k's under twenty kites, I stood with him on the forward deck, watching the wide gibber plain that flanked the Road on all sides, from time to time gazing at the slender figure beside me.

It was easy to tell from his remarks that he was the Anonymous Son, the younger son kept hidden at the tribal capital, with only the year that had lapsed in the company of Summondamas and the other Clever Men to ready him for what was soon to happen.

On some matters, he was still too innocent and uninformed, and there were moments when I forgot about his sheltered life, when his impatient questions became tiresome. Iain Summondamas tried to be there to spare me such moments, but John Stone Grey sometimes insisted, and angrily, that the Clever Man leave us alone together.

"My crime is being young *and* inexperienced, Captain," the Prince said on one occasion when Iain had left us. "What Iain forgets is that I must measure myself against as many strangers as I can. You, your crewmen, anyone we meet. He must not always be a filter to the world I see."

"That makes good sense, John. But Iain is the last of your bodyguard. Naturally he feels . . ."

"He is my only bodyguard," John Stone Grey said. "The others came to me when *Baiame* went into the salt. As Anonymous Son I had one andromorph and one Clever Man — Iain. The Ajaro are not a great tribe now. We must win or we will become extinct like the Wagiri."

"Chian chose you. That will force a great alliance with the Chaness."

"If we win at Air," the Prince said. "And Chian chose Iain Summondamas. Three years ago when he was Ajaro envoy to the Chaness for a time, they were close. She accepts me completely because he is my dear friend. Iain says this is not true, but I know better."

"Complex."

"What life is. Cleopatra, Helen of Sparta, Guinevere: men's love of women makes history. People dare things for power, wealth, ideas, all manner of reasons, but they sometimes do extraordinary things just for another person."

I watched the gibber flats, studied the kites, and brought my thoughts back to our journey. Even as we ran along the Aranda-Aidalay, I knew that in the south arrangements were being made with Buchanan and perhaps other renegade sandsmen to be ready for any ship changing course for the Roads leading near the Air.

With the Prince aboard, we had dispensation for constant comsat scans of the deserts we crossed. Several times during an hour, one of the crew — Rim or Strengi — would key in the Ajaro code and data would appear, telling us of any traffic in the region. We knew of the three Chitalice charvolants which passed us at 1042 on the second day a full hour before we met the vessels as they headed north.

It was reassuring that the tribal charvis barely bothered to acknowledge us, just a single banderole from the poop of the closest ship.

Iain Summondamas came on deck when the newcomers had gone. John Stone Grey followed.

"They knew a Clever Man was on board," Iain said, explaining the flag. "I sensed theirs — two. I wonder what they know."

"What can it matter?" I said. "We've carried Clever Men before. Even royalty. A registered ship carrying a Clever Man to his tribe is nothing to cause concern."

"Perhaps, Captain Tom. I cannot stop being my Prince's protector. He is all I have."

More and more clearly now, despite the bickering, I saw how strong the bond was between the young Prince and his adviser, bodyguard, weapons-master. And it was a two-way thing, a constant learning for them both.

When a look of concern crossed Iain Summondamas' face, I saw John rest a hand on his Clever Man's shoulder.

"We will be in time, Iain. It is our destiny." Then he faced me. "Captain, tell me of Lake Air."

"Lord, we have spoken of it . . ." Summondamas said.

But the youth cut him short. "Iain, I know what *you* have told me."

The Clever Man nodded and moved away, to stand by Shannon and Scarbo who were tending the controls.

"The ancient name for Air is Eyre," I began, "E-Y-R-E", then realized that as Anonymous Son, limited by the year of grace, John had never been to the fighting ground, that it was Iain who had seen *Baiame* die. I went on to tell him what many people did not know, that the vast salt lake was almost twenty metres below sea level in some places, and was even now the 'dead heart' of Australia that Professor Gregory had once spoken of, not the burning gibber and sand deserts further north. I could not tell what was new to him and what was known, but plainly my telling of it was as important as what I said.

One thing did fascinate him — when I spoke of how the 10,000 square kilometres of burning salt was the ancient flood plain for the river systems of the Diamantina, the Warburton and the Cooper, and told him how once all the inland rivers had sought to end there. Only twice in living memory had the Air flooded, and many suspected that the more recent Ab'O terraforming projects had interfered with the drainage systems and the great artesian table that fed the area. Now the Inland Sea to the north took most of the run-off from the northern and eastern rains, and the Air remained a terrible waste, almost totally empty of life.

John told me things in turn. He had seen recordings taken during the Air battles conducted by his tribe; he had the scans from his old Ajaro satellite of other actions on the lake. He knew the wrecks sunken into the salt, scattered across the immense glaring fighting ground. He even recited the names of all the Ajaro charvolants which had been found amid the mirror-ships and rammed, left crippled and abandoned to the lake.

He said their names as he would a litany, and as he spoke them I turned to see Iain Summondamas watching his dutiful Prince, his eyes glittering with quiet pride and other hidden emotions, his own lips ghosting the words being said exactly as he had taught them. Too young himself to have done much fighting for his State, kept at the tribal capital by the side of a younger son except for his brief time among the Chaness and on the Air, he was thrust now into the affairs of the world: a chase, a vital mission, a pending battle to determine the future of one small world.

I understood more and more what was happening here, the completion of a forced growth, the dramatic changes, the levels of fulfilment being met and satisfied in both men.

At 1125, we turned off the Road and headed into the southwest towards the ancient course of the Cooper. The winds made it difficult for kites, so with John's consent we took the luxury of running on solar power. Scarbo put our silvered inflatables in the sky, four long wide sun-snares that kept the accumulators humming.

At noon, the pirates came.

We were on an old battle road, running between claypans and long steep sandhills red with ferric oxides and scoured by endless winds. We had scan going, and Strengi read an intermittent signal, the sort of indistinct reading that can mean anything from a freak power flux to regional interference to insulated vessels in hiding.

"Broken signal!" he cried, and we acted at once. In two minutes, Scarbo had the sun-snares down and had sent up death-lamps. Rim, Iain, John and I uncovered the deck lenses and harpoons.

"You know tribal policy, Iain," I said as we adjusted the deadly glass frames. "Will Buchanan's men use hi-tech?"

Iain shook his head. "No! Laser gives too clear a trace to the satellites. They dare not risk it. The Chaness could not allow it either. They would be incriminated and made to forfeit."

But no more discussion was possible. The Airmen pirates were suddenly there, two sixty-foot vessels in sand-ochre camouflage coming at us from either side down long open wadis. They had been waiting, primed and ready, but needed to gather speed, so we were past them before they reached the battle trail. All the same, they scored hits with their lamps, lenses and ballistics, and we were smoking at the bow and trailing a land-anchor hanging by its cable from an Airmen harpoon lodged near our stern.

Once the anchor's barbs caught on an outcropping, *Rynosseros* would be lost — capsized or badly crippled.

But, fortunately, for a time, the battle trail was straight and reasonably smooth, and Shannon steered a careful central course, though the Airmen did not mean to let that happen for long. With no other kites aloft than their twisting, flashing death-lamps, the low armoured and powered ships gathered speed and started closing. Behind us, the anchor dragged, bouncing and sending dust curling up. That at least was in our favour, for it concealed our position and gave Iain and Rim time to cut at the cable.

Above us, one of our death-lamps exploded, a direct hit, and another drag-line harpoon glanced off the starboard edge of our travel platform, then bounced back.

The Airmen were careless to have risked such a shot in the dust haze, for one of the raider ships ran across that deflected land-anchor and damaged itself. Strengi reported one of our pursuers dropping back. Meanwhile, Rim and Iain sawed at the cable.

While they worked, John Stone Grey, still dressed in the fatigues of Buso the deck-boy, came to me on the poop.

"Can we pull that anchor in?" he asked. "Ease the cable tension?"

"A major gamble, John," I said.

"They will not get it free in time. Your ship."

Gamble against gamble. I considered the Airmen strategy: a stretch of flats to get harpoons in, then rocks to catch their anchors afterwards.

"Tell them!" I said.

The youth ran to Iain and spoke. The Clever Man glanced up at his Prince, then immediately changed actions. Rim fed the harpoon line through an open two-hand winch while Iain guided it.

The anchor came towards us as the line shortened.

Both men worked in a frantic double-handed motion about their cranks while John Stone Grey guided the line. Scarbo gave assistance too once tension was off the harpoon shaft, working it back and forth so that if it pulled free it would tear out less of our hull. Though the spring-barbed head had opened on impact and would still cause us great damage, it might pull free rather than turn and capsize the ship.

Shannon steered; I managed the lenses on the poop and sent flashes of burning light back at the unseen Airmen ships.

"Rocks on scan!" Shannon cried, loudly so Iain and the others could hear. "Five k's."

Now we would know. Iain and Rim winched furiously; John Stone Grey fed in the cable and hacked at it with Iain's short-sword; Scarbo pulled at the shaft. The anchor was four metres out, sending up a great cloud of dust which boiled along the battle trail and hid our attackers, though all our death-lamps had gone now and there were two more burn points where the light metal plating was buckled and the paint blistered.

There were shouts at the winch. The anchor was clear of the desert, ours to use as a weapon once the line was free. Scarbo immediately returned to the cable-boss, fitted two more lamps and our old Javanese fighting-kite. Iain and Rim hoisted the anchor up to where they could aim it, while John still worked at the cable.

I felt the uneven terrain under our wheels and sighed with relief.

"One ship only!" Strengi called up from scan. "They've definitely lost one."

We could see that was so with the anchor no longer raising its trail of dust: one Airmen raider still closing, its companion somewhere far behind amid red dunes, no doubt with a crippled travel platform.

I fired a small hot-pot harpoon back at the pirate vessel. It went wide, and the Airmen captain increased speed, obviously wanting to get in range of another land-anchor shot or their own hot-pots before we could prime and fire again.

"Now!" John cried, as the cable gave way, and the captured anchor went over the side.

Through the dust from our wheels, and the sun's relentless glare, the Buchanan crew may not have seen our retrieval of that iron claw earlier. Now they saw it coming back at them, and there was a choice of seconds: to go over it or swerve aside.

The raider swerved, but the battle trail had narrowed and the ground was broken and uneven with sand-drifts. As the craft began to topple, the captain applied more power, but it was too late — the Airmen craft disappeared into the sandhills. We barely heard its death roll above the roar of our own wheels.

"Scan clear!" Strengi called, and we relaxed at last, dividing up into our different watches as *Rynosseros* ran on through the harsh terrain.

The Chaness had tried subterfuge and failed. Now there was only the lake.

We approached the Air on its eastern side, along the graded battle circuit beside what had once been the Cooper. We ran between sandhills, below salmon-pink sandridges and knolls flashing with gypsum. Now and then we crossed remainders of the ancient Cooper watercourse, wide flat gullies, some green with lignum and samphire amid the white sand-crests, showing where an Ab'O bore had been sunk in the old way, others ragged with saltbush and nitrebush and strange clumps of never-fail.

Halfway through the afternoon, the sandhills cleared at last to reveal the immense glaring expanse of the lake itself, stretching to the horizon. There was no chance of seeing the Airships in this seering haze, with the sun a lid of burning mercury above a chrome land.

I brought up my old National map, a yellowing laminated facsimile, and placed it with the new map Summondamas had provided.

To the south, hazy in all this space and light, lay the vast sweep of the Madigan Gulf, and other landmarks with their ancient National names — Sulphur Peninsula, Pittosporum Head, Artemia Point, Jackboot Bay.

I turned the deck-scan fully on macro, trying to find any trace of those magical places. Such names had replaced far more ancient, prehistoric tribal names, I realized, just as those on Summondamas' chart had banished ours almost from memory.

Beside me, John Stone Grey surveyed those same distances unaided. "It is a place of lies," he said, and I wasn't sure how to take his words.

On the poop's port side, Iain Summondamas was using the other scan to examine the land ahead. Before I could ask John what he meant, the Clever Man stood back and pointed to a beach of sand and salt seven or eight kilometres away around the flat shoreline, where the road started to dissolve in the odd suffused light of a mirage. "There!" Summondamas said. "Go there!"

Scarbo had the helm and silently obeyed, shifting our course from the main road so we ran along another battle trail on the edge of the Air, travelling north to the Ajaro rendezvous.

A hot dry wind blew in off the lake, and sent sand hissing in sudden plumes from the domed white sandhills and shifting sandridges on the shore.

We dared not trust our vision. Shannon and I used the scans, while Scarbo wore his desert glasses and steered us between the crests of fuming sand.

It was indeed a place of apocalypse. Bad enough when it filled with water in those rare times. Now, but for the bores and sinks, the condensation posts and the lonely clanking tribal windmills I had not seen but knew would be out there, it was a bone land.

I watched that beach for ten minutes, mesmerized by the wall of image-ridden light just beyond it, the ever-receding mirage.

Then there was a movement at my elbow. I looked up, and for a moment thought it was Iain Summondamas — the figure had that indefinable presence — but saw instead John Stone Grey. The lake was changing him. How could I have taken this light-skinned Ab'O for an outcast deck-boy? That identity had gone. Now John wore fighting leathers under his djellaba, and the twin swords were thrust into his belt. I dared not say it but he resembled Iain in so many ways, ways that were dear to them both and unspoken.

"You have been here before?" he said.

"Yes, John. A few times. Once I was allowed to witness mind-war on the Sulphur Peninsula. Big corroboree. Many Clever Men, many dragons. No media could attend, but they wanted National accreditation for the outcome. I came by tribal ship then."

Iain Summondamas had come up on deck also.

"Neo-Dieri?" he asked.

"Yes," I said. "The outcome made it possible to raise the new tribe. The Neo-Dieri."

"They are false men," Iain said.

"They did not ask to be cloned," I reminded him. "The Ulla are responsible. They found the Dieri mummy and they gave the dead tissue. They won the right to proceed, to restore that people."

Iain turned his dark eyes on me.

"They do not bring ships to the Air. The Neo-Dieri are not allowed ships yet."

"Worse than Nationals," I said, trying to make my point obliquely.

"Worse than most Nationals, yes," the Clever Man said.

I tried to change the subject. "The Neo-Dieri care for the lake, Iain. They sink bores and grow things. Sometimes the birds even come. The hammon-eagles," I added pointedly. "The kings of the sky."

Iain stared at me. He might have said: "Vat-bred creatures!" were not that new strain his Prince's sign. He returned instead to the main point. "They are the corruption of an ancient people."

There was silence for a moment, then John Stone Grey spoke. "When the Neo-Dieri come, Iain, we will give them honour."

"They will have honour," Iain said. "Spoken honour is easy."

We discovered that the Ajaro fleet was already in position 20 k's or more out on the lake to the north. Only one ship waited at the rendezvous, standing quietly on the salt a hundred metres from shore. This was *Kuddimudra,* the one-hundred-and-forty-foot Ajaro flagship, an eccentric painted and armoured charvolant with a stern coloured with dramatic orange flashes. Through half-closed eyes or at a distance, that stern did indeed resemble the tail of a hammon-eagle, though the vessel was named for the ancient water-demon of Air, a different beast entirely.

Waiting on the shore across from the big charvi were the Neo-Dieri, four very dark, shorter-than-average Ab'Os wearing long desert robes. They stood near their modest camp — two wurlies, a battered condensation tower and four camels. John Stone Grey and Iain climbed down to the hard pan and went to greet them formally. They talked awhile out of our hearing, then John returned.

"It is hard for Iain," the young Prince said. "Sometimes he forgets. He tries to be an Elder for me, the father I did not often see. I have left him to make the arrangements with the Neo-Dieri. Can we see the Airship wrecks together?"

"I think we can," I said. "The light is less harsh now."

We left *Rynosseros* and walked several metres out upon the glaring surface of the Air, listening to the silence. The incredible emptiness made us lower our voices, brought awe, almost a reverence, welling up inside us when we did speak. I raised my pocket glass and peered down the hot metal tube at the horizon. At first there was nothing to mar the desolation, just the endless waste of white salt meeting a hot sky so pale a blue as to be an uncertain stained white itself.

I moved the glass from north to south, adjusted the magnification and tried again. Now what had been half-imagined darker motes dancing in the lake's searing shimmer resolved into the hulks of long-dead ships lifting out of the salt, curving lunate sections of hull, long skeletal prows thrusting into the sky, rusted broken stern assemblies. The sun and the wind had reduced them to ciphers and strange totems, had taken all meaning from them. At night the winds would race across the dead lake bed and whistle and thrum about the wrecks, lifting the loose deck plates, slamming them back and forth, soughing and crying through fused and shattered ports, whispering down the empty passageways, bringing salt and sand and a fleeting ghostly semblance of life.

In those rare years when the lake still filled itself from artesian springs and coastal rainfall, the wrecks would sit in a vast sheet of shallow water that glistened with a startling difference under the burning desert sun and moved to the ruffling breezes. Then the wrecks would be lonely twisted reefs painted with faded war-signs, crusted with verdigris and salt, and would for a time resemble sea-going vessels, the detritus of Salamis, Actium or Lepanto, shapes and forms from other places and other ages brought here to this ancient salt-sea, discarded from time.

I handed the glass to John but continued to stare out at where the wrecks were. Saying they reminded me of primeval land and sea animals, whales, dinosaurs, was not true. There was that other comparison, more recent, which always came first whenever I saw the postcard renderings.

"Aircraft," I said. "They're like aircraft."

"I know this," John said, hearing the term his way.

"No. No. Aircraft. Old hi-tech flying machines. I once saw pictures of a bomber aircraft buried in the desert. Big tail vanes like on some of those hulks out there. But with wings."

"I know," John added. "For the sky. Heavier than air, right? Like the shuttles." He sounded accepting but I knew it was an enormous conceptual leap.

"That's right. They are still used in parts of the world. In the great museum collections or as craft of State."

John swung the glass along the horizon.

"There are hundreds of them," he said, marvelling. Though he had seen pictures and recordings and knew the statistics, he was seeing them for the first time in reality.

"You're looking at lifetimes of tribal wars settled out there," I said. "Thousands of men, hundreds of ships. Great open-plan fleets, the new ones navigating around the wrecks of the old, leaving more wrecks behind."

John handed me the glass. "It is some joke, Tom."

"Yes," I said. "I think of aircraft, and here they are in this dry lake, fighting in the Air."

We laughed, then stood in silence. I had time to study John Stone Grey, to consider him as I did the lake, as part of this world.

There was something about the youth that impressed me, that stirred my admiration, a recognition of the worth in what is new and young and untried.

"Most people lack any sense of destiny," he said and caught me watching him. "But not you. Why?"

I began speaking of my time in the Madhouse and how it had changed me. I told him how I had made an oath when I was incarcerated there, coming to self-awareness and objective time-consciousness, of how I vowed quietly, in spoken words, there in my dark place that linked me to all times, all places and possibilities, that I would live as Alexander the Great was said to have lived, for the moment, for the instant couched in the promise of forever. I would take risks, be reckless when it felt good and vital, that I would never be afraid to feel. I explained how it was an easy promise to make then, with all of my life coming back to me like that, but it wasn't simply the sort of pledge the reprieved man makes, a temporary provisional thing, short-lived and insubstantial.

I knew I would dare things, do things, strive at least, and knew that this would equip me to deal with not just the Ab'Os but all men. It was a divine moment, the sort we all have but often cannot fully grasp; a moment when the psyche is balanced and eloquent to itself, when it sees and knows what cannot be said. Having unlocked the door of my madness, I had such an instant. I knew how it had to be.

John Stone Grey listened, not speaking, not challenging, but seeming to accept that I believed what I said, measuring me as he did anyone he met. He thanked me afterwards and gave me an inquiring look.

"Do you think I am a man of destiny also?" he said.

"I have no doubt of it, John."

"How do you know?"

"Heart knows," I said, which he accepted as he had the rest.

Iain Summondamas had come out on to the lake and was standing a little apart, talking softly with the Neo-Dieri headman, Si Akara, and his three tribesmen. Now the young Prince turned to him.

"Iain?"

The Clever Man turned at once. "Yes?"

"Tomorrow you must stay with *Rynosseros*. You must wait until this action is done."

"No, Prince! I must . . ."

"Iain! Si Akara and Tom Rynosseros are listening. I have good reasons. You will stay with *Rynosseros*. Please accept this."

Iain did, but it caused him anguish. I watched the salt, not wishing to add to his shame, and only turned back when John and Iain, Si Akara and his men had gone.

At 0600 the next morning, *Kuddimudra* lofted twenty-four display kites and moved out onto the Air. We watched her grow smaller until nothing was visible without glass or scan.

Three hours later, in the sharp morning light, the Chaness fleet came. At first there was just a strange edge to the silence, so that we peered out among the wrecks, feeling rather than hearing something across the salt. Then, through scan, low against the horizon, appeared a dark line, a jagged crust between brilliant white and blue, widening, thickening, starting to move forward through the scattered, lonely ship-reefs.

A great fleet under full ceremonial display, advancing to the sound of drums and bullroarers. More than a hundred ships, possibly two hundred, with nearly sixty core-ships, a great array travelling close together, more closely than charvolants normally dared. It was how the Spanish Armada must have looked, or the converging galleys at Actium, only here the sky was filled with kites insulated against mirror-flash, riding lines coated with powdered glass or with tantalum alloy edges. The air thrummed and throbbed with their approach.

Then, from the north, came the Ajaro fleet, smaller, much smaller, and with a great many replicant ships considering the eighteen core-ships the Ajaro had.

It was a dreamlike scene. In the glare and the hot dry wind, the ships began to lose their sharpness as the lake surface heated and the air shimmered. It was already 55° Celsius.

Si Akara came aboard and climbed to the poop carrying two letters. One he handed to Iain Summondamas, the other he gave to me.

"Do not open," Si Akara told me. "Open later, when this is done." He turned to Iain. "You open this when it is clear in your heart how this business goes, you understand? Only then."

Iain nodded, and the Neo-Dieri went back to where his tribesmen stood with their camels on the hard salt-pan. Iain studied the sealed letter, then put it inside his djellaba. He gripped the rail, put his face into the hood of the macro-scan and watched the ships out on the lake. I did the same, slipping my letter into my own desert robes for later.

The fleets were very close now. Kites were changing, a fascinating thing to see. Most of the brightly-coloured top-kites and parafoils were pulled down. Drab battle-kites took their place, and sparkling death-lamps gorging on deadly sunlight, flashing and spinning across the approaching lines.

On our scans, we started to see some of the ghost-ships for the enantiomorphs they were, which made the sight even more dreamlike and unreal. Now and then a charvolant would approach a wreck buried in the salt and pass through it, dissolving around the hulk and resolving again on the other side as substantial as before. I could not help but get a sense of intersecting realities, of two worlds merging, as if the wrecks scattered across the salt waste were the future remains of today's battle or, conversely, the ghosts of those dead and broken charvolants were re-enacting their final moments yet again, restless in death.

The Chaness and Ajaro ships met. Even where we stood, the air throbbed with sound, with the drone of bullroarers and war-didjeridoos, the constant boom boom boom of the damning-drums, with the chanting of warriors and the deeper roar of so many wheels travelling on salt-pan and sand-flat.

And then, as if in a dream, like so much heat-born mirage on this ancient sea of illusion, the fleets passed through each other.

"First pass," Iain Summondamas said. "Nothing."

Which was not quite true. On the lake surface behind the parting lines of ships were tangles of kites and cables from the hidden core-ships, snared out of the hot sky by long boom-gaffs and spring-powered boomerang snares fired at random into the canopies of the enemy.

But it was an easy pass, as Iain said, and as good as nothing. This early in the engagement, kites and cables could be replaced, new snares and booms set.

The fleets cleared one another by several kilometres, slowly turned and began moving together again, gathering speed.

Near me, Iain did not move from the macro-scan. He knew the configurations of the Ajaro ships well, could probably tell which of the twenty or more flagships replicated out there was the real *Kuddimudra* with his Prince aboard.

The second pass was slow and deadly. Before the ships met, harpoons and hot-pots arced out from the advancing armadas, death-lamps flashed concentrated light into the overlapping canopies. When a burn point on a hull showed fire, or a kite went up in flame, the gunnery crews plotted carefully the likely position of their target ship amidst the myriad random and instantaneous replications that occurred.

It was a complex business. So many ships were attacking at the same time, causing damage and trying to monitor the replications of their own successful hits in the endless search for core-ships. Distribution patterns were the first priority but any worthwhile captain knew what a distraction that could be. They posted spotters and samplers, but for the most part took their chances with any vessel that came at them. Weapon strikes first, if possible, then ramming.

No ships died on that exchange either, but both fleets took smoking hulls with them and the ground between was littered with burning kites, dumped fragments of smouldering superstructure, and bodies.

Another pass followed, and another, and with each one the captains gained a better idea of the enemy's disposition, the pattern of ship details being reproduced. It did not take the Chaness long to know how thinly-spaced the Ajaro ships were.

As the day wore on, we watched the next six passes, saw four Ajaro core-ships rammed and left burning, saw how sections of the Ajaro fleet winked out, leaving large gaps that made safe travelling spaces for the Chaness on the next pass.

The Ajaro were fighting fiercely. Eleven Chaness were either burning on the salt or trailing their formations. It meant approaches came less frequently as the Chaness used the recoveries and turns to re-position their ships. The damaged vessels simply missed a pass to tend to their wounds; the Chaness formation tightened, which they could easily afford to do. The Chaness fleet may have looked smaller than when it first appeared, but it was still many times larger than the moving patchwork of the Ajaro.

I was awed by the spectacle. Here was what I had seen in the postcards and simulations, the reality of so many charvis working together, not allowed to use their comp systems or scanning equipment, their stored power or hi-tech armament, just the mirror-ship projectors; forced by their own tribal rulings to rely on code weaponry and the constant burning winds of the Air.

On the other side of the sky, looking down on this waste painted in ochre, red, gamboge, mustard and chrome, were the unseen tribal satellites, monitoring the silent com frequencies to see no-one transgressed, reading energy levels and recording every phase of the operations.

There were four more passes that day, and we watched each one of them till our eyes ached. The Ajaro fleet remained an open lattice, the mirror-ships duplicating every hurt suffered by the vessel giving them their existence, the core-ships trying to protect the hidden ship of their Prince by not gathering too closely about him. The lake was dotted with burning hulls and broken travel platforms, some ships toppled on their sides, others standing upright, burning or crippled.

At sunset, the fighting stopped. Si Akara and the other Neo-Dieri watchers around the shore lit bonfires of canegrass to tell the fleets that they must disengage for the day.

The ships did so, gladly, returning in the deep silence of growing dusk to their ends of the lake, moving as dreamlike as ever, phantom silhouettes against the westering sun.

It was 40°C and cooling, and around us the land was changing. The dunes along the shore glowed furnace red, antique gold and salmon pink, flashing with flecks of lime and gypsum. In the strong wind, the sandhills fumed at their crests like newly-born volcanoes. Canegrass and spinifex along the ridges soughed and rustled, and the sun sank like a vast red dish through a chameleon sky: one moment burnt copper, then a stained smoky lavender, and finally, before evening fell altogether, a deep and mournful grey, the colour of wounded angels.

Iain left the scan only when the visibility had gone. He stood away from it, his hair stirring in the wind from the west, and seemed half in trance, staring at the darkness.

"Iain?" I said, knowing better than to interrupt but too concerned for him to stay silent.

The eyes turned to me. "I was not with him," he said.

"Then you have obeyed your Prince well. You have given him his chance."

The Clever Man stared at me. Then he walked away, climbed down to the salt-shore and went to sit with the Neo-Dieri. It was an irony that he should take solace there with those dark revenant folk, but our best silences were still questions and theirs were easy with ancient understanding. I heard voices talking over the soft grumbling of the camels, then the chanting started as the beacon fires burned low. During the night, the hot wind continued to blow out of the west, to set the lanterns creaking and the lines thrumming and bringing salt and sand and little sleep.

The next morning made the darkness of the night seem an illusion, another lie, a promise which had been broken. Again there was the salt-sea shimmering in the clear relentless sunlight, the strong dry winds, a world resolved into a fierce duality, the startling twin registers of blue sky and blinding white salt-flat. The landscape hurt the eyes, even through our glasses. At 0950 it was already 50°C.

Iain Summondamas was back from the Neo-Dieri camp, and stood on deck in fighting-leathers and djellaba, plainly a replenished man, his swords and an ancient Dieri war-boomerang thrust in his belt, a great honour. A peace of sorts had been made, and it was easy to speak to him as if nothing had happened.

At 1000 the ships came with drums and pulsing bullroarers, the Chaness in a vast concentration, the Ajaro in a carefully-spaced grid, hoping to divide their enemy and see replication patterns. Again the first pass was a cautious thing, a tentative sounding-out of ghosts and distributions. No strikes were made.

On the second pass, an Ajaro ship was hit with a hot-pot, and instantly across the Ajaro formation twenty mirror-ships wore the same plumes of smoke.

Death-lamps flashing, some Chaness ships closed in on where the hot-pot had landed, and soon they had crippled the core-ship which was left burning on its travel platform. Moments later, the vessel exploded and took its ghosts out with it. Across the salt came the racket of snaphaunce fire that meant close deck-fighting, a steady prickle of sound almost lost in the roar of the wheels and the damning-drums.

Then, with the suddenness of dream, it seemed that half the Ajaro ships were burning. Billows of heavy black smoke folded out from them, which told us that John Stone Grey had semaphored for smokescreens. It was a sound gamble for a smaller fleet to take against a larger — though it meant there would be no more coordinated moves until the smoke cleared and the semaphores could be read again. Now the ghosts were useless, hidden in the pall that rolled across the waste.

For several hours we watched the dark smoke haze, using the scans to see which vessels came and went out of the billows. I shared my instrument with Shannon, Scarbo and Rim, and Strengi too when he came on deck, leaving Iain alone with the other scan.

All of us on *Rynosseros* had studied the accounts of smokescreen warfare; we could guess what would be happening on the lake. Tactics had changed. For a start, the Chaness had accepted the Ajaro's strategy and were adding smoke of their own, having no doubt decided that they need only manoeuvre as a moving barricade, close together, to catch the Ajaro core-ships or at least foul their kites and cables.

We saw only the black cloud now, deepening, swelling forth, distending and being replenished as the winds of the lake drew it into streamers and eddies. Under that mantle, the desperate contest continued. With visibility reduced to fifty metres in places, it had become a much slower affair. Now the passes did not happen at all. The ships remained in the boiling cathedrals of smoke they had erected for themselves, so many fuming chalices waiting for encounters, ready now for prolonged deck-fighting as much as fire and ballistic strikes and ramming. We waited to see what was resolved, feeling excluded and helpless, in a separate world.

Then, near the end of the day, Iain cried out and staggered away from the macro-scan, to stand steadying himself at the rail.

"Iain!" I cried. "What is it?"

"Mind-war!" he said. "I felt it. A ship came close to *Kuddimudra.* With many Clever Men. As they passed, they went into trance and killed four of my Prince's Clever Men. They know his ship."

"Are you sure? Could it . . ."

"The ship that did this is called *Kurdimurka.*"

"I don't understand."

"It is chance! 'Kuddimudra' and 'Kurdimurka' refer to the same mythic water creature — the ancient serpent of the Air. It is the same matter the tribes ruled on before. If that ship takes my Prince, there can be his death but no victory. The contest must be fought again a year from now, with fewer ships and fewer men. All we do here will have been in vain."

Without saying more, we went to our scans, though nothing could be seen but the palls of smoke along the horizon.

"Where is John's ship now?" I asked him.

"The extreme left of the Ajaro line," Iain said, not needing his eyes to know such things.

"And is *Kurdimurka* going after her?"

"They are going to try! Their Clever Men are searching down the mind-lines for Ajaro shapes."

I exchanged glances with Shannon and Rim who stood by the scan awaiting their turns.

"Open your Prince's letter, Iain," I said.

The Clever Man brought his head from the hood and looked across at me. "No!"

"You know how this is going to go," I told him. "If the similarly-named ships collide, you will lose both your Prince and the victory. Those ships must be kept apart! Open the letter!"

The Ab'O hesitated, then reached into his desert robes and pulled forth the document. He tore it open and read.

"No!" he cried. "No!"

I reached for the paper and he let me take it. Then, while Iain moved to the rail, I looked at what the young Ajaro Prince had written.

Iain,

This is my final command to you. At the moment you read this, you are Prince of the Ajaro.

Remember that everything I now do is to confirm this fact. It is the Time of the Star and all things can be dared. Chian must be yours.

John Stone Grey.

There were tears in Iain's eyes, and anger and bewilderment. "What can be done?" he asked. Then, as if deciding, he shouted down to the tribesmen crouching on the shore. "Bilili! Bring camels!"

Bilili, the Neo-Dieri jackman, came running, Si Akara with him.

"I want camels!" Iain said when the revenant Ab'Os were on deck.

"No, Summondamas," the Neo-Dieri headman said. "No camels on the Air. It is law!"

Iain turned to face me. "Captain Tom?"

"Iain, we can't! No ships can be added!"

"You read it," he said. "I am Prince of the Ajaro! It is the Time of the Star. All things can be dared!"

"The satellites!" I reminded him.

Iain snatched the letter from me and thrust it at Si Akara. "Read!" he said. "Go to com and call the satellites for us! Tell them! Time of the Star. Tell them!"

Si Akara read the letter and muttered to Bilili in dialect. Then Shannon led both men below to our comlink.

Iain turned back to me. "Go, Tom! Go now!"

"The Neo-Dieri!" I said.

"Go! They are true men, you say? Then they are tribal people. Let them get honour. Go! Go!"

It was madness, but I went to the controls, brought life to the circuits. Scarbo hurried to the cable-boss. On the commons, Strengi and Rim began hooking on kites.

"Use power!" Iain cried. "Kites and power! This is now the flagship. But we must be in the battle. Go! Go!"

Rynosseros moved forward, down the salt-pan on to the lake itself. The big wheels ground the sand and salt crystals, gaining speed.

I had never feared for my ship so much. I expected a strike at any moment, a quick decisive death from the comsats in orbit, the Chaness and Madupan especially, but from any of the units appointed to watch the Air.

When the strikes did not come, I added more power from the cells. Our canopy strained out above, the photonic parafoils drinking in the hot light, the death-lamps building their charges. Scarbo put up five colourful top-kites so we would not appear as a pirate to those watching above.

Rynosseros gathered speed, running at 90 k's, then 100. On the commons, Shannon, Strengi and Rim were bringing out weapons — the harpoons and hot-pots and big deck lenses. Scarbo tended the cables, jockeying the kites for greatest pull.

Si Akara was on deck too, yammering in dialect at Iain Summondamas, demanding to know what was happening, while Bilili remained below at com, sending our message to all who would listen.

"Si Akara," I heard Iain tell the Neo-Dieri. "You are pariah people. Do you accept that? Here is your chance to be a tribe. The Ajaro are nearly gone. The Ajaro-Dieri may be here on *Rynosseros*. Here!"

Si Akara was as uncertain as we all were, as no doubt the arbitrators of the Air contests were at this moment. But it was an appeal that worked, that spoke to the pride and secret hopes of the revenant headman.

"We will talk later," Si Akara said, which was as much of an affirmation as Iain Summondamas needed.

We ran across the lake on a surface smoother and harder than any Road we had ever used before. Ahead, the smoke seemed to be thinning before the hot winds but it was an illusion. The ships manoeuvring in those swirls and eddies were adding to the billows at the level where it was still the most effective tactic, creating a storm-light to fight in.

On the quarterdeck of *Rynosseros,* Iain Summondamas went into trance, questing for concentrations of enemy Clever Men he could engage in mind-war, or use to locate *Kuddimudra* and the Chaness *Kurdimurka* before it was too late, before similarly-named flagships engaged and the contest was voided. The rest of us used the time to don fighting-leathers and prepare our personal weapons.

Ten kilometres remained. Iain came back to us and saw we were suited and ready. He went to speak but hesitated, then flung aside his djellaba to reveal fully his suit of lights underneath, the small mirrors sewn to the leather catching the fierce sunlight so that he was a blinding figure to look upon.

At three kilometres, we were already in the pall of roiling smoke, and our display kites were hauled down ready for battle. The lowering sun had become a sharp-edged coppery shield, as one sometimes sees it during a sandstorm, suspended a handspan above the horizon.

We could see the first of the ships, hazy shapes, ghost-ships or perhaps the core-ships themselves, we could not tell which. It was a navigator's nightmare — constant half-seen forms, startling in their sudden arrivals and departures, making us edgy, ready to fire at anything.

We had no damning-drums to warn of our position, to signal our allies among the Ajaro, no horns, didjeridoos or bullroarers. We ran along in increasing gloom to the last-known position of the Chaness *Kurdimurka,* trusting to Iain's reading of the whereabouts of enemy Clever Men to lead us to the Chaness Prince, to save John Stone Grey if we could.

Drums sounded ahead. In the boiling funereal haze, we saw a charvi approaching, two, three, a small formation of Chaness ships. As they saw us, the drums stopped, to deprive us of an accurate bearing.

"No Clever Men aboard!" Iain cried, which meant there was probably only one true ship, but which meant too we had to trust our own judgement.

Scarbo made that decision, confirming my own. "The one on the left is it!" he cried, and at that instant three hot-pot harpoons left our guns, trailing snare lines. There were two hits, one went wide. The Chaness ship flared into flame at the bow and on the starboard edge of its travelling stage, our good fortune for it hampered both steering and gunners. The damning-drums started again, a summoning rhythm, enemy strike, Ajaro core-ship engaged, come to us Chaness.

We veered away at once, not having enough fighting men to engage in deck-war using spears and snaphaunce fire, and not wishing to get caught up with other Chaness ships.

I knew yet again how mortal *Rynosseros* was, how completely vulnerable, and how untried in fleet fighting we were.

The burning ship tried to use its flames to stop us, but with drive cables afire, it manoeuvred too late. I ran *Rynosseros* through one of the holoforms, an uncanny thing, then corrected our course for *Kurdimurka.*

Iain had readings, more mind-war a kilometre ahead. I steered blindly, with the pall hanging across the sky, fed by a furnace-red sunset now, and Iain Summondamas, the new Ajaro Prince, half in trance, murmuring directions in my ear. Mind-war was ritual war, but in this blind fighting it had a new vital role, to let Clever Men track other Clever Men, and the greatest concentrations were naturally attending the Princes. So *Kurdimurka* was hunting *Kuddimudra,* so we were seeking them both, by the mind-fields of their own searching Clever Men.

Another ship crossed our bow, an Ajaro sixty-footer, *Jusu,* trailing smokescreen at the stern. The small ship saw our colours and the command pennon and changed course to follow *Rynosseros.* At the same time, Iain flashed into trance and told her Clever Man captain who we were. *Jusu*'s damning-drums started up and on the poop, clear of the cables, crewmen swung their bullroarers in droning accompaniment, calling ships, Ajaro come to us, Prince formation here.

Now the gamble started in earnest, for there might be conflicting signals, two flagships calling, dividing the Ajaro fleet, though I doubted the problem would arise. John Stone Grey, paradoxically hampered by his ritual entourage of Clever Men, would have stopped calling. The brave youth would be gambling that Iain had read the formations, read the Chaness Clever Men, and knew of *Kurdimurka*'s quest for the Ajaro flagship. There were technical breaches here that possibly the Star could not excuse, but there was so little to lose and so much to be gained.

Another ship darted past, a low insulated hull painted in sand-ochre camouflage, slipping by us under six photonic parafoils.

"Pirate!" I cried, but the vessel vanished down a smoke tunnel of its own making, drawing coils and wisps after it like hungry hands.

Buchanan's men again, after more photographs, more provocative and contraband footage for the souvenir kiosks and archives of the coastal cities, for the curiosity-seekers of the world. The Eagle's men may have assisted the Chaness for a time, but now we had reached the Air, they were back to their usual operations, capitalizing on what had to be a sensational development — the presence of a National ship in all this. Comp estimates were seven chances in ten of that raider making it off the lake back to Buchanan's eyrie, four in ten at that speed of colliding with an ancient wreck or another core-vessel, but that was a considered risk. Many Buchanan pirates had become wealthy men.

"*Kurdimurka* ahead!" Iain Summondamas cried.

Before us, shapes were moving in the gloom. Iain went into trance, gave a mind-command for *Jusu* to rush ahead, the least he could do for *Rynosseros* and her crew. Then he turned to us.

"The Chaness know what we have done," he said.

"How? Clever Men?"

"Who can say? A powerful Clever Man read it. Buchanan may have told."

"What of *Kuddimudra* and John Stone Grey?"

"We are too late. His ship is down."

"Survivors?"

"I cannot tell. I believe all the Clever Men with him are dead from mind-war. *Jusu* will lead us there, but it is very late now. *Kurdimurka* has gone. I get no readings. All the Chaness ships have gone. Tomorrow will be the end of it."

When we found the broken and smouldering hulk of *Kuddimudra*, the sun had dropped below the line. The smoke haze had vanished before the dry desert wind and the sky had lost the last of its soft rose and lavender twilight. The horizon was rimmed with the deepest verdigris where the copper sun had set.

Kuddimudra had collided with an ancient Airship wreck, not at great speed but with enough force to snap the drive lines, sheer the main pins and cripple the leading wheels. The hundred-and-forty-foot Ajaro ship had toppled across the ancient hulk and wedged there, and the Chaness flagship and its escort vessels had simply halted and sent hot-pots then warriors across.

There were three Ajaro survivors, all crewmen, and one of them told us how the Ajaro Clever Men had faced their enemies, greatly outnumbered, and died in savage mind-war. Then most of *Kuddimudra*'s complement, John Stone Grey included, had fallen to Chaness swords and spears, a sad and futile end to the day.

But instead of a voided war, another year of grace, a re-engagement, and one more chance for the Chaness to put an end to the Ajaro tribe forever for their impudence, the battle would continue tomorrow. For better or worse, we had that much.

Jusu's damning-drums began once more, a forlorn sound, and led the remaining Ajaro ships to us. Slowly, moving carefully, the survivors came kiting in the darkness on a refreshingly-cool change of winds, steering by starlight and moonlight, manoeuvring in around *Rynosseros* and *Jusu* and the wreck of *Kuddimudra.*

In all, there were only five tribal ships left, and one of these, *Emu,* was crippled and would not be repaired in time for battle. Still, Iain gave her captain honour and did not order his vessel from the lake.

For an hour the exhausted crews of the ships helped to move the Ajaro dead and wounded on to *Emu.* Then we trudged across the salt in the relief of the cool wind for a meeting on the canted but largely intact commons of *Kuddimudra.* The captains and their weary crews gathered on the sloping deck, watching the lanterns swinging and creaking in the wind, waiting for Iain Summondamas to tell them what was to happen now.

The young Clever Man climbed to the damaged quarterdeck and introduced himself, for most of the veteran sandsmen had never been to the tribal fires and seen the Anonymous Son's bodyguard, this man John Stone Grey had committed them to honouring.

Iain began softly, but as he explained how he had become Prince, how the similarly-named flagships had almost voided the whole engagement, his voice took on a greater and greater presence.

"Tomorrow we will win!" he said finally, and left a silence.

"Tomorrow finishes it!" one shipmaster said. "Unless we are cunning and greatly fortunate."

"You are Pina," Iain said, identifying the man, name-claiming him before them all.

"Yes."

"Then if what you say is what you believe, Pina, you can do no worse than trust me as John Stone Grey did."

"John Stone Grey is dead," Pina said.

"And gave us a day. And an unvoided war, do you understand? Tomorrow is his."

"Who are these others?" an old Clever Man asked.

"You are Bel," Iain said, and name-claimed him too. "Tom Rynosseros and his crew you know, as I've explained. The others down on the lake there, waiting for us, are Si Akara and his jackman, Bilili, from the Neo-Dieri. Our friends and brothers."

There was muttering and many hard looks. Several tribesmen peered through the darkness at the figures on the cooling lake.

Si Akara and Bilili did not seem to care. While Iain outlined his plan for bonding the tribes, the Neo-Dieri were studying the lake surface, Si Akara crouched on his haunches running a handful of salt crystals through his fingers.

Iain came to the end of his proposal. "I ask for a ruling on this," he said, and discussion began.

This was tribal business so I went down to where the Neo-Dieri communed with the lake. Si Akara looked up.

"Do you trust us older Ab'Os, Captain Tom?" he said, his dark eyes catching the lamplight from ruined *Kuddimudra,* the barest hint of a frown visible on the weathered face.

"This is your land twice over," I said. "I trust you."

Si Akara squeezed salt through his fingers. "The Ajaro must go from here. Twenty kilometres. There!" He pointed in the direction of the Neo-Dieri camp, where we had entered the lake.

"Why?"

"Nothing is lost if we do it," he said. "We will still be on the lake. Trust."

"In the morning. These men are tired."

Si Akara stood. "Too late. Now!"

"Tell Iain Summondamas."

Si Akara shook his head once. "The Ajaro will not accept it from a Prince who is still unproven. They will not accept it from dead men made hot again."

"Me?"

"*Rynosseros* is the flagship until Iain orders you from the lake, which he will do soon now to save you from tomorrow's battle. You made this possible, this chance, as much as the boy did. You must persuade him."

"There is so much to lose."

"Trust," Si Akara said, and gave me what was left of his handful of salt. The lumps and flakes felt moist, oddly frangible to the touch, and spoke their silent message clearly enough.

I went to Iain Summondamas. The captains and Clever Men were still deciding on the Neo-Dieri brotherhood, talking as if this was the tribal home-fire and there was a future for the Ajaro beyond the setting of tomorrow's sun.

In a low voice, I told the young Prince what Si Akara had said. He hesitated less time than I had.

"Enough!" he cried, and drew his sword, an echoing, superbly-deft action, so that all eyes locked on him at once. "I have ruled. It is done. We go to the shoreline and we launch our attack from there. Follow *Rynosseros.* Pina, sit down! Any man who disputes this may fight me, here, now — warriors with sword, Clever Men with mind-war. I am your Prince or I am not."

Everyone stared at the figure on the quarterdeck of *Kuddimudra,* where so recently John Stone Grey had fought and died. Iain's suit of lights shone through the front of his djellaba. His sword was a mirror curve of reflected lamplight.

The simplicity of the fierce ultimatum was inspiring. Iain had owned his Princehood. I looked to where Si Akara was standing with Bilili and saw the Neo-Dieri headman nodding with what I took to be approval.

Iain strode across the canted deck, through the assembled warriors and Clever Men. "We move in ten minutes," he said. "Follow my drums!" Then he went back to *Rynosseros,* taking with him four drummers and seven of the remaining Clever Men.

At the end of the allotted time, the drums and bullroarers began, and the small Ajaro fleet moved away from *Kuddimudra.* The twenty kilometres to the eastern shore took several hours due to the pace of the damaged hospital ship, and because of the dark wrecks which loomed like flattened twisted skulls, silent death totems, in the searchlights striking out from the atropaic eyes in *Rynosseros'* bow.

The salt under our wheels told the same story as Si Akara's handful earlier. The lake surface was more powdery than it had been. Our wheels made grooves rimmed with flashing crumbling salt crystals.

What the Chaness would be thinking, what the comsats understood, we could not know, but they were reading six charvolants moving in convoy under non-photonic parafoils, driving across the Air with searchlights ablaze and drums pounding.

With five kilometres to go, there was water under our wheels at last, the beginnings of the flooding that had nearly spelt our doom.

Iain remained with the body of John Stone Grey during our journey across the salt, chanting softly at times, paying his final respects. But when our searchlights picked out clumps of spinifex and hummocks of canegrass on the sandridges, he abandoned his vigil and came up on deck to supervise the landing.

We did not leave the Air. Manoeuvring with difficulty in the darkness, our tiny fleet moored a hundred metres out from the Neo-Dieri camels and huts at the shore-camp, our wheels half-covered by water, with winch-lines fixed to posts hammered firmly into the hard pan, ready to haul our vessels to safety.

"How did you know?" Iain asked Si Akara.

The Neo-Dieri laid a finger along his temple. "The wind. The salt. The Star is here." He shrugged.

And that was the end of it. There would be the scientific explanations — news of rains in the far north-east, a blocked or broken subterranean conduit to the Inland Sea, or accumulated waters from the sandstone catchment areas on the western slopes of the Great Dividing Range feeding through the water table, overloading the Great Artesian Basin underlying this most arid part of Australia.

When the sun rose the next morning, we were in the shallows on the edge of a glittering desert sea, with a strong warm wind blowing waves against the upper edges of our travel platforms and spray cooling our faces.

Out in that windswept expanse of water, the broken Airship wrecks were like strange ocean creatures, barbed, finned and vaned, their toppled hulls spired and arching in the bright sunlight. And in the distance, our scans showed the Chaness fleet swamped and stranded. Most vessels were in five metres of water at least and would never move again. Others, on hummocks of silt, could be given new travel platforms and other lives. But when the flood waters drained back into the hidden chambers of the earth, not one ship would be able to move from the lake on its own. Technically, they belonged to the lake now, though the Chaness were a powerful tribe and there would be negotiations with the arbitrators and special pleas made at the great corroborees, claims for Star dispensation. But most of the ships would stay all the same.

The Chaness had lost, and to the real kuddimudra of this waste, the enduring water spirit of this primeval inland sea.

We waited all morning, until the confirmation came through that the Chaness had forfeited and the Ajaro claim was to be upheld. Then and only then did our ships winch themselves ashore, the successful vessels helping to drag in the others until we were safely on the salt-pan before the sand-ridges facing the new sea.

An Airmen pirate ship, unseen in its ochre markings against the shifting dunes, suddenly came to life and, risking power, moved from where it had been recording our beaching activities.

This raider was not so lucky. The satellites were watching us closely and they received readings. There were flashes of hard light, the distinctive tearing sound of sky-born laser, and the Buchanan vessel exploded and rolled burning into the dunes, a final drama in all that had happened.

* * *

At 1400, we were checking out the electrics and cleaning *Rynosseros* down when Iain Summondamas and Si Akara came aboard.

"We should go," I told the new Prince.

He nodded. "My hand will always be open to you, Captain Tom."

"I value that greatly, Prince."

"Iain."

"Iain," I said, and smiled.

"One day," he continued, "I may send you a deck-boy, a younger son, to be taught the National ways. Will you accept this?"

"I will gladly, Iain."

Iain Summondamas nodded again. "One thing more. Your letter."

"You wish to know what John Stone Grey said to me?"

"No," Iain said. "While I do not know, my Prince still lives. He has something more to say. But you will read it when you leave here, while you can see the Ajaro-Dieri ships and the lake. Yes?"

"Yes."

We shook hands then, Iain first, then Si Akara, and as we did, the headman slipped something small and hard into my palm, his eyes telling me of its secrecy.

Then the Ab'Os turned and left *Rynosseros*. As they headed for *Jusu*, I examined what Si Akara had given me, then issued the order to move out.

We were running through the sandhills and fuming ridges under the hot afternoon sun when I drew John Stone Grey's letter from inside my djellaba. I broke the seal, opened it out and read.

Tom,

Win or lose, you have survived. I have survived in you and in Iain, for I must believe that he lives also and in great honour. Si Akara has given you a small thing, a stasis-flask with an authorization. The flask contains some cells for cloning.

Grow me this andromorph. In three years he will be my age now, if the program is true: an unwed son's only chance, a father no other way. Let him earn his way on the Starship, where I learned what I needed. Call him Hammon.

I love you for what you have done, and wish I could be there now to tell you so.

John Stone Grey
Ajaro Prince
Anonymous Son
Hammon-Eagle.

I laughed and wept.

The Starship. Of course, the Starship. Airships and Starships!

Rynosseros moved at speed amid the dunes, with twenty kites in the sky and a strong lake wind at our backs. When I turned to look behind me, it was as much to hide the tears falling on to John Stone Grey's final words as to see *Jusu* and the tiny flashing mirror-figure of Iain Summondamas.

"Yes," I said. "Yes."

Everything we do is to complete our destiny, everything, word or deed, and as I held the stasis-flask firmly in my hand, it seemed that this fact could never be more true than at that moment, as we ran from the Air, safe again, full of the blessings of renewal and a sense of destiny at the Time of the Star.